"What's down there that got you and Dr. Papadopolous killed?"

Lost in thought, Annja stood and stared at the lake so long her legs ached from not moving. The moon came out from behind a cloud, reflecting against the tiny waves and making it look as if sequins had been scattered across the water's surface.

This setting seemed wrongly tranquil and falsely placid, looking on one hand as if it could be on a postcard, and on the other as if it could appear in the next Stephen King movie.

"Come to Rock Lake," Annja murmured. "Enjoy the scenery and watch your step." In her mind she saw Edgar's body broken and twisted at the bottom of the stairs.

Movement along the shore caught her attention. It was someone with a flashlight, not tall enough to be Detective Rizzo. She couldn't tell whether it was a man or a woman. The beam of light swung toward Annja, picked her out and then the flashlight went dark.

Annja peered into the shadows, trying to separate them and make out the figure in the mist.

The prickling at the back of her neck told her this wasn't a tourist....

Titles in this series:

ROGUE Angel™

Alex Archer

SUNKEN PYRAMID

A GOLD EAGLE BOOK FROM

W★RLDWIDE®

TORONTO • NEW YORK • LONDON
AMSTERDAM • PARIS • SYDNEY • HAMBURG
STOCKHOLM • ATHENS • TOKYO • MILAN
MADRID • WARSAW • BUDAPEST • AUCKLAND

Recycling programs
for this product may
not exist in your area.

First edition November 2013

ISBN-13: 978-0-373-62165-1

SUNKEN PYRAMID

Special thanks and acknowledgment to
Jean Rabe for her contribution to this work.

Printed in U.S.A.

The
LEGEND

...THE ENGLISH COMMANDER TOOK
JOAN'S SWORD AND RAISED IT HIGH.
The broadsword, plain and unadorned,
gleamed in the firelight. He put the tip against
the ground and his foot at the center of the blade.
The broadsword shattered, fragments falling
into the mud. The crowd surged forward,
peasant and soldier, and snatched the shards
from the trampled mud. The commander tossed
the hilt deep into the crowd.
Smoke almost obscured Joan, but she continued
praying till the end, until finally the flames climbed
her body and she sagged against the restraints.

Joan of Arc died that fateful day in France,
but her legend and sword are reborn....

1

"Nahkom, *īaq enakah āēsīyan?*"

Nahkom spun to face the craggy-faced youth who'd spoken. She knew Cha-kau-ka had been following her, showing himself now only because the trees had yielded to a stretch of barren ground and there was nothing left to hide in.

She wanted to be rid of him.

"Nahkom, *īaq enakah āēsīyan?*"

She wrapped her mantle tight when the wind gusted and stared defiantly at him. Nahkom was confident that she was as good a hunter as any man in her tribe, and she would serve her people best pursuing game, not tending to simple chores.

"Nahkom, *īaq enakah āēsīyan?*" He'd said it louder this time.

She answered, explaining that she intended to gain pelts for trading, and waved her stone ax for emphasis. Then she hurried south, where beyond this great clearing the pine forest thickened and rose to blot out the bright blue winter sky. She looked only once over her shoulder, seeing Cha-kau-ka shake his head in obvious dismay.

He would not follow her into the dense section of

trees. The people from her village did not hunt there, in part out of respect for a band of Hochungra who lived in the area. But mostly they avoided it because the elders believed that the Anamaqkiu lived under the section of canopy where the light could not reach. The Anamaqkiu were the dark spirits of the underworld, and she recalled a tale from her childhood about them stealing the life breath from babies.

The Anamaqkiu had been very active lately, setting the ground to tremble fiercely. Days past, the quake was so strong it took down her father's lodge. Today the earth was quiet, though, and the snow cushioned her feet and chilled the soles through her moccasins.

Nahkom had slipped away into these same woods at the end of Blueberry Moon and had not found any dark spirits—she'd found nothing but trees and trees, though admittedly she had not gone far. Tales, nothing more, she decided, and words would not keep her from hunting where surely game was plentiful and where Cha-kau-ka would not come. Young, he believed all the stories.

Now she decided to go much farther, and under the thick canopy she was not disappointed. Within minutes Nahkom was carefully skinning a large fox. As she worked, she listened to the branches shushing against each other in the breeze. She tipped her face up to take in the fragrant scent of the pine—preferable to the pong of blood from her kill. Seasons past she would have never hunted fox—only deer and only because her tribe ate them and used their hides. But the French had come, and they wanted fur. Dealing with the French was beneficial to her people, who had moved from their northern territories in pursuit of pelts for trade.

Finished, she admired the fur, so thick and soft. She rolled it, tied it with a cord and slung it over her back. The wind shifted, and in its whisper she heard birdsong. For several moments she did not move.

It was musical and wholly unfamiliar, and she wanted to see what bird made it. She wove her way through the pine and birch trunks and followed a frozen stream. If she was lucky, she'd find a beaver mound and so would sate the French's desire; they seemed to prefer the beaver pelts above all else.

When she caught a glimpse of feathers, her heart sank. Nothing more than a *kākākēw,* a common raven that was hiding behind a cluster of pinecones. But when it moved along the branch, she realized she was mistaken, and she had no name for this bird. It was singular.

The bright morning sunlight touched it, setting its feathers—that she had first thought black—to sparkle an iridescent, intense green and blue. It was as if the bird did not know precisely what color it wanted to be. It had a long tail plume that shimmered like stars reflected on night-dark water. Its head, neck and chest were the rich shade of wet ferns, and its lower belly and beneath the tail was bright crimson. There were violet streaks in its plumage, and when it turned, she saw that the outside tail feathers were snow-white.

She gasped at its startling beauty, spooking it. The bird lifted from the branch, its wings glittering with bits of silver, and glided away. Captivated, Nahkom dropped her pelt and followed. Then she lost track of it, finding something else to steal her attention—a broad, massive stone building on the edge of a lake. The water was not frozen, and it should have been. Perhaps it was new, just born, and so had not had the time to ice over. Maybe the dark spirits had called it up from the belly of the world with all the quaking the earth had been doing. Maybe the dark spirits wanted to drown the massive stone building, which had challenged the trees in height.

Had the French built the structure? The moment that notion came to her, she dismissed it. The French were intelligent, with their guns and fine, complicated clothes, their difficult language and all the trappings of their society...but they had not been in these lands long enough to build this.

Who lived here?

The Anamaqkiu? Their enemy? If the latter, no wonder the dark spirits were rocking the earth to get rid of it.

Nahkom padded forward.

The stone was worn, indicating its great age, but the years had not erased all the intricate carvings on the bricks. Her fingers traced images of creatures that were half beast, half men, and of the bird that had drawn her here. There were several depictions of the bird, the largest with its wings spread wide and head held up toward the sun.

There were sun carvings, too, and of people bowing down. And more of the bird, so very many of the bird. She heard it, still chirping melodically. Perhaps the beautiful creature had flown to the other side. Nahkom climbed up to a ledge that appeared to wrap around the entire structure. She followed the path, rewarded to find an entranceway on the opposite side and steps that led up to it…and amazed to find more buildings stretching toward the horizon, their bases cocooned by the frozen lake. Was all of this a city? And was the lake growing to swallow it?

There were no tracks but hers, no scents or sounds of people. No one had lived here in a very long time.

She glanced up at the opening. It was framed by an arch with numerous etchings of suns and birds. At the top, the stone head of a creature with small ears and long fangs protruded. A warning to stay out? A shiver flitted through her. Was this totem an image of a dark spirit?

She could still hear the bird. It had flown inside, and its song continued to tease her. Listening, she could hear more than one voice. More of the beautiful birds!

Nahkom pulled in a deep breath and followed the melody up the stairs and through the arch. The interior smelled moldy, reminding her of plantings that had been left too long in the ground and had started to rot. It was warm in here, the stone stopping the winter air from coming inside and holding on to the sun's heat. She shed her deerskin mantle.

The sunlight stretched the length of a corridor filled with still more decorations on the stone. But these were painted, everything at the same time lovely and disturbing, the images fantastical and grotesque. Nahkom studied them slowly as she went, still listening to the birds.

Her course took her into a room filled with totems emerging from the walls, nests rested on the tops of those carved stone heads. She gulped in the turgid air and saw more than a dozen of the amazing birds

perched. There appeared to be an equal number of
males and females, the droppings thick on the floor.
The sunlight did not reach quite far enough for her to
see the entirety of this chamber, and so she relegated
herself to only where the light touched the ground. A
part of her worried that the Anamaqkiu—or something worse than the Anamaqkiu—might indeed be
hiding in the thickest shadows, and that her chief's
stories might be true.

There were trinkets scattered everywhere—bowls,
vessels, beads and tools, and she fell to examining
them, all the while listening to the birds. The great-
est singers of her tribe could not match the wondrous
chorus. The birds must stay well here in the winter, she thought, the building protecting them from
the brunt of the snow and cold that always came
with Anāmaehkatwan-kēsoq, Shaking Hands Moon.
Maybe the birds would share this place with her. She
would bring seeds and pinecones in trade for their
music and company.

Some of the bowls were as red as blood, and she
shuddered to see that they were filled with finger
bones. She pushed them against the wall and continued her exploration, moving aside rotting strips of
fabric and discovering small skulls. If the Anamaqkiu
stole the breath of babies, perhaps they also stole their
heads.

But there was beauty amid the clutter of death. Jewelry the likes the French and the artisans of her village could not have fashioned. Intrigued, and fighting
down a rising worry of the dark spirits, she probed
farther, coming to the very end of the sunlight and seeing the laid-out form of someone who must have been

important. Lengthening shadows kept her from all the details, but she could tell he was wrapped in what had once been beautiful cloth. An impressive headdress crowned him, and her questing fingers tugged it loose.

She nearly put it on, but it was heavy, and she did not want to tempt the spirits. Nahkom settled on removing a disk that was around his neck and prying a knife from his dead grip. His hands broke with her act of theft, and the cracking sound silenced the birds. There were tiny figurines around him, more of the half beasts. She decided not to disturb these, but only because she did not have any pouches to put them in.

She noticed the light had retreated behind her. She took a last look around then hurried out with the disk and the knife, stumbling down the corridor and scraping her face against the wall. She picked up her mantle and wrapped it around her. Outside, she saw that the sun was lower, the morning long gone and the day deep into its afternoon. Nahkom had lost track of time inside the building—*her building.* But the sun was still bright enough, and it set the disk in her hand to practically glowing. It was so shiny and smooth, and the image of one of those beautiful birds had been pressed into the center of it. The disk had a comfortable weight to it, and it was pleasantly warm against her palm.

There was a hole at the top, where a piece of rotted leather had held it to the dead man's body. She took a strip of leather she'd brought for tying pelts, strung the disk and hung it around her neck. No doubt the French would offer her a great deal in trade for it. No! She shook her head and slipped the disk beneath the fold of her blouse. The French would want to know where she'd gotten it, and she did not intend to share the knowledge of her ancient building with anyone.

She stopped and examined the knife closely. The blade was long and curved, made of a sharp, pale stone, thin and impossibly hard. The edge of it was encrusted with something brown that flaked off as she worked at it. The handle was also some kind of stone, a mottled green like the hues of the forest melting together, and carved to look as if lizards had curled themselves around it. There was a strip of fur where the handle joined the blade, a piece of spotted, soft hide that had somehow defied the years. She wrapped her fingers around the handle and made a slashing motion. It would serve her better than the ax.

Nahkom retraced her steps around the ledge. The beautiful birds were singing again. She walked back into the woods and retrieved her dropped fox pelt. It would be wrong to abandon the fur. The creature had died to yield it to her, and the French might give her another blouse in trade for it.

When she reached the far edge of the woods and looked out on the stretch of barren ground, she spotted Cha-kau-ka. Had he waited all day for her?

He'd been busy, she realized as she drew closer. Next to him was a mound of hides he had collected, several of them beaver pelts. Her lone fox fur was pitiful in comparison. Certainly he would claim that he was the better hunter and that her rightful place was taking care of children.

"Nahkom, *āq nakah wāēpīyan?*" he asked.

She told Cha-kau-ka the truth, that she was coming from the darkest part of the forest where the

Anamaqkiu and other spirits danced and sucked the breath from babies.

His mouth opened in a mix of surprise and disbelief. She pulled the necklace out from beneath the folds of her blouse as proof, and the rays of the setting sun caught the disk and made it look molten. Then she displayed the knife, which she'd tied to her belt. Cha-kau-ka reached toward it, and she obliged him.

A quick slash across his arm, another against his neck. The blade was sharp and sank into his flesh as if it was water; his draining life turned the snow crimson.

She'd wanted to be rid of him.

Nahkom added her pelt to his…a fine showing for a long day of hunting. Her father would be so proud of her. She tucked the disk back under her blouse, adjusted her mantle and headed toward her village, struggling under the weight of all the fur.

If anyone in the village asked about Cha-kau-ka… she'd tell them that she hadn't seen her young brother. There were wolves in this area, and they would eat the evidence during the night.

She would return to her ancient building as soon as she traded all of these skins to acquire fine, complicated clothes from the French. Then in the chamber of finger bones and baby skulls she would listen to the song of the colorful long-tailed birds and search out more of the ancient treasures.

She would not stay out of the shadows this time and would never worry about the Anamaqkiu again.

Nahkom knew she had become one of the dark spirits.

2

Thursday

> I have quite the monster for you to chase, dear
> Annja. We must meet for dinner tomorrow so I
> can give you my notes.

Edgar Schwartz hit Send and leaned back in the uncomfortable chair. He closed out his email and called
up a news page to skim a few headlines.

Amazing what people were capable of doing to
each other. Edgar decided not to read any of the par-
ticulars and to instead indulge in something pleasant.
He reached for the phone and dialed room service,
ordering the cabernet-braised short ribs and a bottle of Shoofly Shiraz. The Madison Arms Hotel had
a delightful menu, and he intended to work his way
through as much of it as possible during his stay.

Thirty minutes, the man at the other end of the
phone announced. Just enough time, Edgar thought,
to take a peek at his son's Facebook page and catch
up on the grandchildren's vacation pictures, and then
maybe surf one of his favorite archaeology sites. He'd

just clicked Open on a folder labeled Disneyland when his cell phone chirped.

"Oh, bother." One of his colleagues, he guessed. The conference started tomorrow, and he'd be talking to plenty of his fellow archaeologists then. It was no doubt someone wondering why he didn't go on the pre-conference tour today. He didn't want to admit to the caller that his feet hurt.

The phone stopped chirping. A pause, and then it started again. Persistent, eh? Edgar thought, still deciding to ignore it. And yet... He stretched across the desk just to see who was calling. The hair prickled at the back of his neck. He picked it up. "Yes?"

He scowled and pressed the phone close. "I'm not changing my mind, damn you. I should have never told you about this, never should have showed you. I should've kept my big mouth shut and...What? Speak up. I—" The words came at him in a hiss. "Papa? Really? When?" More hurried words. "Dear God. And we'd been so careful, Papa and I." A pause. "Not careful enough, apparently....Of course. Of course. Did you say anything? Anything to anyone?...No? Are you certain? How could anyone else have found out?...Oh, Papa, I suppose....No, he wouldn't have told...Doesn't matter, does it?...All right, I'll call you when I can."

Edgar closed the phone and shoved it in his pocket, lumbered to his suitcase and felt around on the inside flap until he came up with a jump drive. He hurried back to the desk and shoved the drive against the slot in the laptop. He pressed a few keys and tapped his fingers, waiting.

It wasn't connecting fast enough.

He should call the front desk, shouldn't he? No. No

one there could help, and it would take too long to explain. The police? No on that account, too. Doubly no, in fact. He patted his pants to make sure he had his wallet, looked at his watch and tapped his fingers faster.

"Come on." A return trip to his suitcase, and he dug into the flap again, coming away with a half-inch-thick folder filled with paper and a heavy envelope. Edgar considered himself both old and old-fashioned, and though he embraced computers, he still kept a little hard copy around. He shoved the folder and envelope in between the top mattress and the box springs and smoothed the spread down over it. They might not look there, and if they did, it wasn't complete. There was only his suitcase and the laptop, right? They might be content with just searching those, and maybe with tossing the room a bit, opening all the drawers. That was what they did to Papa's place. Gave it a tossing and then covered their tracks. They wouldn't check the mattress. They wouldn't! Had they found anything at Papa's? Well, certainly. But Papa hadn't had *everything,* only pieces and a couple of old, ancient things. Edgar had the whole puzzle between the folder and his computer and what rumbled around in his brain. And Edgar had that "icing" for the cake, the one thing that would prove him right and make him famous. His crowning achievement in archaeology.

"Oh, hurry up, will you!" he scolded the laptop. There! It was finished. He pulled the jump drive out without hitting the button that said it was safe to remove it. His thick fingers pounded across the keys. A few missed strokes and he had to start over. "Hurry up. Hurry up."

The pictures of his youngest granddaughter holding hands with Mickey Mouse flickered then blinked out. The screen went blank. There, the hard drive was erased!

Edgar was panting, likening himself to a bulldog that had been forced into too much activity. He didn't wear panic well, too many years and too many high-calorie restaurant dishes followed by too many bottles of wine. His chest felt tight with worry, and he tugged his shirt collar open. Eyes wide, he took a last glance around the room. Was he forgetting to cover any other tracks?

Forgetting anything important?

Wallet, jump drive—which he would hide in one of those fake potted plants in the lobby—car keys. He'd come back for the jump drive when it was safe, and the folder between the mattresses, if they didn't find it. The relics were small, so they were in the folder, too. He patted his pockets again to make sure, opened his cell phone and tossed it into the toilet so it would be ruined. Then he trundled toward the door, knocking over the desk chair in his hurry.

"Steady on, old man."

He looked out into the hallway.

Empty.

He could hear a few television sets playing from behind closed doors. The song "Wanted Dead or Alive" thrummed from the nearest, accompanied by the *whoosh* of a wave, suggesting that the guest was watching a Discovery Channel crab-fishing program.

Should he knock on someone's door?

Ask for help?

No. Nobody here could help him. And he wasn't about to put a stranger at risk.

He headed to his left, hoping he'd guessed correctly that the elevators were in that direction. The Madison Arms was a large hotel, and he had trouble sometimes finding his way in these big places.

Another left. He panted faster, making a chuffing noise.

Success! A bank of elevators waited.

A light blinked on above the center door, someone coming up to this floor.

It might be room service, with his cabernet-braised short ribs and Shoofly Shiraz. But it hadn't been a half hour, had it? Maybe another guest with a room on this floor. But maybe it was someone else. He swung around and retraced his steps, chuffing louder. Right at the next corridor. He passed the door to a suite and heard a blast of canned laughter—someone inside watching an insipid sitcom. A right again and he saw the exit sign for the stairwell at the end of the hallway.

Edgar was on the tenth floor. He could do ten flights, couldn't he? It would all be downhill. Edgar knew he would damn well have to manage it if he wanted to save his fat hide. He patted his pocket again, feeling the metal bulge of his car keys. Find a spot to stash the jump drive, retrieve it and the folder when it was safe, he repeated to himself. Couldn't keep the jump drive on him in case they caught up to him. Old, out of shape, he wouldn't be outrunning anybody. And he'd watched enough thrillers in his day to know if they caught him they'd search him...or worse.

"Dear God." Then he pushed open the metal door and heard it clang loudly shut behind him as he trundled down the steps.

3

Annja Creed breezed into the spacious lobby of the Madison Arms Hotel, duffel slung over her back.

"Swank for the land of the Cheeseheads, eh?" Rembert said. He was a few steps behind her. "Downright ritzy."

Annja raised her eyebrows. "*Swank? Ritzy?* Using your grandfatherspeak, Rem? Old-man words." She instantly regretted the jab when Rembert scowled and turned red. The "grandfather" bit was a sore spot. She knew her cameraman had just celebrated his thirty-ninth birthday. But he'd become a grandfather before that. He had a teenage daughter at home, unwed and with a child just turned two. She opened her mouth to apologize.

He waved away any further comment and shuffled to the front desk, where two men in department-store suits were in a heated discussion with the manager.

"Checking in." Rembert got the attention of a desk clerk. "Rembert Hayes." He tugged out his wallet and handed over a credit card. "This is for incidentals, though there won't be any. The room's already marked as paid, right? I'm not paying for the room."

The clerk tapped some keys on her computer. "Yes, your reservation is covered. Room eight-fourteen. Three nights, queen. Checkout is by noon on Monday." She took the offered card and ran it through a slot. She returned it and gave him a key card protruding from a small envelope. "Complimentary appetizers and glass of wine from five to seven." She passed him a voucher. "The bellman is—"

"Don't need one." Rembert lifted his suitcase in one hand and hefted his camera bag with the other. "I can save five bucks and carry it myself."

"Enjoy your stay," she offered.

Annja stepped up and put on a polite smile in contrast to Rembert's sour expression. "Annja Creed." She handed over her credit card. She was paying her own way, as this was passing for a vacation.

Her producer, Doug Morrell, had offered to pick up the bill when he decided to send a photographer to get footage for all-purpose promos, but she declined his generosity. Her idea, her dime, her time. Doug was going to have zero say in how she spent the next three days.

She initially hadn't even wanted the cameraman. She'd told Doug no but he pressed the matter, saying that filming her appearance at this conference would help add a scholarly air to their cable-television show *Chasing History's Monsters*. She relented. But next time she wouldn't cave. Next time…

"Miss Creed, I love your program!" The desk clerk beamed. "May I?" She produced a cell phone and opened it.

"Of course."

The clerk snapped a picture and returned the phone to her pocket. "Just a little proof I met a real celebrity today."

Rembert tapped his foot and made a sound as if he was clearing his throat.

The desk clerk's lips formed a thin line, and she passed back Annja's credit card along with her hotel key card and wine-and-appetizer voucher. "Eight-ten. One of our nicest suites. The bellman—"

"I've only the one bag," Annja said. "I'll manage. Thanks."

"Enjoy your stay," the clerk said.

"Fancy suite, huh?" Rembert headed toward the elevator. "La-di-da. I'll just drop this off in my non-fancy suite, and then—"

"You're in quite the mood," Annja said, watching him punch the up button with more force than necessary. "I'm really sorry about the grandfather—"

He let out a hissing breath and stabbed at the button again. "The baby needs an eye operation. Found out three days ago."

Rembert hadn't mentioned that on the flight here from New York City. In fact, Annja recalled that he hadn't talked about much of anything, losing himself in a movie on his iPad and pointedly ignoring her during the entire trip.

"I see."

"It's not one of those elective things. If the kid doesn't have it, he'll go blind. Gonna be expensive, the operation. Real. And the kid—Colton… She named my grandchild Colton after some contestant on a reality show. Colton isn't covered—"

"—by your insurance."

"No. My wife's insurance, yes. Or what used to be my wife's insurance. Colton was on a rider, *had* been covered. But she got laid off, part of the pink-slip-athon that hit the loan division of the bank. Didn't think to change my insurance to cover the baby, and she didn't think to sign up for Cobra." A pause. "We just didn't think."

The elevator doors opened and Annja let him go first. Inside, he stabbed at the eight button.

"So now my life is a sitcom," he huffed.

Annja waited for him to continue.

"Sitcom, you know—Single Income, Two Children, Oppressive Mortgage. Sitcom. A real laugh."

The reason for Rembert's last-minute presence at the conference dawned on her. Annja hadn't imagined that the top-notch cameraman would normally put in for such a routine assignment as filming a few segments of archaeologists blustering on about their topics of choice—all of it to be mashed into a commercial or two promoting Annja as the host of *Chasing History's Monsters*.

Rembert had been avoiding working with her ever since their trip to France to film an episode about the Dog Men of Avignon. He'd been beaten and shot at and had pronounced Annja risky company when their stint in Paris ran them afoul of a madman who thought himself Charlemagne's heir. Rembert had told her then he would never work with her again.

But he needed the money, Annja realized. He was taking any assignment that came along and bumping junior camera operators to get gigs like this one.

"Thanks for coming with me," she offered.

He shrugged and punched the eight again, staring at the ceiling until the chime signaled they'd arrived at the correct floor. "Don't mention it." The door opened; he exited first and found his room halfway down the hall.

"I'll meet you downstairs, at the conference sign-in. Rem?" Annja's room was just past his.

He mumbled a yes, fumbled with the key card and disappeared inside. He poked his head back out. "Give me a few, okay? I think I'll take a shower first."

And hopefully cool off, Annja thought as she set her duffel on the sofa inside her suite and freshened her face in the washroom. "Don't mention *grandfather* ever again," she told her reflection. "Ever, ever, ever again." If Rembert didn't cheer up, it would be an uncomfortably long weekend. But she didn't have to share his company for the entire conference, did she? In fact, she wouldn't.

She would be having dinner tonight with an old friend—Edgar Schwartz—and tomorrow she had scheduled a lunch meeting with another longtime colleague, Peter Chiapont, an expert on Egyptian architecture. And in between were wonderful lectures she could get lost in.

She ran her fingers through her hair and smoothed a wrinkle out of her blouse. Besides, there was nowhere to go but up with respect to Rembert's attitude.

A quick phone call before joining the others, Annja thought. She went to the phone and pressed nine. "Dr. Edgar Schwartz's room, please." She hung up when it rang several times and switched to voice mail. She tried his cell phone and got nothing. He was probably downstairs grazing at the breakfast buffet, which kicked off the Great Lakes States Archaeological Conference and where she intended to be a minute from now. Rembert could find her there.

She wasn't the featured speaker of the conference, though when she signed in at the registration table, clipped on her badge and grabbed a program, she saw that her picture was the biggest in the booklet, filling the inside front cover. Annja hadn't sent them one to use when she'd registered a few months back, but they must have contacted her network. It was a stock publicity photo showing her in an Indiana Jones–style khaki shirt, broad-brimmed hat and her hair expertly curled around her shoulders. "Annja Creed of *Chasing History's Monsters*" was printed beneath, along with the name and website of the network that sponsored the program.

She inwardly groaned; her producer, Doug, obviously had paid for it as an ad spot. Annja didn't want to be a star here, just a plain old conference-goer intending to listen to as many lectures as she could fit into a three-day blitz. She'd only agreed to speak when the conference chairman called a second time and begged her to sit on two panels: one dealing with fringe archaeology and the other on antiquities of Tham Lod's spirit cave.

The next time she came across a conference she wanted to attend, she'd do so under an assumed name and certainly wouldn't mention it to Doug.

She looked around. The two men in the department-store suits were still talking to the hotel manager. Interesting. But not as interesting as the scents that wafted out of the nearby ballroom, where breakfast was being served. Annja was seriously hungry and let her nose lead her.

The room was expansive and packed with men and women seated at long tables arranged like a pattern of dominoes. They were all chattering between bites, a few looking up to note her entrance, and then returning to their food and conversation. It was a pleasant buzz. Annja recognized several people, including Peter Chiapont, who was engrossed in conversation with an ample-breasted female companion. She estimated attendance here at better than two hundred. The conference itself would draw probably twice that by the time it really got rolling this afternoon, attracting professional and amateur archaeologists, and students. But this breakfast was pricey enough to keep some of them away.

She suspected that a lot of these folks had arrived yesterday for the organized pre-conference outing at Aztalan State Park, site of an ancient Native American village noted for its flat-topped pyramid mounds. Annja had not been particularly interested and so waited for the first flight out of New York this morning.

She went directly to the buffet table, grabbed a plate and made her choices: pumpkin French toast with apple-raisin compote, a mound of cherrywood smoked bacon, poached eggs on English muffins—all of it barely fitting on the plate—and a bowl of fresh berries for a side. She might make a second trip for the granola waffle with cranberry-lemon butter…if the other attendees didn't raise too many eyebrows at her first trip. Annja had an unusual metabolism and a corresponding appetite.

Edgar had emailed her a few days ago about the hotel's celebrated chef and overseer of banquet functions. She didn't spot Edgar in the sea of faces, so she took a seat in the middle of the closest table.

No empty seat nearby for Rembert. Good. She suspected he would pass on this buffet anyway; it would probably strain the expense account Doug had allotted him. With the first bite of the French toast, Annja decided she would also celebrate the chef.

"Amazing," she said. The man across the table from her nodded. He was eating the French toast, too.

"So you're the famous Annja Creed." This came from a hawk-nosed woman a few seats down on the opposite side of the table. "I've seen your show—once. That picture in the program book doesn't do you justice."

Annja came up for air and mumbled a thank-you around a mouthful of poached egg. She definitely was going back for a second plate—a heaping one. On that trip she'd look around for Edgar; she'd tell him their dinner date would be in the hotel restaurant. No need to go outside with food as delicious as this.

Speaking of Edgar…she heard his name pop up in a few of the nearby conversations. She took a large pull from a glass of fresh-squeezed orange juice a server poured, and met the gaze of the man directly across from her.

"Dr. LaVerne Steger, right? I think we spoke a few years ago at—"

"The Society for Medieval Archaeology Colloquium in Belguim. Yes!" His lopsided grin showed he was happy that she remembered him. "I'm looking forward to this afternoon's lecture on the cultural contexts of medieval Britain and how it pertains to archaeological studies in America. Are you going to it, Miss Creed?"

Annja craned her neck this way and that, not seeing Edgar but hearing his name mentioned again.

"Edgar," she said, not answering his question. "Dr. Edgar Schwartz. Have you seen him this morning?"

Dr. Steger paled, and the people seated around them stopped eating. Someone tipped over a water glass.

"Oh, you don't know?" Dr. Steger's face showed shock.

"I'm surprised you didn't hear." This from the hawk-nosed woman. She put down her fork and folded her hands in front of her. "Dr. Schwartz is dead. He fell in the stairwell last night and broke his neck."

Annja felt the color drain from her face.

"The poor dear," the woman went on. "He'd been dead a few hours before someone came across him. He'd be eating with us now if he'd only taken the elevator." She paused. "He would have loved the French toast. Well…he would have loved everything here."

Annja's thoughts shot to the two men in the lobby in the department-store suits. They were police.

"Excuse me," she said, pushing away from the table, her appetite dissolving in a flood of grief. All of a sudden the murmur of conversations and the clink of silverware that had sounded so pleasant moments before became a thunderous wave pounding at her senses. Annja focused on keeping her breakfast down and stumbled from the room, just as the keynote speaker came to the podium and addressed the gathering.

"Welcome to Madison, Wisconsin, for the annual convocation of the Great Lakes States Archaeological Conference. We hope you—"

The two detectives were still talking to the manager, the taller jotting something in a notebook, then closing it and putting it in an inside jacket pocket. Bright light spilling out from the hotel's restaurant off the lobby haloed them.

Both men were lean, broad shouldered and had short hair. There the comparison ended. The tall one was somewhere in his sixties, with long fingers and a long face that reminded Annja of the Lenny Briscoe character from Law & Order. She placed the shorter one at thirty…at the outside. He had boyish features, and his eyes met hers when he turned toward the bank of elevators.

She stepped up to intercept them. "Excuse me…"

"Annja Creed," the older detective said.

She nodded, then realized that he'd read her name off the badge she'd pinned to her blouse. "You're here about Edgar." She put her hands in her pockets. "Dr. Edgar Schwartz."

The older one gave her a visual up and down and stepped around her and to the elevators. Annja now had a clear view into the restaurant. Rembert was there, eating a plate of eggs and looking at something on his iPad.

"I'm a colleague of Dr. Schwartz's," Annja offered. "Edgar and I go back some years."

She received a nod in response from the younger detective.

She waited, hoping he'd volunteer some information. When that didn't happen, she continued, gesturing with a tip of her head toward the ballroom. "The people in there, they said Edgar died last night."

"Broke his neck when he fell in the stairwell." This came from the tall one behind her who'd punched the up button. "That's what the M.E.'s initial report says. Pretty clear-cut accident, she says. Chief sent us out just to confirm."

Annja fixed her gaze on the young officer. He had a handsome, angular countenance and animated earth-brown eyes. She felt an instant connection, and she took a step closer. He had on a hint of soft, musky cologne that agreeably tickled her nostrils. "Clear-cut. But maybe you don't think so. Do you, Detective?" she asked him. It was a guess, and she tried to get a reading from his expression.

"Yes, actually, I do think so. Accidents happen all the time. But we caught the call and so we're look-ing into it to be certain, Ms. Creed," he continued, his face turning hard and shattering that connection she'd felt. "This is a police matter. Routine, sure, but a police matter nonetheless. You can learn about it in the newspaper tomorrow or the day after. We're not at any liberty to discuss it. Regulations, you understand."

"Please tell me something," Annja pleaded. There was a quiet intensity in her voice.

"Sorry," he cut back. "Contact the coroner's office. Maybe she'll cave and release something to you." The elevator chimed, ending the conversation. He gave Annja a curt nod and brushed past her.

"You didn't ask me." This came from the older de-tective, who was holding the elevator door open for his

4

Annja impatiently watched the light above the elevator; it indicated the detectives stopped on the tenth floor. She pushed the up arrow and waited for the next one.

Murder.

Annja was on intimate terms with death, a macabre partner that had held her dance card ever since she'd mystically inherited the sword that once belonged to Joan of Arc. The blood on her hands would never wash off—not that any of the men she'd killed had given her a choice.

But Edgar wasn't part of that world. He was just an archaeologist, her friend and colleague, inoffensive and retiring.

Murder?

The elevator chimed and a door opened.

Annja stepped in, hitting the button for the eighth floor.

Murder? Edgar?

Edgar Schwartz was a lifelong resident of New Mexico. Annja had met him quite a while ago filming a segment for *Chasing History's Monsters*. Tourists claimed to have seen chupacabras south of Albuquerque, and it was a ripe topic for her show. Edgar's specialty was the Anasazi, which history had mysteriously swallowed. He'd indulged Annja and took her out into the desert to where the chupacabra was reported and where his students were sifting at a kiva. Annja had liked Edgar immediately, and their friendship strengthened through the years. They reconnected at archaeology conferences and at southwest digs she visited on her own or for *Chasing History's Monsters*. They'd corresponded often through emails, sometimes chatting about archaeology news, always discussing dishes they'd sampled and favorite restaurants. Edgar's appetite matched or exceeded Annja's, though while she remained slim and athletic, he had not.

She exited the elevator on the eighth floor and returned to her room, where she tugged her laptop out of her duffel. A quick search showed nothing about Edgar Schwartz's death, but she found a blog posting he'd made early yesterday, about arriving at the conference, passing on the tour because he was tired and perusing the menu. The last entry mentioned how much he was looking forward to dinner with the TV archaeologist Annja Creed.

She closed the laptop down and left the room, turning toward the elevator and then spinning and heading instead to the stairwell. Indeed, she was on intimate terms with death—she just hadn't expected to be touched by it in Madison, Wisconsin.

Her stairwell landing was shadowy, but the landing below and the one above were lit. Annja shivered involuntarily as she leaned over the railing, looking down. They said Edgar had been found dead at the bottom. Sucking in a deep breath, and finding the air a redolent mix of stale odors and antiseptic floor cleaner, she took the steps up two at a time and came out on the tenth floor. No sign of the police detectives, no open hotel-room doors.

But the Arms was a big place, and the hallways branched in different directions. She turned left, made another left at the next corridor toward where she knew the elevators would be and heard muted voices coming from an open door. She recognized the voice of the young detective who had been rather curt with her.

For a heartbeat Annja considered slipping up quietly and eavesdropping; she might gain a little more information. But she squared her shoulders, dismissed that notion as juvenile and lengthened her stride to stop squarely in the doorway.

Edgar's room was tidy, almost as if the maid had just readied it or he'd not had time to settle in.

The detectives ceased their conversation and stared at her. In the silence that settled between them, Annja noted the faint chime of an elevator, but it was for the floor above. She heard a siren, a fire truck from the sound of it, in the distance then growing in volume, joined by another before fading as they moved deeper into the city. A radio played from a room or two down the hall. The tune was Stevie Wonder's. A snippet of the closing lyrics came through. "Boogie On Reggae Woman" was the song. From the seventies, she thought. Edgar would have favored it.

The young detective was giving her a serious look. Realizing she wasn't moving on, he shook his head.

"Police investigation, I told you. Wait until tomorrow's paper and—"

"He was a *friend*," Annja said.

"Good to have friends." He stepped between her and the door frame, squeezing out into the hall. "I bet he was friends with a lot of the people at this conference. But they have the sense and courtesy to stay downstairs."

The problem with detectives was they didn't have the little name badges that uniformed cops wore. Annja wanted to address him by something.

"Look—" she started.

"Lieutenant Greene," he supplied.

"Look, Lieutenant Greene, I—"

"—was a friend of the deceased. I get that." His expression softened, but only for a moment before it became stoic again. "And like I said in the lobby, I can't comment on an ongoing investigation, no matter how routine it is. It's policy. If you'll excuse me." He glanced over his shoulder. "Manny, I'm going back down, to talk to this—"

"—Professor Chia something," the tall detective interjected.

"Yeah. I'm going to pull him into the manager's office. Meet me there when you've got this packed to go." Then he was gone down the hallway. He touched the elevator button, and like magic the door instantly opened for him.

Annja was glad to see the door close and the contraption whisk him away.

Chia something? Dr. Chiapont? Peter? Did he know something about what happened to Edgar?

She stepped into Edgar's room.

The older detective was scribbling in his notepad. On the desk next to him was a file folder about a half-inch thick. Edgar's suitcase was open in the center of the bed. It looked as if nothing had been removed from it, clothes neatly folded. She craned her neck, but she couldn't see into the bathroom; the door was halfway closed.

The oldies station aired a brief commercial about a local auto lube service, then Morris Albert's "Feelings" cut in. Annja wrinkled her nose; she hated the song.

"I am... I was—"

"—a friend of this Professor Schwartz," the detective said. "You've mentioned that a few times, if I recall." The detective had a long face, heavily lined more from the outdoors than the years, Annja decided, based on its ruddy color. She thought it made him look like a piece of carved tree bark. His eyes were dark and set wide, his forehead high and his hair thinning and gray.

"I need to know, Detective—"

"Manny. Manny Rizzo." He closed the notebook and sighed deeply, the sound reminding her of dry leaves blown across parched ground and adding to her image of a tree. He shut the suitcase and snapped the latches. "You're not going to give up, are you? Figure I'm the easy mark, eh? A softy. Arnie...Lieutenant Arnold Greene's in charge of this investigation and wouldn't give you the time of day. But me, you figure—"

"He was a friend," Annja repeated.

"Yeah, I heard you the first time."

"A good friend." Annja didn't have too many good friends, and now she was down one.

"Look, Ms. Creed, I know who you are. A beauty queen or supermodel or somesuch who traipses around Egypt and the Amazon pointing out old buildings and creepy—"

Annja felt her cheeks reddening. Her blood simmered whenever people didn't take her seriously, didn't think she was a real archaeologist.

"Listen to me," she cut in. "I know…*knew*…Edgar pretty well, better than anyone here at this conference, most likely."

"You're not a relative."

"No."

"Not sure if they've notified his next of kin yet." Detective Rizzo scratched his nose. "Hope they took care of that, though, from the station. People downstairs are probably tweeting and texting and whatever else they can do on their little telephones. Hate to have his wife find out by—"

"Edgar was divorced."

"—or his kids hear by—"

"—and grandkids." Annja remembered Edgar happily showing her pictures of them.

"Yeah, hate to have them find out on Facebook or wherever. I better check to make sure the notification's gone out." He pulled out his cell phone and punched in some numbers, muttered a curse and tried it again, his fingers seeming too big for the buttons.

Annja blatantly listened in. The conversation took Annja aback. The investigation was indeed very fresh if Edgar's sons were only just being notified now.

He finished and dropped the phone in his pocket.

"Anything else, Ms. Creed? I'm working here."

She took the edge off her voice. "What makes you, Detective Rizzo, think it was murder? I take it Lieutenant Greene doesn't share your—"

"He'll come around," the detective said. "Right now he's going with the M.E.'s preliminary report. All by the book, Arnie is. But he'll come around real soon. Bright boy. Before the rest of the morning's gone, he'll—"

"What makes you think that Edgar…that Edgar was—"

Detective Rizzo picked the suitcase off the bed and rested it next to the desk, then put his back to her, not out of rudeness she realized, but because he was looking around to see if there was anything else to close up and take with him. He ran his long fingers through what little hair he had and let out another leaf-blowing breath.

"Detective." Annja tried again. "What makes you think—"

Detective Rizzo turned, a perturbed expression marking his long face. "Oh, for the love— Seriously? Why would you think it *wasn't* murder, Ms. Creed?"

Annja answered with a question. "Was there a power outage last night in the hotel?"

"No." He shook his head. "We checked."

"Then Edgar took the stairs for some other reason. He wouldn't normally have done that."

Manny offered a wry smile that deepened the crinkles around his eyes. "Lieutenant Greene is a young man, Ms. Creed. And so he doesn't understand old men. We don't take the stairs unless we have to. Especially fat old men like your Professor Schwartz."

"Edgar would have taken the elevator—"

"If he would've taken any way out of the hotel at all. My guess was he hadn't intended to go anywhere. He'd just ordered room service," the detective continued. "Wouldn't think a man like your Professor Schwartz would abandon a fancy meal."

Another siren wailed from out on the street, an ambulance by its tone. It grew until it seemed on top of them, then cut out.

"So someone took him into the stairwell," Annja mused aloud. "Dragged him or forced him or chased him. Someone killed him there and tried to make it look like an accident."

"That's my thinking." He straightened his tie, folded his notebook and stuck it in the inside pocket of his jacket. "Laptop's missing, but the cord is here. Found the cord on the floor. Another clue some amount of foul play's involved. The perp maybe was an amateur because he left the cord. But it's too early to say just what went down. All just guesses on my part." He sighed. "And you shouldn't be saying anything about any of this. I don't need Lieutenant Greene on my wrinkled ass because I talked about a case to a movie star."

Annja nodded. "I won't say anything." She looked around the room for…for what? "I…I want to help." Need to help, she decided. All thoughts of attending the conference had vanished.

"*Chasing History's Monsters,* right? That's the name of your television show."

She didn't answer, still glancing around, eyes recording all the details and searching. There was the laptop cord on the desk, next to the folder. Edgar's folder? "He always brought a laptop everywhere," she said. "Never an iPad or tablet. An *old* laptop, because for whatever reason he liked its operating system and didn't mind its bugs."

"Sounds like you really did know him."

"His laptop. It wasn't in the suitcase? It wasn't with him…in the stairwell?"

She registered his lack of reply as a no.

Edgar was an aging archaeologist, pushing seventy or more likely already past it; she'd never pried about his age. He wasn't into anything controversial that she knew of, hadn't been on a single dig in the past six months because he'd told her his arthritis was getting worse. Why would someone murder him? For money? Edgar wasn't wealthy, but he was reasonably comfortable and very old-fashioned. He preferred to carry cash over credit cards. Would someone kill him for money? Or had he—possibly—discovered something worth getting killed over? Edgar?

"His wallet? Was it on him? Was—"

The detective interrupted her. "Why don't you go back to your conference? There are no monsters here for you to chase, Ms. Creed." He picked up the folder, carefully tucked it under his arm and bent to grab the suitcase, but his chirping cell phone stopped him.

He scowled as he dug for it, then put it to his ear. "Really? Really? This is going to be a long day, Arnie. I'll be down in a few." He returned the cell to his pocket, picked up the suitcase and gestured with his chin to get Annja to leave.

She remembered the email Edgar had sent her yesterday. *I have quite the monster for you to chase, dear*

Annja. We must meet for dinner tomorrow so I can give you my notes.

"Oh, there's a very real monster here, Detective Rizzo. The one that killed Edgar. And I definitely plan to chase it into the ground."

She spun on her heel and headed toward the elevator just as the radio started to play Alice Cooper's rendition of "Only Women Bleed."

5

The elevator doors opened to the lobby, revealing the flashing red lights of an ambulance parked just beyond the hotel's front doors. Paramedics were loading someone into the back of it; Annja couldn't see who.

But from the buzz of voices coming from the people gathered nearby, she picked out a name: Elyse Hapgood. Annja didn't know if that was a hotel employee, a random guest or one of the archaeologists attending the conference. The latter, she decided, when she gleaned more sentence fragments.

"Heart attack, poor dear."

"Keeled over in the middle of the French toast."

"Too young for a heart attack."

"Told Elyse to go on a diet."

"Think she'll make it?"

"Was she breathing? Did anyone notice if she was breathing?"

"She wasn't fat. Elyse just had a big chest."

"Double D."

"Triple."

Hotel employees were dutifully keeping the entrance clear. Lieutenant Greene looked to be holding court over the controlled chaos. He stepped away to talk to one of the paramedics, who nodded and got in the ambulance.

The siren started again and the ambulance pulled away.

Rembert appeared at her shoulder. He had a pensive expression, as if he were considering something. He looked beyond her, toward the ballroom doorway, where the gaggle of conference attendees grew and continued to chatter. Their voices were a buzz, like cicadas nesting, Annja thought, but through it she continued to pick out interesting bits.

"Dr. Schwartz."

"Elyse."

"Deaths come in threes."

"Who's next?"

"Only one death—Edgar Schwartz. Elyse might make it."

"Edgar, Elyse, they should've lost weight."

"Two deaths. Don't forget Papa."

"Why do they want to talk to Peter?"

"Peter's with a policeman."

"Threes, I tell you. Someone else will die."

"Did you…do you…know her, Annja?" Rembert had a small camera in his hand, and he had it pointed at the gathering of archaeologists. He panned with it a moment, then turned it off.

"Elyse?" Annja wondered if Rembert had recorded the woman being taken out on a stretcher or Peter being pulled into the manager's office.

"Yes, her. Did you know her?"

"Never met her. I don't even know who Elyse is," she told him. "And I don't know what happened."

"It wasn't a heart attack." Rembert kept his voice

low. "I've seen a few heart attacks. That wasn't one of them."

Annja recalled that he used to work at one of the big New York news stations and probably had seen a lot of things, heart attacks included.

"I was getting shots of the breakfast," he continued. "Just background stuff. A little color. I saw her go down. By chance, I saw it. Got it." He tapped his camera and smiled. "Fortunate I was aimed right at her. There's nothing in my contract with Doug that says I can't shoot stuff on the side. He knows I still do some freelancing, doing more of it now. Got her going down, collapsing, the reactions of the people around her. Choice stuff."

Annja waited to pick up more news through overheard conversations. The archaeologists continued to talk, some of them moving back into the ballroom, one starting up the lobby's impressive sweeping staircase, a few heading to the bank of elevators. One of the elevator doors opened, and Detective Rizzo came out carrying Edgar's suitcase. He walked past her and around the corner of the registration desk. Annja assumed the manager's office was back there. Lieutenant Greene followed him.

"No, I certainly don't think it was a heart attack," Rembert repeated. "I'd bet money on it…if I had some money to bet. It was just…weird. And I don't think she choked on anything, either. That biddy over there—" he tipped his head toward the hawk-nosed woman who had been at Annja's table for breakfast "—thinks she swallowed too big a hunk of French toast. But it wasn't choking. It was…weird."

Annja was beginning to lose her patience. She faced Rembert. "Then what was it?"

He shrugged. "I just know it wasn't a heart attack. Her eyes got all big and her mouth started opening." He made an O with his lips and tapped his camera again. "She looked sort of like a goldfish." He paused. "We got a fantail a couple of weeks back for Colton. She was breathing, too. You don't breathe if you're choking to death. Sweating like a pig. She was really sweating, like instantly sweating. Really weird."

Annja's thoughts whirled. She didn't know Elyse, and so the woman wasn't her concern, but Edgar was, and she wanted...*needed*...to pursue that. She glanced toward the corner where Detective Rizzo had vanished and she tried to shut out the incessant drone of conversations.

It wasn't working; the voices continued.

"Are they arresting Dr. Chiapont?"

"Peter? Going to jail?"

"No! Peter's friends with Elyse. Maybe the cops just need information about her."

"But he was arguing with Edgar yesterday, Peter was. Dr. Schwartz. Red-faced. I saw him. Peter and Elyse and Dr. Schwartz, right here in the lobby."

Annja looked away from Rembert and tried to see who had made that last comment. She couldn't catch it. But now Elyse had suddenly become her concern, too.

"Peter wouldn't hurt anyone." The statement was made multiple times.

"He was hot about something, though," Dr. Steger said. "Really angry at Edgar. And he didn't seem all that pleased with Papa on the tour."

"Maybe Peter's just having a bad day. We're all entitled to bad days."

"Bad day? Peter made threats."

She saw who made that comment, a round-faced man with a shock of red-brown hair. She'd talk to him later.

"He wasn't mad at Elyse," Dr. Steger added. "He was with her just before this happened."

"Elyse is married."

"That doesn't mean anything. Peter plays around," the hawk-nosed woman interjected.

A door shut loudly somewhere behind her. A moment later Detective Rizzo walked by and fluttered his long fingers at the group. Like a conductor directing an orchestra, he got them to quiet. Annja watched him pull out his notebook. Next to her, Rembert was recording again.

"Show of hands," Detective Rizzo said. "Who was sitting near Mrs. Hapgood?" He was looking at name badges and scribbling furiously. "What did she eat?" More scribbles. "Did any of you eat the same thing?"

"Poison," Rembert said just loud enough for Annja to hear. "He's thinking poison. Someone tried to kill that woman."

Detective Rizzo was separating the conference-goers based on their answers and trying to herd some of them back into the ballroom.

"Poison." The word came out flat. Annja's head throbbed. "Poison, here? This is just a conference."

"There's death wherever you go, isn't there?" Rembert mused. "Paris, France, and Madison, Wisconsin."

The crowd chattered again; and once more Detective Rizzo got them to stop.

"I might have a juicy story here," Rembert said. "Something I can sell to one of the local networks. Got some great video."

Annja's lips curled. Rembert was thinking about a paycheck, not about the woman who'd been taken away in the ambulance, not about Edgar…whose death he hadn't even learned of yet.

"Threes, I tell you," one of the archaeologists repeated as he was nudged into the ballroom. "Deaths come in threes. There'll be another one."

The hawk-nosed woman put a finger to her lips.

"There's been three," Dr. Steger said, ignoring Detective Rizzo's admonition to be quiet. The detective gave up and disappeared from Annja's sight, going farther into the ballroom.

Annja spotted Dr. Steger standing just inside the ballroom entrance. "Didn't you hear about Papa? Gregor Papadopoulos, a local fellow? He was on our tour yesterday. But he never made it to the hotel for the breakfast. Died in his sleep last night. So there's been three. Well, three if Elyse dies."

Annja's throat tightened. She thought about her sword, hanging in the otherwhere, waiting for her to summon it to her hand. She pushed the image away.

Rembert muttered, "Maybe even one of the big nationals will pick up the story if it's a slow news day. I can hear the headline now: Archaeologists Drop Like Flies."

Annja walked at a snail's pace toward the ballroom. What the hell was going on in Madison, Wisconsin?

6

The next hour added to Annja's headache. She sat at a table in the middle of the ballroom, absorbing the activity and sorting through the details she'd gathered. She watched Detective Rizzo methodically talk to one archaeologist after the next, always writing in his notebook, which seemed to have inexhaustible pages. She couldn't hear his questions or their answers; she wasn't close enough and there was too much competing noise. But she studied expressions, and from that she decided who she would speak to later.

As Detective Rizzo dismissed them one by one, some remained in the room, hovering nearby to overhear what the others said, while some left for elsewhere in the hotel. At the other end of the room, the conference organizers massaged the speaking schedule. She could hear them a little better, but she chose to shut it out.

A small cadre of busboys entered and started clearing the tables, trying to be quiet, yet still managing to clink and clunk plates and cups and rattle silverware. Rembert came in a few minutes later. Annja turned so she couldn't see him; she didn't want to watch him record more pieces for potential sale.

Annja didn't know Gregor Papadopoulos, hadn't heard of him before the scuttlebutt she'd picked up minutes ago…but then she didn't know most of the archaeologists she'd seen at the breakfast. There had only been a dozen or so familiar faces. Perhaps it was time she attended more of these conferences and broadened her circle of contacts in the field face-to-face. Her internet contacts were many, but it wasn't the same.

Of course, if she did attend more of these things, more of her contemporaries might die. Rembert's words festered: "There's death wherever you go, isn't there?" Her macabre dance partner wasn't about to abandon her.

She shook off a little of the melancholy with a long breath that fairly whistled between her teeth. Her presence had nothing to do with Edgar's death, she told herself. Or with this Gregor, whom she'd never met and whom she doubted simply died in his sleep. Her being here had nothing to do with whatever happened to Elyse Hapgood…whom she also didn't know and who wasn't dead—yet, at least.

But all three incidents were somehow related; Annja felt it in her gut. And she suspected that Detective Rizzo thought so, too.

So what was the common thread?

Them being archaeologists, sure.

But it had to be more than that.

"What can you tell me about Gregor Papadopoulos?" Annja asked Dr. Steger. The detective had finished with him, and it looked as if he was not one to stick around and eavesdrop.

He stopped short, surprised, as if he'd been lost in thought and hadn't noticed her sitting there. "What?"

"Gregor Papadopoulos? I heard you talking about him."

"Oh, Ms. Creed." He pulled out a chair and sat next to her, glancing away for a moment as a trio of bus-boys clattered by and picked up more plates and cups. One of them dropped a glass on the floor and muttered a profanity as he picked up the pieces.

"I knew him, most certainly I did. But I didn't know him all that well," he said. "If you take my meaning."

Dr. Steger had a kind face, but his cheerful demeanor from breakfast was gone, replaced by a rueful expression.

"I didn't know him at all," Annja told him. "I've realized I'm not terribly familiar with a lot of my Midwest contemporaries. I know far more archaeologists on the coasts and overseas. And lately, I've stayed in touch over the computer rather than in person."

"Ah, the computer. It keeps people close and at bay in one fell swoop." Dr. Steger steepled his fingers and appeared thoughtful. "This conference pulls them from all over, archaeologists—professionals and hobbyists, a good mix of students from the local university and the University of Chicago—but the glut come from the middle of the country," he admitted. "Gregor was from right here in town. Heard he was Greek. Born there, schooled here and stayed. Never married."

"Tell me some more about him," she urged again.

"I don't know all that—"

"Whatever you know. Anything."

He raised an eyebrow. "Well, I don't know much more than that. We weren't friends, but we were friendly. I'd see him every year at this conference… except the one that was in Saint Louis, but that was a while back. He specialized in the indigenous peoples of Wisconsin and northern Illinois, from the sixteen and seventeen hundreds, if I recall correctly. Helped with exhibits at the Milwaukee museum—a nice place, you should go—and at a little museum down in Kenosha. It's a good spot, too, but not worth your trouble unless you're local. Anyway, he was real chatty on the tour yesterday, but then he must've known the mounds like the back of his hand. He told us to call him Papa. Wasn't an old man." He paused. "Not young, either." He paused again. "Oh, maybe fifty. I'm five years past that. Makes you think about your own mortality, eh?"

"Of course," Annja said.

"Oh, and I heard he taught a course every semester at the University of Wisconsin."

Dr. Steger got up to leave, and Annja reached out, touching his wrist. "What about Mrs. Hapgood? What was…*is*…her specialty?"

His face pulled forward, eyebrows touching in the middle. "You think this is somehow related…Dr. Schwartz, Dr. Papadopoulos, Elyse?" He gave a soft laugh. "Dr. Schwartz died from a fall in the stairwell, Dr. Papadopoulos in his sleep. Probably a heart attack. Heard he'd had a bypass after last year's conference. That was the early rumor at this morning's breakfast, his bad heart. We were talking about that right before you joined us. So you think this might be related, eh? A big game of Clue? Gregor Papadopoulos in the library with the wrench. Mrs. Hapgood in the study with—"

Annja frowned, lying to him. "No. I don't think that. I don't think they're related. All coincidence, I'm sure. Just…I'm just curious. Do you know Mrs. Hapgood?"

"Nope. But Dr. Chiapont does. They showed up together. And her specialty?" He reached into his back pocket and pulled out the conference program, unrolled it and flipped through a few pages. "Lots of lectures on the Midwest and Plains indigenous peoples this year. Lots… Oh, here she is. Doesn't have a doctorate, but she's scheduled. Specialty? Probably something to do with Mesopotamia. She was supposed to lecture on her research on the fabled Hanging Gardens." He rolled the program and put it back in his pocket. "Nice picture of you inside the cover."

Annja drew her lips into a thin line. "Thanks."

"They're moving some things around, but the lecture on the cultural contexts of medieval Britain and how it pertains to archaeological studies in America is still on for one o'clock. See you there, Miss Creed?"

She politely nodded, but she was lying again. Annja's plans for the weekend were changing. She couldn't let questions go unanswered or a mystery slip by her…especially if it involved a friend, like Edgar. It was just a matter of where she would start.

Maybe with Peter. She got up and turned to go back to the lobby, to wait there until Detective Greene had finished questioning Peter. She'd ask Peter some questions of her own.

"Ms. Creed!"

She hadn't noticed the conference chairman approaching her.

"Ms. Creed, do you have a moment?"

She was going to say no, but he barreled ahead.

"We've moved some things. Dr. Chiapont's seminar. Mrs. Hapgood's canceled, of course. Hopefully, Peter can make his lecture this evening. Dr. Schwartz's panels, naturally, off the docket. We've moved yours up." He had a program in hand. "The one on the spirit caves in Tham Lod. It's in one of the smaller conference rooms." He pointed to a map in the program. "You've got a half hour before it starts. You don't mind, do you?"

She was going to say yes, but he continued.

"We're running the changes on the screen in the hotel lobby and printed up a sheet to distribute. Tragic, all of this. But with all of these people here, the conference must continue."

A woman behind him had a stack of papers, which Annja guessed were copies of the quickly amended schedule. She handed a sheet to Annja.

"Awful, just awful, all of this," the chairman went on. "And on my watch. Imagine. Not a single health problem the past three years, and now this."

"Things come in threes." The woman tutted.

Annja mulled over how to politely decline.

"You're the only speaker on the Tham Lod topic," the chairman said.

Annja had an obligation to Edgar, but she also had an obligation to the chairman. "All right." She did have thirty minutes before the lecture, so she'd at least let Peter know she wanted to speak to him as soon as possible. The lecture would be easy; she didn't need notes. She'd experienced so much in her explorations of the Thailand caves that she could easily fill the time slot.

And then she would delve uninterrupted into Edgar's death.

She felt an urge to summon her sword. Maybe a hint that trouble was going to find her?

Out in the lobby, she stopped in her tracks to see Peter Chiapont being led out the front door in handcuffs, prodded along by Detective Greene.

Just what the hell was going on in Madison, Wisconsin? she wondered again.

"Annja—" Rembert was right behind her, camera bag on his shoulder. He was filming Dr. Chiapont being helped into a squad car. "Just heard you're up next. I think I should—"

"—get a clip? Yeah, Doug would appreciate it." Before you go shopping the rest of your footage, she thought. "Upstairs, first conference room on the left."

She took the stairs two at a time, welcoming the brief activity and pleased to put some distance between herself and Rembert. Between herself and everyone, actually, if only for a few moments. The hall upstairs was empty, and she breathed deeply, appreciating the scented air courtesy of a grand arrangement of flowers on the table—a mix of orange lilies, small pink carnations, yellow solidago and purple iris.

This place was indeed swanky, she thought. Ritzy, to use Rembert's grandfatherspeak.

She stared at the flowers; they could have passed for an elaborate funeral arrangement. She scolded herself, unable to keep thoughts of Edgar's death at bay even for a little while. Was one of his sons coming here? To claim the body? Or would they have it—

"I should've taken the elevator." Rembert was with her again, huffing from his jaunt up the steep staircase. He took a comb out of his pocket and used it on Annja. "There. Perfect."

She gave him a smile that didn't reach her eyes.

"After you," he said, extending his hand toward the conference-room doorway.

She stepped past him, expecting an empty room, as it was twenty minutes before the hour and her topic was originally scheduled for tomorrow. But the room was close to full, easily eighty or ninety people waiting for her words of wisdom. She doubted that it was the subject that brought them, most likely the picture on the inside front cover of the program. Her celebrity had lured them here.

She would start a few minutes early. Better than sitting quietly at the front, locking eyes with the attendees and continuing to ruminate about Edgar. A deep breath, the air still tinged with the flowers from the hall but also filled with the various colognes and perfumes the men and women wore.

Voices were low, some of them talking about Mrs. Hapgood keeling over at breakfast, some of them mentioning Annja and her photograph in the book. One noted that a videographer was present.

"Will we be on television?" This from the hawk-nosed woman. Olivia Rouse, her badge read. She was sitting on the end of a row near the middle of the room.

"Maybe," Rembert answered. He put on a wide-angle lens and filmed the audience while Annja took her position at the podium.

Annja gave a brief introduction and started discussing her adventures in Thailand and discovering spirit caves that had been lost to the centuries. Rembert changed lenses and recorded her. The talk was actually doing her a little good, she realized, helping shake off a smidgen of her sadness. She truly loved archaeology.

More people filtered in, some standing at the back because there were no more empty chairs.

One man in particular caught her eye.

She swallowed hard and forced herself to continue the lecture.

He was more than six feet tall, with the broad shoulders of a swimmer. Impeccably dressed in a black leather jacket over a vanilla-colored shirt, eyes and hair as black as a starless sky; he had a square-cut jaw and was ruggedly handsome. His age was difficult to determine, but Annja knew he was at least five hundred years older than her.

He'd been one of Joan of Arc's protectors, though he'd ultimately failed to save her from her fiery death. Annja knew he had no interest in Tham Lod's spirit caves or with archaeology in general. But he had a vested interest in her—when he was not distracted by his own machinations—because she carried Joan's sword. They crossed paths frequently, but never before at a function such as this. It couldn't be good news to see him here.

Annja did her best to avoid him when the lecture was done and she attempted to leave the room.

Too many people, too many questions and a press of bodies that was difficult to work through thwarted her plan. He was there, just beyond the doorway, waiting, his face implacable, eyes aimed at her.

He let most of the attendees filter out before stepping forward to block her way.

"Annja Creed," he said.

"Garin Braden," she returned, noting that his conference name badge read Gary Knight. "What brings you to Madison, Wisconsin?"

"I've always wanted to attend the Great Lakes States Archaeological Conference," he said.

She noted the blatant insincerity in his otherwise appealing voice. "I don't want you here, *Gary,*" she said, half-surprised that she'd spoken that aloud where others might have heard her.

"That's funny. I don't want you here, either." Garin's eyes twinkled darkly. "In fact, it would probably be much healthier for you if you packed your suitcase and went back to New York. There's nothing for you here, Annja. Nothing but things that don't concern you. And nothing, if you listen to all the gossip in the halls, but death."

He politely nodded and turned away, pausing at the flower arrangement to pluck out a pink carnation, snap off the stem and slip the bloom into the lapel of his jacket.

7

"The Thai salad with lobster and shrimp cakes, and the club sandwich on sourdough." Garin folded the menu and handed it back to the waitress. "And a glass of white soda, whatever brand you carry, no ice."

She filled his water glass and took his order to the kitchen. The restaurant was upscale and understated at the same time; a place he could recommend if the food lived up to its hype. Linen tablecloths everywhere, linen napkins expertly folded to look like swans, instrumental music so soft it was just above a whisper to not intrude on the diners' conversations. He stared at the lemon impaled on the rim of his glass.

He'd chosen a table off to the side, but where he could still have a view of the lobby. Annja had left the hotel minutes ago, her cameraman on her heels. Apparently he wasn't fast enough to catch her or persuasive enough to share her company as the man had returned, shaking his head and disappearing out of sight.

Garin took a sip; the chilled water felt pleasant on his tongue.

It was a mistake, he thought—not by any means coming to the conference, but showing up during her lecture, announcing his presence. And then saying such ominous things. He hadn't intended to do that. But seeing her picture inside the program book, hearing people talk about "that Annja Creed," had made him act impulsively. He was amused, listening to the gossip, some admiring Annja and thinking she was a great role model for young people considering careers in archaeology, others saying she was a sham specializing in fringe topics and shouldn't have been given speaking slots.

None of them, he suspected, knew just how intelligent and talented…and how dangerous…Annja Creed really was. He certainly didn't underestimate her.

"Damn it all," he said and downed the water in one long pull, then sucked on the piece of lemon. He'd allowed his ego to come to the fore. He could have let the weekend pass quietly, meeting with his contacts under her nose and out of her sight, all the while keeping tabs on her to make sure she didn't interfere with his plans. He hadn't needed to stand at the back of her room so she would be certain to spot him.

Nothing but things that don't concern you. And nothing, if you listen to all the gossip in the halls, but death. Yeah, that statement would surely get her to leave Wisconsin—not.

Coincidence that they both were in Madison this weekend? A divine accident? He *needed* to be here, that was given. But her?

She was here…for what? To speak to peers, many of whom didn't respect her? To escape *Chasing History's Monsters* and her television-host duties for a time? Or could she—possibly—be aware of what might transpire in the shadow of this conference?

Had she caught on to it, and was that the real reason she was here?

To foul his plans?

The server placed the soda and salad in front of him, added a little ground pepper. He drank the soda quickly, thirsty for whatever reason today. Nerves? Over Annja? Hardly, he thought. Garin speared a lobster cake and chewed on it slowly, letting the flavors seep onto his tongue. He appreciated a good meal, among the other fine things his long life had afforded him.

And Garin had been enjoying his life immensely. He'd been *cursed* with eternal life ever since he'd failed to protect Joan. A curse? He'd only considered it that in the beginning. Now it was a blessing, one he didn't want to give up. If he had his way, Annja's sword would be broken up again if it would guarantee he'd never die. He wanted her alive, so that someday that might come to pass. Dead, who knew where the sword would end up? He was as much tied to it as Annja.

But why did she have to be here? This weekend?

"The salad is quite good," he told the server when she brought his club sandwich.

"One of our specialties," she said, smiling kindly.

"And another soda, please."

She took his empty glass and disappeared.

Maybe it hadn't been a bad play after all, revealing his presence to Annja and making the quip. If she didn't already know about the dark side to this conference, his appearance might rattle her enough she wouldn't catch on and discover why he was really here. And she had these deaths to deal with; he'd never known her to let something like a little mystery just sit. One of the victims apparently had been a friend of hers. She'd be focused on solving that, leaving Garin to his business.

"Pity," he said as he wrapped his mouth around the sandwich. "Pity to be forced to mourn a friend."

However, if, by chance, she knew why he was really here, knew about the shadowy bits, all the more fun he might have. Garin enjoyed a good game and the opportunity to outplay Annja Creed.

And he especially enjoyed winning.

He was nearly finished with his meal when he saw a particular fellow cut through the lobby.

Garin dropped two twenties on the table, dabbed at his lips with the napkin and sauntered out.

8

Annja paced in the lobby of the police station. It had taken her a few calls to find out where Peter was taken, and then she had to hail a cab to take her there. Madison boasted five police districts, and he was at the one on South Carroll.

"Good thing it's tile and not carpet," said a young officer at the desk. His badge read Phillip deSpain. "You'd have a strip wore off."

"Sorry." Annja stopped in front of a bulletin board. She read one of the announcements:

> The Madison Police Department's Traffic Enforcement Safety Team (T.E.S.T.), in addition to other enforcement efforts, will be specifically addressing traffic violations this week in the following areas: Tuesday, East District, Atwood Ave. at Oakridge Ave. (Detour Area Enforcement); Wednesday, South District, 3800 Block Speedway Road (Speed Enforcement).

There was more to it, but the words swam in front of her eyes.

"I have your information, ma'am," the officer said.

He replaced his phone in the cradle. "Peter Chiapont was brought here about an hour ago. They just finished a preliminary interview, so now he's across the street."

"What?" Annja said.

"At the sheriff's department." He paused. "For fingerprinting."

"So he's actually been arrested?"

"I don't have that information, ma'am. It's part of an ongoing investigation, so I don't expect to have anything for a while. The blotter gets updated in the afternoon. But you can go across the street to the Dane County Sheriff's Department and—"

Annja was out the door before he could finish.

They were not quite as helpful or friendly as Officer deSpain, but she soon learned that the city police department, though it had holding cells, used the sheriff's jail. Annja talked to one deputy after the next, finally finding someone who could both assist her and was a fan of *Chasing History's Monsters*. Her celebrity was convenient sometimes.

"I'll give you a few minutes," a deputy told her. "We don't usually do this so early in a case, but Detective Rizzo gave the okay."

Detective Rizzo? Was he here? Annja would try to find him after she talked to Peter.

The deputy put her in a small room divided in two by a thick piece of Plexiglas. She sat at the counter on an uncomfortable stool, stared at the phone in front of her and waited. Putting her wrist to her nose, she could smell what trace of perfume she had left. Not enough to mask the smell of this place. It had the pong of previous visitors, cleansers that weren't used often enough and desperation.

A tap on the Plexiglas roused her.

Peter was disheveled and looked tired and quite a bit older than his forty years. He slumped on his stool and gestured to her phone, picking his up awkwardly because he was handcuffed.

"Peter, what's going on?" There were a dozen other questions churning in her head, but she started with that. "What have they arrested you for? What's the charge?"

His voice was thick. "Good to see you." He paused. "But why…why did you come? Were you appointed, to bring back the scandalous news to the conference?"

Maybe he hadn't heard her. She tried again. "Peter, what's going on? What have they arrested you for?"

He held the phone away from his face for a moment, as if considering his answer. She was afraid he'd put it down and walk away, leaving all of her questions unanswered.

"They think I killed Edgar," he finally said. "They think I—"

"Preposterous," Annja cut back. Someone killed Edgar, certainly, but it wasn't Peter Chiapont. "Whatever would make them suspect you?" She remembered the comment someone made about his arguing with Edgar. "You and Edgar are…were…friends. Have they officially charged you with murder?"

He shook his head, again holding the phone away. He closed his eyes and let out a breath that steamed the Plexiglas. "Annja—"

"What?"

"They've not arrested me for that…yet. And of

course I didn't kill Edgar. I wouldn't kill anyone. And…Edgar, he was a friend."

"What are they holding you on, then?" He was in an orange jumpsuit; he'd been charged with something, hadn't he?

More waiting. "I have a…" He scowled, clearly uncomfortable with what he was going to tell her. "I have a previous assault charge against me. I was… am…on probation. They can hold me because of my priors. At least hold me for a while."

Priors. More than one. Priors…a term someone used who was either in law enforcement or the courts, or who was on the other side—like the other side of this Plexiglas. She realized she didn't know Peter Chiapont as well as she thought. More questions warred inside her. Annja wanted to ask him about those "priors," but that would have to wait. Besides, she could probably find out via public records and an internet search.

"What were you arguing about, you and Edgar?"

He sat forward and dropped the phone on its cradle. Annja furiously tapped the glass, and his shoulders sagged. But he relented and picked up the receiver again.

"Ridiculous stuff, Annja," he said wearily. "Really ridiculous, unbelievable stuff. Edgar thought he was onto something because of what he found at one of his New Mexico digs. I don't know what. Or because of what he heard from another archaeologist visiting there. Something to that effect. Thought this 'great thing' was tied to up here."

"In Wisconsin?"

"Yeah."

"The Anasazi? In Wisconsin?"

Peter shook his head.

"No, the Mayans. Edgar's specialty was the Anasazi, but he got onto an ancient Mayan kick because of what he heard or came across when he and Papa were together. He was like a father to Gregor, you know? Edgar's the one who encouraged him to go after his doctorate. They go way back."

Annja straightened, cradling the phone against her face with both hands. "And you argued about… Mayans?"

"In Wisconsin."

"You argued about Mayans *in* Wisconsin?"

"No. No. No. Not exactly. We argued about fringe archaeology. About not being taken seriously. Edgar thought this Mayan revelation would be his glorious find, get him into the history books, get him on television, in *Newsweek* and *Archaeology Today*. Make him and Papa famous. What was it he said to me…? Something to mark his presence on the planet, something to prove he mattered, something to leave behind. I told him it would make him a laughingstock. That's what we argued about. I told him everyone would call him a fool."

"How bad of an argument?"

He shrugged.

"Bad enough to be overheard, obviously, Peter."

"Well, yes. Or I wouldn't be sitting here and wearing this. I stupidly said I ought to bash his fool head in, or was going to bash his fool head in. It was the heat of the moment. That the medical examiner is claiming a cracked skull killed him doesn't look too good for me, huh? They tell me she's changing her report from accidental death to homicide."

"You have no alibi?"

"Depends on what time they think he died, I guess. I was with…someone…for part of last night. And it depends on whether she'll admit she was with me." He hunched forward, like a turtle tucking into its shell. "She's married."

"This Mayan thing, Peter, do you think someone would kill Edgar over that?"

"Ha!" Peter rolled his eyes. "Seriously? Edgar was an old idiot. It was crazy stuff. He and Gregor thought they'd—"

"He's dead, you know, Dr. Papadopoulos."

"Papa, I know. Of a heart attack in his sleep. He should've watched his diet, exercised."

"What about Mrs. Hapgood? Does she have anything to do with Mayans in Wisconsin?" Was she Peter's potential alibi?

Another burst of laughter. This time Peter threw back his head and his shoulders shook. Annja couldn't tell if he was laughing hard or if he had started to cry.

"Peter…Edgar is dead. Dr. Papadopolous is dead. And your friend Mrs. Hapgood is in the hospital."

"Coincidence," he said, head still back. "All this in one weekend, coincidence." He sucked in a big breath, held it, then released it in a whoosh. "My friend Annja Creed. My dear friend Annja Creed wants to connect dots when there's nothing to connect. Coincidence. My dear friend Annja Creed wants to know about the Mayans and Edgar's mysterious find. I'm here in a damnable jail cell, maybe facing murder charges, and she wants to know about the Mayans. What a dear, dear friend I have in Annja—"

"Peter!" Annja spit his name out furiously. "I'm here to help you! But I can't help you if I don't know what's going on. I had to know what the argument was about. Why the police suspect you. I can't help you—" and I can't avenge Edgar, she thought "—if I don't have enough information."

"Fair enough. No, Elyse Hapgood has nothing to do with Mayans and she'd just met Edgar in the lobby yesterday. Coincidence. An unfortunate coincidence." Peter looked at her. "Also unfortunate is me being here." His eyes were red and puffy. He swallowed hard and nodded. "Sorry for barking at you, Annja. Bad mood. Jail does that to you. False accusations do that to you."

And my aching head isn't helping me, she thought. "Do you have an attorney?"

"I picked one out of the Yellow Pages. Nice advertisement. Nice picture. On the young side, probably good judging by her fees. She'll be here in—" He looked at the clock on the wall. It was covered with a mesh cage. "About an hour."

"Do you need me to call anyone for you?"

"I'd like to know if Elyse is okay." He snickered, but it was a sad, nervous laugh. "Other than that, no. I think enough people already know all about this. A few hundred of them back at the hotel. And their wives and husbands and children and neighbors. Probably my neighbors by now, too. Soon they'll all be passing my mug shot around. Ain't the internet grand?"

"I'll see if I can find out anything about Mrs. Hapgood for you." She gave him a rueful smile and picked through the rest of her questions, deciding what to pose next. "Peter, I—"

But she didn't have the opportunity. A door opened on Peter's side of the room, accompanied by a loud, nasally buzz. A deputy walked in and motioned to him.

"Gotta go," Peter told her, hanging up the receiver.

Annja hung up and stared at the phone.

Where next?

Back to the hotel...

"Miss Creed?"

She turned too abruptly and winced, adding to the ache in her head. "Detective Rizzo."

"Manny'll do." He gave her a lopsided grin. "Your friend tell you much?"

Had he been listening? "Too much and not enough." She shifted on the stool so she could look directly at him. He'd changed clothes since this morning, a different shirt, no jacket. "Can you recommend a car-rental place, Detective?"

"Going somewhere?"

Yes, she thought. But where? What was her next step? "I prefer it to calling another cab."

"I can give you a lift. Save you the time and the money."

"Back to my hotel?" She intended to poke around there for clues and answers.

"Actually, I was thinking Lakeside." His face took on a serious mien.

"Lakeside? Where is—"

"Professor Schwartz was there, stayed for a couple of days before he ended up at the bottom of the stairwell. Hotel records said he'd been a guest of theirs on and off over the past year."

Annja stood.

"A fellow by the name of Gregor Papadopoulos was there with him this last time and one time before," Detective Rizzo continued. "Damned interesting, eh? So I think I'll check it out. Not far from here. Care to join me?"

"What about your partner, Lieutenant Greene?"

"Arnie's back at the hotel. The conference breaks up Sunday night, Monday morning. Only got two and a half days before all those archaeologists spread to the winds. He's giving me what he thinks is the grunt end of this. He's taking the cushy side in the air-conditioned hotel."

"Lakeside," Annja repeated.

"It's about thirty-five minutes from here, less if I push it. Just off I-94. And I tend to push it. I won't ask again."

She nodded. "Absolutely."

He thrust out a folder. It was the one that had been in Edgar's room.

"I'll drive. You can read." He held the door open for her. "And you can buy us a couple of sodas from the machine on the way out. I want one with caffeine."

Annja gladly reached into her pocket for a handful of coins. A dose of caffeine might be good for her, too.

9

The Asian woman in the tight green dress was not here for the conference. She clung to Garin as they stood on the lawn across the street from the Madison Arms, pretending to admire the capitol building.

"I'm hungry," she told him, clicking her manicured red nails against his plastic-coated name badge. "You went to lunch without me."

"You were still in bed, sweet Keiko. And you eat so little anyway. Like a bird."

She pouted. "I'm bored, Gary. You said I'd have something to do while you were at this convention. All these anthropologists—"

"Archaeologists, Keiko."

"They're boring. So many of them are…old."

Not nearly as old as I, he thought.

She playfully entwined her fingers with a loose strand of his hair. "Can't we go see something?" She leaned close and whispered into his ear. "A movie? A dirty one? Is there a zoo? I adore penguins." She sucked in her lower lip. "No, not the zoo. It might rain, and I just had my hair done. We could go to a mall with boutiques. I love to shop. Somewhere, Gary. Please?"

He'd met Keiko in Chicago, where he'd been for the previous two weeks on business. A waitress at a restaurant he frequented, he'd taken her back to his hotel one night, and she'd been returning there ever since.

Garin appreciated athletic and inventive young women, and so Keiko had been a fine distraction. But he didn't need her to be a distraction now. He reached deep into his pants pocket and pulled out a small clear envelope filled with white powder. He pressed it into her hand. "This should ease the boredom."

She smiled wickedly. "Share it with me?"

"Not now. I'm meeting a man here, and then there are a few lectures I intend to catch."

She pouted, but he could tell it was a put-on face. "All right, Gary. I'll go to our room and *ease the boredom*." This last she said trying to parrot his voice. She tilted up on tiptoe and kissed his ear. "And then maybe I'll go shopping by myself and spend a lot of your money."

He listened to the gentle *shoosh* of traffic behind him, slowing, probably due to the light changing, and then in the lull he heard Keiko's shoes *click clack* across the pavement as she returned to the hotel.

Garin stood motionless for several minutes and took in the other sounds. A jackhammer started up somewhere out of sight, chewing into asphalt; honking—taxis everywhere had the same tone, it seemed; the faint burst of a siren that just as quickly stopped; the laughter of a child playing nearby on the grass in the shadow of her mother. Madison sounded "wholesome," at least on this cloud-scattered day. Wholesome and a little…he used Keiko's favorite word… boring. But he read the news and knew that here, in front of the capitol building, there were rollicking protests…over government, taxes and whatever other causes stirred up the residents. Campouts in the rotunda. Often they played out on the national networks. And there was the university, with its notorious Halloween weekend to consider. Still, the city seemed rather decent; the kind of place boring people could raise boring families, could grow old and die and decay beneath the earth.

He watched the little girl. She'd scooped up a long green beetle and studied it, smiling and letting it walk from one of her fingers to the next. A burst of giggles, and she squeezed it between her thumb and forefinger, and brushed the pieces away.

"Over there." A man who'd crossed from the hotel strode past Garin, indicating a bench under a sad-looking honey locust.

Garin waited a few beats before following him.

The mother called to the little girl, took her hand and left the lawn to follow the sidewalk deeper into the city. A cloud overhead brightened with a sliver of lightning, followed by a quiet rumble of thunder.

"Willamar," Garin said as he joined the man on the bench, a comfortable space between them. The other benches were occupied, these with capitol employees who had brought their lunches outside.

The man's name tag read W. Aeschelman, marking him as a participant at the archaeology conference. He saw Garin looking at the badge and unclipped it and put it in his pocket. "I don't suppose I need this here."

"No," Garin agreed, taking his own off and palming it.

"I recognized you immediately from the description they sent me," Aeschelman said. "You stand out in this crowd, Gary Knight. My associates said you have attended our gatherings in New York and overseas."

"I've been to a few." Garin had not signed up for the conference with his real name, nor had he given it to Keiko. "Aeschelman." Garin drew out the surname. "Your family is from the Aeschel Valley at the Swiss–German border."

"My grandfather," Aeschelman admitted. "How would you know that?"

"I know Germany." Garin pinched the bridge of his nose hard, as if that twinge of pain might push away a memory. Garin was born in Germany, bastard son of a knight who had little to do with him. He found more of a father figure in the company of an old man who sometimes claimed to be a wizard. *"Wir Deutschen tun unsere arbeit im schatten hell Wisconsin sonne, ja?"*

"I don't really know Germany," Aeschelman returned. "And I don't speak German."

"Pity. Though some consider the tongue guttural, I think it the most beautiful language." And a beautiful country, though Garin thought it better five centuries ago.

They sat quietly as a woman leading a dozen teenagers walked past. She pointed at the capitol building. It was probably one of those tours students were forced to take at the tail end of the school year, Garin mused.

"The capitol's architect, George Browne Post, graduated in 1858 from New York University." Her delivery was monotone, as if she'd spoken it too many times. "It remains the tallest building in the city."

Garin thought of Keiko, who would have called the tour guide boring.

"Many pieces are being exchanged this weekend, most of them small and easy to transport. Several of them quite rare and exceptional. I'm looking forward to this auction," Aeschelman said after the tour group was well beyond them. "Some very rare things, actually."

"I'm looking for one item in particular. I emailed you about it."

"And I am assured it is among what has already been secured."

Garin's palms itched with anticipation.

"What you want is likely not the most costly of the offerings this time, but pricey nonetheless, I'm sure."

Money didn't matter to Garin. It came and went. He'd lost and gained fortunes and was currently flush. "I want to see it first, a private viewing before it's up for auction."

"The pieces are coming in tomorrow. Though hopefully, what I am looking for will be acquired today."

"How many buyers?"

"Only eight besides yourself and myself, so ten in all. Two of them are attending the conference as we are. One is acting as a broker, doesn't have the resources himself. But his patron is well-heeled. I have nothing to sell this time. Like you, I am just buying." Aeschelman leaned forward, elbows on his knees. "There was to be one more buyer."

Garin knew the number of buyers would be low this venture; the fewer people involved, the less chance their illicit business would draw attention. In larger cities, especially in Europe and in Japan, a few dozen serious collectors would be invited, and the bidding wars could be fierce. Garin had attended several of the "meetings" and had purchased small, expensive things to ingratiate himself with the market and the people who ran it. Nothing he particularly wanted, but it was all a means to get him in deeper and thereby eventually get what he was really after, which according to Aeschelman would be within his grasp tomorrow.

"One of the archaeologists who died?"

Aeschelman didn't answer.

Garin waited a moment, then asked, "Where will this take place? The auction?"

Aeschelman lowered his voice. With the traffic sounds and the jackhammer and a radio one of the picnickers had turned on, Garin could scarcely hear him. He leaned closer. "In a large hotel suite, Governor's Club level, during the banquet. Not everyone at the conference attends those things, meal functions—expensive and dull and only three choices of entrées."

"Enough people there, enough people absent," Garin observed. "So none of those actually attending the conference will be missed either way."

"Precisely."

"You said there was to be one other," Garin pressed. "What about—" He raised an eyebrow, always curious, leaving his question hanging. He wanted to know which one of the fallen attendees had been involved in—and now removed from—the competition.

"A mistake, Mrs. Elyse Hapgood," Aeschelman returned. "She made a mistake."

"The woman from this morning?" Garin watched the tour guide lead the teenagers up the capitol steps.

She was still pointing to this and that, still lecturing. Thunder rumbled again. "Who took—"

"I took care of her."

"Poison? Did you use poison?"

"It's only detectable in autopsies, tissue samples, and only in the best labs if it is done quickly. Never shows up in the blood. It degrades fast, and so it will be gone by the time the Madison coroner makes the first cut. Usually they chalk it up to a heart attack or stroke."

"So she's dead, this Mrs. Hapgood."

"Not yet. Two more hours at best, I should think." Aeschelman flexed his fingers. "That's the beauty of it. The stuff draws the death out long enough—"

"—so that the poison is gone by the time it is over."

"Yes," Aeschelman said. "There is nothing for the coroner to find. I've used it a few times before. I use any means, Mr. Knight, to get what I want."

"And you poisoned her…why?" Garin rested the back of his neck against the top rung of the bench. Aeschelman was dangerous in daring to admit this to him. Garin nearly asked why he would do such an imprudent thing and draw the attention of Annja Creed. "Why eliminate Mrs. Hapgood's pocketbook?"

"Pity I had to do it. She had provided many items for our auctions in the past. I purchased one of her Babylonian demon jars a year ago. She provided us another demon jar this weekend. Intact. She was more of a provider than a buyer. She knew how to acquire things and give us leads for rare pieces."

"Then why—" Garin persisted. He wouldn't ask again, not wanting to provoke Aeschelman. Yet he had the sense that the man wanted to talk about it.

"In the end, I felt we had more to lose by keeping her. I wanted to be rid of her, that's all. I just wanted to be rid of her." Aeschelman stood and rubbed his hands on the sides of his pants, retrieved his name tag and looked toward the hotel. Then he squinted up at the darkening sky. "I wanted to be rid of her because she was talking. Talking. Talking. Talking. I was the one who invited her into our circle, and so it was on me to do something about her. She had connections and leads, most certainly. But she also had a big mouth. I overheard her discussing with a few of the other archaeologists yesterday on the mounds outing, dancing much too close to the topic of our circle. Couldn't let her keep talking, you understand."

"I completely understand," Garin said. So Aeschelman's confession was actually a warning to him: play by the rules or don't play at all. Keep the artifact smuggling ring a secret or die. But Aeschelman didn't know Garin had his own set of rules, and poison or guns or any other sort of lethal weapon would not truly hurt him. "I understand completely, Willamar."

"Good, Mr. Knight. You were recommended to me, but I do not know you."

"Some of your associates do."

"Yes, they say you favor medieval relics. I just want to make it clear that we are a clandestine group."

"Crystal." The dying woman was of no concern to Garin, but he suspected Annja would meddle. Three deaths at the conference would be too much of a mystery for her to ignore, and she would wrongly think that they were connected. "I want a good look at it. Beforehand. I want to make certain it's real before I spend my money."

"Everything within our little circle is real, Mr. Knight. You should know that by now." Aeschelman reached under his collar and tugged out a leather cord. A gold disk hung from it, twice the size of a silver dollar and thick, gleaming despite the gloomy day. Similar in appearance to an Olympic medal, but clearly made of real gold, Garin imagined it must feel heavy hanging from the man's neck. It was shiny and smooth, and the image of a beautiful bird had been pressed into the center of it. "This is real. I acquired it Thursday night from an archaeologist Mrs. Hapgood told me about. He was not able to come to the conference this weekend, but a few of his acquisitions will be available. Not this one, though. This one I am keeping for myself."

"The medallion is striking."

"And genuine. Everything within our circle is all real, I assure you."

"Your medallion, is that—"

"Mayan, Mr. Knight." Aeschelman tucked it back under his shirt and extended his hand. Garin shook it. "I will let you know when the items arrive tomorrow. You will get a close look at what you're interested in. A private viewing, as you—and your money—have requested." He turned away and walked toward the Madison Arms, pausing only to wait for a break in the traffic.

Garin waited several minutes, listening to the thunder, watching the people gather up the remainder of their lunches and scurry into the capitol as the first big drops of rain fell.

Garin didn't mind the rain.

He crossed the street at a leisurely pace, his palms still itching in anticipation.

10

The soda went down fast, the caffeine lessening her headache, but not chasing it away entirely. Food—that would do the trick. Annja was famished, having eaten little at breakfast and not yet found time for lunch. She was so hungry her fingers faintly trembled. Hopefully, she and the detective would stop for a bite in Lakeside. "Linner," Rembert called it, a late lunch/early dinner. It would give her an opportunity to better look at the material in the folder. She'd call Rembert then, let him know where she was.

It was onerous to read in the unmarked Impala. The rain had started just as they left the station, intermittent big fat drops plopping heavily against the windows. They hadn't traveled more than a handful of blocks before the sky opened up. The hammering rain and slapping, dragging wipers—which were in need of replacing—made it difficult to concentrate.

Some pages were printouts with food smudges in the margins; some newspaper clippings with tiny type—about two unsolved murders, judging from the headlines; an assortment of note paper of various sizes—all with Edgar's handwriting on them and more smudges. There was a photocopy of an old fishing map, with words scrawled on it that were so small they were impossible to read with the car moving and the rain coming sideways now. Difficult to read practically anything at all except the large print, the way Detective Rizzo kept changing lanes and speeding and slowing, tires sluicing with the deluge.

But what she could make out intrigued her—sketches of Mayan symbols—birds, creatures that were half man, half jaguar, feathers, suns—and Edgar's annotations all around them. *Lakeside* was circled at the bottom of one page, along with names and phone numbers that at the moment were undecipherable.

"Why are you letting me see this?"

Detective Rizzo didn't answer immediately, changing lanes instead and adjusting his rearview mirror. They were a few miles beyond the edge of the city now, headed east. "I figured you'd want to…being a close friend of Professor Schwartz's and all. I remembered you telling me that, more than once, about the 'close friend' part."

"What about your regulations and Lieutenant Greene?"

He shrugged, his shoulders seeming too broad for the car.

"Are you going to get in trouble for taking me with you?" She liked the detective and it concerned her that her presence might cause problems for him.

"'Cause I didn't bother having you sign any papers for a ride-along?" He snorted. "I've filled out more than my share of paperwork."

"I'd just hate—"

"For me to get my wrinkled ass handed to me? Lady, I'm sixty-six, the oldest officer on the whole damn force, and the higher-ups have finally coaxed me into retiring. Suggested I be reassigned to nothing but desk duty if I don't hang it up. So I put in my request. I've got exactly two weeks until my retirement party, where I'll—"

"—turn in your badge and gun."

He grinned. "Nah, the badge is a keepsake. Once you get a badge with a number on it, well, it stays with you through your whole life. It gets retired along with you. And as for the gun." He patted the one in his shoulder holster. "The Glock is my personal sidearm."

"I bet it will be a good party." She returned to examining the contents of the folder.

"Same day as my birthday—sixty-seventh. Saves them the expense of two cakes. No, I'm not too worried about regulations at this point." He paused and changed lanes again. "I do, however, give a very big whoop about solving the murders of two archaeologists…maybe three depending on what happens with that Mrs. Hapgood. Nice note to go out on, don't you think? Solving a double? Or a triple? Might get me a commendation or some such, picture in the paper and all of that. Might show Lieutenant Greene that age and smarts can win out over youth and pigheadedness." His expression paled slightly. "No offense to you, Miss Creed, about the youth part. But this'd be a fine note for my swan song."

"Call me Annja, Detective Rizzo."

"Only if you call me Manny."

"All right, Manny." She pawed through more of the documents, finding a yellowed dot-matrix printout that seemed to have some age to it. A sentence was highlighted, and when she gripped the paper hard and brought it up to her face, she managed to read: "Three Mayan pyramids at the bottom of Rock Lake." Then she and the words were bouncing again, as Detective Rizzo swerved the unmarked Impala around a semi and stomped on the accelerator.

"Where is Rock Lake?"

He smiled. "It sits right next to Lakeside, which is the town. Rock Lake is the…well, Rock Lake is the lake. And from all this rain, I'd say it's turning into a huge lake."

She tried to read more of the printout, but it was a lost cause. She would insist they stop for "linner" so she could get a better look at the material.

He leaned down to reach a small computer that rested low on the dash between the front seats. He typed in some numbers, all the while dividing his attention between the screen and the highway ahead.

"Damn computers." He looked ready to punch it, but he shut it off, grabbed the radio and brought the mic up, calling the central dispatch. "Run a check for me, will you? It's an Iowa plate." He dictated the SUV's plate number.

Annja noticed that Detective Rizzo's gaze shot back and forth between the rearview mirror and the road ahead. "We're being followed?" She'd been so absorbed, trying to read Edgar's folder.

"Have been since we left the station a block or so behind. Wasn't sure about it, though, until we were out of the city. Car stays with us with all the weaving, matches my speed."

The radio crackled a couple of seconds later with an answer, the woman's voice taut. "Queried the plate and got a hit on NCIC. I'm showing that as an active stolen out of Cedar Rapids, date of entry on the twelfth. Vehicle should be a white Chrysler Sebring convertible."

"Interesting," Detective Rizzo returned. "Louise, those plates are on a gray Ford Explorer that's dogging my wrinkled ass. Request backup ten-eighteen from either the county or state patrol, whoever has the nearest marked units."

11

Detective Rizzo spoke louder into the mic again as thunder boomed. "I'm on I-94. We're…oh, hell, I can't read the mile marker for all this rain…. I'm approaching the Marshall exit. Copy?" He thumbed the mic again. "Copy? I'm in a blue Impala." He put the mic back, placed both hands on the wheel and changed lanes again. "Don't know if she heard me. Nearly out of radio range here."

Annja tried to decipher the chatter on the radio, but it sounded like static. She shut the folder, slid it under her seat and craned her neck to see out the back window.

The Ford Explorer was the shade of gunmetal. There were two men inside, the driver tall, his head brushing the roof of the SUV, the passenger shorter, his face fully visible but the features barely discernable because of the rain and the wipers. He had on sunglasses—despite the gloom—and a Milwaukee Brewers baseball cap; she could see the logo because the Explorer was so close it rode the Impala's bumper. The men had to be connected to all of this, right? The image of her sword appeared in her mind and again she almost had the sensation of the pommel in her hand. A warning? Intuition? She thought of Edgar, Gregor, Mrs. Hapgood, and her throat tightened. And the presence of Garin…that was disturbing, too.

"I don't have enough of the pieces yet." Annja hadn't meant to say that aloud, thinking of a giant jigsaw puzzle. She needed more information to get a better idea of what the puzzle should look like when completed.

"Well, either they—or we—are going to be in pieces," Detective Rizzo spat. "Unless the sheriff or state police get some units here fast." He flipped on the Impala's sirens, the light on the dashboard pulsing with an eerie bounce against the torrent of water. "If nothing else, this should get traffic out of our way. Don't need anyone getting hurt."

The Explorer's front bumper slid up over the top of the Impala's rear one and gave it a violent shove.

"Damn it," Detective Rizzo cursed. He reached for the mic again. "Dispatch, I need those units ten-thirty-three. Copy?"

There was a squelching sound.

"Copy?"

"Oh, for…" He put the mic back.

Annja saw the Explorer driver smiling, big white teeth under a dark mustache; a shiver danced down her spine. She was about to offer the detective a driving suggestion, but then realized she didn't need to.

The detective veered to the right, breaking free of the Explorer, and floored it. There was a stretch of highway ahead with no cars on it. There were, however, cars pulled over on the shoulder, the drivers waiting out the worst of the storm and observing the siren and lights.

Annja knew that driving in weather like this was treacherous, magnified tenfold by the Explorer's maniac driver.

"They're faster. Those SUVs," he said. "Higher center of gravity. I should've taken one of the Crown Vics. I like a heavier car." He jogged to his right, then left, the car spinning sideways, doing a one-eighty before he turned it around and headed straight east again. The Explorer slowed to keep the Impala in front of it. "Not enough fast, these sedans." He slapped his hand on the steering wheel, cranking it right when there was a long gap between cars. "Not letting me get behind her, either. If I could get behind her…"

The Impala slid, water spraying up on the passenger's side as if they were taking it through a car wash. Annja couldn't see out the back anymore, just a glow from the Explorer's headlights, and she barely made anything out through the front. She wasn't immortal. She could bleed and die…and could very well do that here on a highway in Wisconsin. Again she saw the sword hanging suspended in her mind. But Joan of Arc's blade couldn't save her from this hellish car chase. What would happen to the sword if she perished here?

The Explorer rammed the Impala again. Annja's head whipped forward, her chin hitting her breastbone and the seat belt digging into her chest.

"Good thing the air bags haven't popped yet. We'd be toast." The Impala roared forward, sending water flying in all directions, the tires barely holding to the pavement. Manny was as far forward as the seat belt and steering wheel allowed. The fingers of Annja's hands gripped the dashboard, knuckles bone-white.

She'd been frightened before so very many times, but this time she wasn't in control of the situation. She could do nothing but sit back and worry. Her heartbeat thundered in her ears, and it felt as if her stomach had jumped up into her throat. Annja realized what an expert driver the detective was. She would be doing no better under these horrid conditions.

Actually, she was quite certain she would be doing worse and that she and the Impala would be scattered bits being washed away by the pounding rain on I-94.

He let up on the gas as they approached a low spot on the highway that looked as if it had a river running across it. Once through the deep puddle of water, he accelerated again.

"Where's the damn sheriff's department?" The detective reached a hand toward the mic and then stopped. The Explorer bumped the Impala again. He grabbed the wheel with both hands, but the Impala skidded at an angle, slipping off the highway and hitting the shoulder, gravel spitting against the undercarriage. He fought with the car and got it straightened out again and brought it back up onto the road. "Do you hear sirens?" he asked Annja. He flipped off the Impala's siren. "Other than ours?"

"No." She ground her teeth together. This time when the Explorer struck them, the Impala veered toward the left.

He turned his siren back on. "You got a gun, Annja?"

Why would the detective think that? "No!" Annja shouted to be certain he could hear her.

"Can you shoot?"

"Yes!"

"Well?"

"What?"

"Can you shoot well?"

"Yes!"

"Behind the seat. There's a rifle. Can you shoot a rifle?"

He banked the Impala right and drew the Explorer into the left lane and away from the cars parked on the right shoulder. Annja undid her seat belt, twisted and reached behind the seat, fingers searching and finding a case. She twisted farther; her knees on the cushion, she reached over the back and unzipped the case, tugging out the rifle carefully.

She rolled down the window, the rain angrily hitting her face like hundreds of pinpricks, and leaned out, leading with the rifle and trying to get a bead on the Explorer.

"No cars here! Go for it!" the detective shouted, still pressed as far forward as he could manage. He took the Impala into the left lane now, drawing the Explorer to Annja's side. "Shoot out a tire! Try not to shoot them. Too damn much paperwork if you shoot them! A tire!"

Annja took aim, holding the gun tightly, and fired. She held steady as the rifle bucked. Missed, but close. A spark of light showed she'd hit the bumper.

"Damn it all to St. Louis!" the detective spat as he struggled to keep the car on the road. At the same time he tapped the brakes, and the Explorer shot past them. "Finally," he said. "Finally we're behind her. Don't drop that gun!"

Annja heard a siren. "There's a—"

"Yeah, yeah, I hear it. Old, not deaf," he quipped. "Oh, will you look at that—"

The Explorer had cut across the median and was swinging around to come up behind the Impala once more. So fast and reckless a U-turn the detective elected not to try to stay on its tail.

Annja regained her purchase out the window as the detective steered the protesting Impala far into the left lane. If the Explorer wanted to run them off the road, it would have to come up on Annja's side again.

She was soaked, and her eyes were mere slits against the rain and wind. Still, she managed to focus just enough. One shot, the recoil and the wind nearly making her lose her perch. The second shot hit a front tire, but again she saw the wide white smile.

And the Explorer kept coming. Annja was ready for it, and despite wet fingers, kept a firm grip on the gun. She fired at the same tire. The Explorer came up farther on the Impala's right. The detective turned the wheel hard into the SUV, and Annja fired one more time—on the mark. Its tire finally blew, pieces of rubber stripping away from the rim like snakes flailing madly.

The Explorer rocketed out of control across the lanes and vaulted over the shoulder toward the guardrail. The Impala slowed and slid to the side of the road, the detective pumping the brakes.

Annja heard the metal guardrail scream before it snapped and gave way to the crashing SUV. She leaned farther out the window to watch the vehicle carom down the small, steep embankment, the front end striking the bottom and causing it to flip at an odd angle, like a child's toy tipped onto its side. The detective drove onto the shoulder and put on his flashers, the police lights continuing to pulse.

"Sheriff or troopers should find us now," he said.

The sirens were louder and she caught a glimpse of flashing lights coming up behind them through the sheet of rain. Annja pulled herself back into the car just long enough so she could reach down and open her door. The detective grabbed the rifle from her and tossed it into the back.

"You never fired this," he told her. "Understand?"

She was outside before him and sliding fast down the embankment, heading toward the Explorer, sword appearing in her hand. Had she called Joan's legendary blade? Or was it reflex? No matter. Racing into trouble, it had joined her. The pommel felt good against her skin, the blade hidden in all this rain; she didn't worry that the detective would see it.

The Explorer was lying silent. There was no sound, no movement. It took only a second before Annja smelled the gasoline.

"The fuel line!" she hollered, not bothering to look behind her to see where the detective was. The busted fuel-injection system must be pumping gas onto the hot engine. Spirals of smoke rose in the rain. "Stay back, Manny! Stay back!" In spite of the downpour a fire began. "Stay back!"

She ran what she judged to be a safe distance away and dropped to a crouch, mud oozing up around her ankles. From her vantage spot she saw the Explorer explode, the driver's side door flying up as if it had been shot out of a canon. Pieces of glass flew through the air, glittering red with blood. Chunks of metal also flew, propelled like deadly shrapnel as the fire fought against the storm to eat through what remained of the SUV.

Annja had expected screams from the men trapped inside the fireball, but the crash and explosion had happened so fast. She hoped they had perished before the flames got them, though at the same time she was furious that she couldn't get a close look at them, that she couldn't have saved them and demanded they tell her what this was about.

She dismissed the sword. Her fingers fluttered over the tall plants and grass. There was something oddly pleasant in the sensation. She watched the flames lick at the metal husk, the rain batter everything. In the back of her mind she pictured Joan of Arc burning in fire.

Steam rose from the car and spread out over the field like a blanket of early-morning fog. She listened to crackles and pops, hisses, the tat-a-tat of the storm, to the siren…two sirens, three, four…that grew louder still and then stopped. In fact, it hadn't taken the sheriff's deputies and state patrol long to get here. Everything had happened so quickly.

Two lives snuffed out in a handful of minutes. She stood, the mud grabbing at her feet. Detective Rizzo huffed up beside her. Out of breath, he leaned forward and put his big hands on his knees.

"Too old for this," he said. "Forget what I said about the sheriff being able to find us now. Aliens from space could see this fire. Too damn old for all of this."

"But at least we're going to get older," Annja told him. "You're a great driver, Manny. I thought we were going to get plastered on the highway."

He nodded toward the burning car. "It's going to be

some time before we find out who they were. Dental records, stolen plates, all of it black." He turned and slogged back toward the highway, his breath coming out ragged.

Annja watched the fire for a few more minutes. The rain was slowly winning out. She looked over her shoulder and saw the detective struggle up the embankment, pulling himself by grabbing onto vines and weeds. She waited several minutes more while he talked to the sheriff's deputies and state troopers. Another state police car pulled up; six cars total had lights bouncing around through the gloom. Then, satisfied that gaining any information right now from the Explorer and the charred bodies was useless, she returned to the highway.

Surprisingly, the Impala hadn't suffered a lot of damage.

She scraped her feet against a piece of guardrail to pry off the mud.

"I suppose we're headed back into Madison," she said.

"Yeah," Manny replied. "Medical examiner is on the way. This is a crime scene, and that means we're actually not going anywhere until we've answered a whole lot of questions."

Annja overheard a state trooper on a cell phone talking to the Madison Police Department. "One of your officers, a Detective Manolito Rizzo, has been involved in a lethal-force incident outside his jurisdiction."

"Oh, hell," Manny said. "We're gonna be here forever. I hate paperwork." He pointed to the thick scratches on the Impala and the crooked and dented rear bumper. "Gonna have paperwork for this, too. A big damn tree worth of paper for all of this."

Annja's stomach rumbled, but she knew no one could hear it over the radio chatter and rain.

12

A reporter from the *Wisconsin State Journal* was the first to arrive. His photographer was in tow, a thirty-something redhead Garin thought attractive enough to approach…were the circumstances a little different. The reporter was immediately shooed out of the ballroom, which had been divided by ceiling-high accordion panels into three lecture halls.

Garin was taking it all in and watching it unfold. The conference organizer had established the rules. He wouldn't let any reporters into the seminars—unless they purchased a full conference membership, and then they were to observe a modicum of professionalism. But they were welcome to remain in the lobby, hallways, the restaurants and the sidewalk out front, interviewing whichever conference attendees were willing to give them the time of day. The organizer himself declined to comment.

The *Journal* reporter went to work, hitting up one after the next—anyone with a conference badge—and taking notes, indicating who he wanted the redhead to get shots of. Garin had not yet put his own badge back on, and therefore was apparently not a viable target.

As the minutes ticked by, he noticed an unusually

large number of cars and vans pull up. Local television reporters from the look of them, making sure each hair was in place and that they got as little rain on them as possible.

The logo on the side of a VW Beetle that stopped out front was small, *Althouse,* and Garin almost missed it. He found out minutes later it was a local blogger, as was the woman from *The Critical Badger* who arrived soon after. Young, thickset and dressed in browns, he mused that she looked like her blog's namesake.

Something must have hit the scanners about the deaths at the conference, or maybe an item had appeared on the police blotter that caught the media's hungry eye. It didn't matter what had drawn them—Garin considered the very presence of the media inconvenient…and wholly to be avoided on his part.

Garin noticed that most of the archaeologists looked put off by all the media attention, several of them grumbling that it was ruining the conference.

A television news reporter announced herself to a hawk-nosed woman, who had apparently emerged from one of the divided rooms to see what the commotion was.

"I am Katrina Jacoby here at the Great Lakes States Archaeological Conference in Madison, and I am speaking this afternoon with—" She put her recorder under the woman's hawk nose.

"Dr. Olivia Rouse."

Garin took the staircase up to the second floor, stepping past a fresh-faced, gangly-looking reporter trying to interview unsuspecting guests. The newsman looked young enough to be delivering papers rather than writing for them. Garin was both amused and irritated by all the activity, and hoped it would go away soon. Ahead of him, a prudish-looking woman in her late forties held a notebook. He couldn't tell if she was a reporter or with the conference. She opened her mouth to say something to him, but he brushed by.

He went down the hall, found the room he was looking for, slipped inside and put on his badge. A few minutes late, he'd missed the start of the session. He selected a seat in the last row as far from the door as possible. There were two speakers: the program listed them as a husband-wife team from Milwaukee who had just returned from France, part of a dig team from a small site.

Joan of Arc had been burned within a few miles of their Rouen workplace. Garin pinched the bridge of his nose; another memory he tried to unsuccessfully push to the back of his mind.

"She remains a significant figure to all of Western civilization," the woman lectured. "The French, from politicians to clergy to writers, all invoke her name. Even our own Mark Twain—"

Garin studied the other attendees. He thought he might see Annja here, the topic hitting close to home. Perhaps she thought it all old hat and that this pair could teach her nothing that she hadn't already learned on her own or from Roux or himself.

There were only two dozen men and women in the chairs, though the room could hold easily three times that many. According to the revised program, this lecture was up against seminars about Native Americans, Early Mississippi River Culture and Technological Tools for Today's Archaeologists—perhaps topics more appealing to the bulk of the attendees.

Garin moved up a row, directly behind someone he vaguely recognized.

"Yes, our own Mark Twain wrote about Joan of Arc," the woman continued. She hit a few keys on her laptop, and a scene from their small dig appeared on the screen. "We had the pleasure of working with French archaeologists just outside Rouen, where Saint Joan was burned at the stake for being a heretic."

The rest of the speaker's words did not hold Garin's attention. He had known Joan personally, had served under Roux to protect her, and no matter how deep historians and archaeologists dug and researched, they would never be able to paint a true picture of the Maid of Orleans.

Garin leaned forward, tapped the man's shoulder and whispered. "Are you Annja Creed's cameraman?"

Rembert turned and whispered back. "I'm *a* cameraman. I wouldn't call myself 'hers.' She's not here. She's down at the police station. You'll have to—"

"I don't want to talk to Miss Creed," Garin returned. "I'd like to talk to you. I'll buy you a drink. In the bar downstairs." He looked at his watch. "Say, in two hours. Actually, let's make it an early dinner, an hour from now." There shouldn't be much of a crowd in the restaurant then.

"I saw you talking to Annja earlier. You are—" Rembert's voice rose a little too much and he drew a "Shhhh!" from a man nearby and a stern look from the speakers.

Garin turned his badge so Rembert could read: Gary Knight.

"I may have quite the story for you," Garin whispered. He leaned closer still, so he could read Rembert's badge. "I have something far more interesting than what the media circus is trying to ferret out, Mr. Hayes."

"One hour," Rembert said. "Sure." A pause. "You're buying, right? Dinner and drinks?"

Garin nodded and left as the picture on the screen changed to broken pots the dig team had discovered.

13

"You're buying, right?" Rembert took another glance at the menu. "I'll take the grilled New York strip and a bottle of Guinness stout."

"The glazed ahi tuna," Garin decided. "And bring a bottle of your Laetitia Pinot Noir…with my meal."

"I'll have my Guinness now," Rembert cut in.

The restaurant was busier than Garin had expected it to be at five o'clock. Perhaps the older archaeologists were used to eating early, all those senior-citizen specials that restaurants around the country advertised. No such specials were advertised here. He handed the menu back to the waiter. Fortunately, they had a table against the far wall, with empty ones all around them. Garin had told the waiter they needed privacy for a business meeting.

"So, Mr. Hayes, you're Annja's cameraman for the weekend, but not usually her cameraman. Do I understand that correctly?"

Rembert chortled. "Look, I thought you said you wanted to talk to me, not Annja."

"I do want to talk to you. I only mentioned Annja." Garin studied Rembert's face, finding a mix of emotions he couldn't quite lock down. "I know Annja Creed, and—"

The waiter brought the Guinness and retreated.

"Well, I know her, too. All too well, and that's why I don't usually work with her. It's a long story." Rembert shook his head and poured the stout into his glass and took a big swallow. His smile showed his approval. "I was with her in France and…well, let's just say sometimes things get difficult and dangerous around her. I have a family to consider. And I'm rather fond of my own skin. But things are tough so I'm here shooting some footage *of* her for the producer. All promo stuff."

"All of it?"

Rembert smiled. "Well, I sold some video to one of the local networks. I was here when—"

"—one of the bodies was wheeled out. I saw you recording it."

"Yes. I got some choice pieces. Right place, right time kind of thing." Rembert drew his features together. "You're a curious fellow. You said you had a story for me. Is this for *Chasing History's Monsters?* I'm not working with Annja, not really. But I do lots of other shoots for the channel, some freelance work on the side."

Garin softened his expression in an effort to put Rembert at ease. "No, this isn't for *Chasing History's Monsters*. A silly program, really, and I rarely catch it. This is something you can sell to a network for news, though I suppose your channel might do something with it. It's topical and could earn you a fine turn of coin. Maybe one of the nationals would pick it up. But no, there's no monster in it. Nothing to interest

Annja Creed. To be honest, I would prefer—I would insist—that this remain between you and me." Garin scrutinized Rembert's eyes. As many years as he'd walked the earth, he'd learned how to read men. "Do we have an agreement?"

Rembert looked dead serious and didn't blink. "I don't have to tell Annja. I don't have a problem with that. But I want to know what this is about before I make any promises about anything."

"Ah, a man of integrity." Garin leaned back to let a silence fill the space between them. Despite his words, he doubted Rembert Hayes had much integrity at all; he'd done a little checking, and the man needed money. The need for money made men desperate. And that would make Rembert easy to manipulate.

Garin picked through some of the hushed conversations several tables away—everything seeming to deal with this lecture or that seminar, or speculation about the deaths of three archaeologists. Apparently the woman from this morning had just bitten that proverbial dust. "I appreciate a man of principle, Mr. Hayes."

Rembert finished the stout. "I'm also a man who could use some money."

Garin was surprised at the frankness. Maybe Mr. Hayes was a little more honest than he'd first thought. That pleased him; he found honest men easier to coerce, because at the heart of everything, they tended to be trusting.

"There, it's on the table, Mr. Knight. I need money." Rembert ran his finger around the lip of his glass. It produced the faintest hum: crystal. "But you know that somehow, don't you?"

Garin didn't answer the question. Annja's colleague was astute. Was this one more misstep he was making this weekend, going with an honest *and* astute man? One more chance to tempt fate? First letting Annja know he was here? Bringing Keiko? And now approaching Mr. Hayes? He hadn't thought the man all that savvy. Had his own bravado overpowered his common sense to approach Mr. Hayes? Or had he just gotten a little too reckless with his goals after so many years? He grinned. Maybe he'd been bored lately and was looking to make things interesting.

No matter. He'd started this. He might as well see how it played out. So Rembert Hayes was perceptive—not a trait Garin was looking for in the man, but he could overcome that.

"Mr. Hayes, I don't care what your financial situation is. But if you're selling footage to the networks over a few…deaths…at an archaeology convention, you could profit more with something of considerably greater interest. Death? That happens all the time. But this—"

The waiter brought salads and cracked pepper over the bowls.

"Another Guinness," Rembert said. Then he edged forward, his voice a conspiratorial whisper. "I'm interested. I wouldn't have come here if I wasn't interested. But I don't know anything about you. And I don't know what this is about."

"And you're going to walk away when all of this is done still not knowing anything about me," Garin said as he speared a cherry tomato and popped it into his mouth. The raspberry vinaigrette dressing was delightful. "Other than that I've a penchant for some very old things. A history buff, so to speak. Do you have a problem with that?"

Rembert picked at his salad. "Fine."

"Good." Garin ate the rest of the tomatoes and nudged the salad plate away. He kept his voice low; there was enough space between this table and the nearest occupied ones. No one could hear; but he was still careful. "There is an artifact-smuggling ring operating under the noses of the conference organizers. Some serious artifacts, and the pieces will be sold tomorrow night."

Rembert coughed and grabbed his water glass, downing it to clear his throat. "Smuggling? Illegal, right?"

"Very."

"Like the stuff stolen from the museum in Cairo in the riots?"

Garin was pleased Rembert kept his voice equally quiet. Both men stopped talking when the waiter returned with their meals. The waiter opened the wine and let it breathe. Garin sampled it and nodded his consent, then paused until the waiter left. He continued, "I can't tell you where the artifacts came from, only that they belong in museums. Taken from digs, I'd guess, pocketed and smuggled when they should have been showcased and cared for elsewhere. Most likely archaeologists involved are making some money on the side by not reporting everything they find, by putting a few pieces up for sale. Most archaeologists are scrupulous caretakers of history—like Annja Creed. But not all of them."

Rembert dug into his steak, his eyes closing in obvious pleasure. "And you're telling me this…because?"

"It rankles me," Garin said. In truth, a part of him was bothered by the whole notion of smuggling pieces of history. The larger part of him just wanted to get one up on Annja, to bring to light something that she would have reveled in exposing…had she the opportunity. To get what he wanted and best her all in the same instant. It would paint him as a hero, wouldn't it? Even though he would remain on the sidelines. But more than all of that, he would be getting one up on Roux.

"How do you know about it, this smuggling ring?"

"Not your concern." Garin tasted the grilled ahi, finding it more than acceptable.

"Why come to me?"

"I can go elsewhere." Garin continued to eat. It was as fine a meal as he'd enjoyed in the best restaurants in New York and Paris. And here…in the Midwest… who would have thought it? "And perhaps I should. A newsman from Milwaukee or Chicago or—"

"No need to do that. I said I'm interested." Rembert took another bite of his steak and a long swallow of the stout. "But you're getting something out of this, right?"

"Of course. I always get something out of my endeavors."

They finished their meals and the waiter took their plates.

"Dessert?" Garin asked.

"Yes," Rembert answered as if on autopilot. "Black forest cake."

"The chocolate marquess."

"So what are you getting out of this, Mr. Knight?"

Garin's smile was tight and thin. "I am buying one

of these smuggled relics. I am buying one and you're not interfering with that or recording that transaction. In fact, you'll help. You'll not videotape me or my purchase…if you want to keep that skin of yours that you say you're fond of. But you are free to cover the rest of the sale, revealing whatever participants and whatever antiquities you want. Artifact smuggling is news, Mr. Hayes. Big news. It is certainly the stuff that newspapers and networks would buy from you. Why, your uncovering such a ring, and I know this one has been operating around the world for at the very least a few years…well, you could practically write your own ticket, couldn't you?"

Rembert stared.

"I've looked you up. You're a newsman at heart. You don't need Annja Creed on this. You don't need anyone."

"I don't like the idea that you're going to buy something. That makes you a crook—"

"It makes me a collector."

"I don't like it, but I'm in," Rembert said. "All in."

Garin sat back as the waiter brought the desserts.

"I hope you have a very small video camera, Mr. Hayes. Tiny."

"I'll get one."

"By tomorrow night."

Rembert waved his hand to get the waiter's attention.

"One more stout," he said.

14

"All of it is connected," Manny said. "Dr. Schwartz's murder, Dr. Papadopolous's supposed heart attack and Mrs. Hapgood…whatever the hell killed her."

Annja had overheard the radio chatter about her dying in the hospital's critical-care unit.

"Everything is connected," he repeated.

"Including the men who tried to run us off the road," Annja said.

"Yeah, them. I'd sure like to know why they were after us. Don't have anything that—" The detective's voice trailed off and he ran his hand through his thinning hair. "Well, maybe I do have something. Just have to connect all the dots, so to speak, before two weeks are up."

Two weeks? Annja thought more like two days, with the conference ending this weekend. She didn't have two weeks. In eight days she was scheduled to fly to Morocco to film a segment of *Chasing History's Monsters*. She'd set up interviews, and she wouldn't change those plans.

"Two weeks and I'm out of here, you know."

Annja thought the detective sounded sad about his upcoming retirement.

They took a booth in the cozy diner and glanced at the one-sheet menu.

"Two weeks, after how many years on the force?" She redirected her attention to their waitress. "Two cheeseburgers, one of them a double, no onions."

Annja didn't want to have onion breath in the car with Manny. "A large order of fries, chocolate milk shake and a piece of apple pie, a big one, with cheddar crumbles." She handed the menu back to the waitress. "Oh, instead, nix the milk shake. Bring me two big mugs of hot cocoa. Do you have any?"

"Sure, sweetheart," the waitress said. "We'll fix you some hot chocolate. Do you want whipped cream on it?"

Annja nodded.

"Cola," the detective said, letting the waitress know that Annja's drink order wasn't for the both of them. "Biggest you have, and light on the ice. And…I think I'll have a bowl of your chicken soup and a piece of pie, too. Pecan if you have it, otherwise apple is ducky." He gestured to the counter, where pies were showcased under a glass dome smudged with fingerprints. "Put a scoop of ice cream on my pie. No, put two."

It was a step above a greasy spoon, but not by much in Annja's estimation. It was, however, the first restaurant they'd come to after being thoroughly debriefed by both the state police and the sheriff's department. It was just outside the Lakeside city limits, its blinking sign Open 24/7 catching their attention in the dimming light. The place had a big faded orange-and-yellow canopy out front that extended partway over a lot that also apparently served as a used-car dealership. That part of the business consisted of an array of old and battered cars and motorcycles, a sign on the side of the restaurant reading Everything Runs. He parked as much of the Impala under the canopy as would fit, and he and Annja managed to get out and into the diner without getting any wetter. The rain was coming steadily still, but the wind had settled down.

"Forty-three years," he said in answer to her question. "Signed on after four years in the army and after two in a community college down in Oglesby, Illinois. Associate of Science degree, took a lot of criminal justice courses and found an opening in Madison."

"I don't know if I could stick with anything forty-three years. Congratulations." She raised a water glass to him. Annja had brought Edgar's folder in with her, spreading the bits and pieces out on their table to sort through, all the while her mind reeling with questions about the men who had chased them. No trouble reading anything here; and the only sounds to distract her were minimal—dishes and silverware clinking and rattling behind the counter, and rain still rat-a-tatting outside. Only three other customers, and they sat several booths away. She and Manny no doubt had missed the dinner rush; it was approaching seven o'clock.

"Interesting stuff, isn't it?" the detective asked. "I made copies of everything before lunch, but some of the printouts were so light not everything picked up. So take care, those're all the originals. I'll have to log them back in tomorrow morning." He growled. "Have an appointment with my chief twelve hours from now. Probably gonna hand my wrinkled ass to me over that…well, over that."

Annja knew he meant the whole ordeal on I-94.

She set all the newspaper clippings aside. In the car she'd thought they were about two murders, but apparently there were several deaths—seven, dating back to WWII, all unsolved and all from Lakeside. Spread out over that many years—almost eight decades—it wasn't odd or untoward, other than the fact Edgar had apparently gathered them together. She had no clue as to what they had to do with the rest of the folder, but a part of her believed what Detective Rizzo had voiced: "It's all connected."

She skimmed the news clippings, then put them aside. Then she went onto Edgar's notes and archaeological assumptions, reading quickly, focusing on the fishing map of Rock Lake and the scrawled notations around its sides.

One of the other patrons got up and dropped some coins in the jukebox. Bon Jovi's version of Cohen's "Hallelujah" came on.

"It's important, what you've got there. Important to solving this," Manny said. "Ah, here we go." The waitress set the drinks down.

Manny took a long pull of the soda. "I know it's important because your Professor Schwartz hid it between the mattresses, clearly didn't want someone to find it."

"But you found it."

"Learned a lot over forty years. First place to look is between the mattresses."

She smelled her burgers cooking, the aroma making her mouth water.

"So he was probably killed over it…over something in it," she said. Fringe archeology, that was what

Peter had called Edgar's research. Ridiculous, he'd said. Indeed it smacked of something incredulous to her, and all the odd notes about the Aztalan Park and people missing the bigger picture. She kicked herself for not coming a day earlier and going on the tour of the Native American mounds. If nothing else, she would have met Professor Papadopolous, who apparently was involved with Edgar's discovery. The squiggles of Mayan symbols, latitude and longitude marks. Mayans in Wisconsin? Unbelievable? Maybe not. Maybe something was real enough to get Edgar killed over it, and Papadopolous, too. Annja had seen some pretty preposterous things in her time.

"Annja, I'd wager everything that he was killed over something in that folder."

She turned the pages faster, skimming now and looking for the most relevant pieces. If she could somehow talk the detective into letting her keep the folder tonight, she'd give it a more thorough read. There was a name and a phone number at the edge of the map, and next to it, "Lake diver, $100 an hour, boat included."

"He had someone dive the lake."

"A lot of people dive the lake." Manny signaled for a refill on the cola.

Annja took a break and downed one of the cups of hot cocoa and reached for the second. "And a glass of water, please."

"He really thinks…thought…" She still had trouble believing Edgar was dead. "He really thought there was something in the lake."

"He isn't the only one."

Annja looked up from the paper.

"There *is* something in the lake. Water." Manny laughed. "Just kidding. There were some fishermen lots of years back discovered mounds in the lake. There are more like them, the mounds—above water—at the park."

"Aztalan."

"That's the one. People still dive the lake from time to time, looking for more of the mounds. You read about it in the paper once in a while. But the lake, from what I've heard, isn't an easy dive."

Annja held up a photo of the park clipped from a magazine.

"Still, aren't the mounds Indian, Wisconsin Indian, not Mayan Indian?" Manny grabbed a spoon when the waitress set the bowl of soup in front of him, sloshing some of it on the table. "I've been to the park."

"Out of vanilla ice cream," the waitress said as she plopped down the pie. "Do you want whipped cream?"

He shook his head. "Can't stand whipped cream. This is okay." He started on the soup. Between sips, he said, "That's a lot of food, Annja. You're not gonna stay so skinny if you have many meals like that."

She didn't reply to his comment. Instead she asked, "What will you do, Manny?" Annja reached for her first sandwich.

He cocked his head, his bushy eyebrows arching.

"I don't mean in this…investigation. In two weeks, when you've retired. What will you do?"

"You mean, after I get all the accolades for solving a triple? 'Cause don't let no coroner's report fool you. I'll bet my pension that Mrs. Hapgood was killed, too." He put his soupspoon down and took another drink from his soda glass. "Move to Texas. Already bought a place. Brownsville. Acacia Drive."

"Do you have relatives there?"

His faced clouded momentarily. "Don't have relatives. Well, a brother in Detroit, but we hardly speak. Never married, no kids that I know of."

"So why Brownsville?"

Manny gave her a lopsided grin that she considered his most endearing expression. "Tired of the cold, Annja. Wisconsin winters can be brutal. Searched on the internet and found Brownsville to my liking. Took a trip down there over Easter and chatted with a Realtor. Picked me out a two-bedroom, two-bath ranch, bigger than my house here. Garage, outbuilding, patio, inground pool even, comes with all the appliances, a washer and dryer only three years old. Central air. It's a good neighborhood, too. Paid a hundred and twenty-three thousand. God bless the housing slump. Gonna sell my house here, all the furniture included. Getting me some new things to sit on down there."

She started on her second sandwich. "It's hot in Texas," she said around a bite as she reached for some French fries.

The lopsided grin grew wider. "Yeah, ain't it? Let me tell you something, Annja. You don't have to shovel hot. And you don't have to mow it, either, lawns so brown down there so I'm thinking my mower won't get much of a workout. That swimming pool will, though."

He'd finished the soup. She noticed he was only nibbling at his pie and was watching her intently, amazed at how quickly and how much she could eat. Annja stuffed a few more fries in her mouth.

"I was so hungry," she finally said as way of explanation. "Breakfast, I didn't really have any, and—" She let the thought trail off and finished the second sandwich and the rest of the cocoa. She stuffed a few more fries in her mouth, looked at her apple pie and picked up a fork. "And I get a lot of exercise."

"I think even Lieutenant Greene could've caught on to the notion that you were hungry."

"Wonder if he found anything out at the conference."

"Listen," he said. He pushed the pie away and finished the soda. "Before you showed up at the station to see Dr. Chia what's-his-name, I'd shuffled through the folder, made the copies, like I said, and I checked with the police in Rio Ranch."

Rio Ranch was a suburb northwest of Albuquerque. Annja had been there once to visit Edgar. She stopped eating and gave the detective her full attention.

"Edgar's place."

"They said his home had been broken into and gone through. Clearly searched, but not a complete tossing like you see on TV. Somebody was careful, if you get my drift. Like they knew exactly what they were looking for. Next-door neighbor said she spotted a man walking through the house really late last night but didn't say anything, thought it was Professor Schwartz's son." He shrugged. "Maybe they found what they were looking for."

"Then why kill Edgar here?" The question was for herself. "If they found what they wanted?"

"Because maybe they didn't find what they were looking for. Maybe they searched his house after they killed him. Didn't find it here, so looked there."

Another shrug. "Maybe they didn't find what they wanted in his hotel room because they didn't know to look between the mattresses. Your friend Edgar was murdered over what was in the folder." He reached into his front pocket and pulled out a small, clear police-evidence bag. "Maybe somebody knew your Professor Schwartz had these, and they wanted them. Maybe this is why those idiots in the Explorer were dogging us, looking for this or wanting to see if we knew where it was. Follow the money—that's what they were doing. They could've killed us easy by ramming us, but they were playing, trying to just knock us off the road. I'm betting they wanted to talk to us. Didn't work out too good for them, eh? Anyway, I gotta get this back first thing tomorrow or it'll be my hide for good."

It made a heavy *thunk* for its size.

Annja pushed her plate away and leaned over it. "Gold."

"Yeah, gold. It was in a plain white envelope inside that folder. Bet it's worth a good chunk. It looks old. Really old."

"Ancient." Annja's heart raced. Without opening the bag, she moved the contents around. Three gold circles, each a little larger than a silver dollar, though twice as thick. One had a froglike creature on it with a bird head, another something that looked vaguely like an insect with a human head. The fine details were remarkable. There were symbols around the edge, which looked to be a language. The third momentarily stole her breath. It depicted an elk—an elk in its body and antlers—but it had a stylized Mayan man's face. She turned the evidence bag over to note images of the sun on the other sides. "These are Mayan."

"Yeah, Mayan, Aztec, Incan, old. Some expert from the Milwaukee museum is coming in tomorrow for a look-see. Coins, huh? Ancient coins."

"Uh, Mayans," Annja corrected, "didn't use coins for commerce. They used jade beads. These were from a piece of jewelry. See." She pointed to each coin. "The small holes. These were part of a necklace or something. All of this is pre-Columbian."

"Pre—"

"Pre-Columbian. From before Columbus came to the New World."

"Guess you really are an archaeologist." He ate more of the pie. When the waitress returned to their booth, he grabbed the evidence bag and put it back in his pocket. "Jeez, I could get in trouble for having these. Serious deep trouble for not leaving these in evidence lockup. Wanted you to see 'em."

"If those belonged to Edgar, they should go to his sons."

"If they weren't stolen. Heavy suckers for their size."

"Edgar wouldn't steal. Those are exceedingly valuable, given their age, condition and workmanship. They look perfect. But Edgar would not have stolen them."

Manny considered that. "Good to know, but we'll be double-checking before we hand over any of his effects from the hotel room."

Annja pictured the image of the last gold circle she'd looked at and burned it into her memory. The detail on the gold was indeed incredible. And the image was definitely an elk. Annja doubted elk herds had ever stretched down into Mexico. They were northern beasts—Canada, Minnesota, Wisconsin.

"Mayans in Wisconsin," she whispered. "I have to find out if Edgar was right."

15

The detective parked the Impala in an open spot in front of the Sweet Autumn Inn, a sprawling bed-and-breakfast that sat on an acre dotted with tall pines. The front-porch lights were ablaze, but with the cloud cover and towering trees, the place looked shadowy and haunted.

"This is where your Professor Schwartz and that Papadopolous fellow stayed a few nights before they both wound up dead." Manny got out and stretched, worked a kink out of his neck and looked up at a sky that had finally stopped raining. "I'm going to chat with the manager. Then I'll be down by the lake, a cabin called Copper Beach Cottage. It's where the two of them stayed a few months back, and Dr. Schwartz rented it by himself twice before that. You can join me or—"

"I'll take a stroll down by the lake, Manny. Catch up with you at that beach cottage."

"Too small of a place to get lost in, this town," he commented. "Just wish we would have gotten here earlier, when we had some light. I'm good for one, two hours here, tops. Then we're going back. I've got an early meeting with the chief. Maybe I can get back out here tomorrow afternoon."

Annja started down the street, signs pointing the way to the lake. It wasn't pitch-dark yet, but it was getting there. Streetlights were on, looking haloed by damp mist. In the distance, toward the small downtown area, she saw the colorful lights of a carnival.

"Don't get lost on me!" he hollered jokingly. "I'm your ride back."

She waved, picked up the pace and tugged her cell phone out of her pocket. She'd turned it off, not wanting anything to interrupt her time with the detective. From the green glow on the tiny screen, she could read that she'd missed three calls, two of them from Rembert earlier in the afternoon, one from Private Caller, which didn't reveal a number.

Instead of calling Rembert, she keyed in the number for the diver Edgar had noted on the fishing map; she'd memorized it. After a half-dozen rings, a man answered. It was a private residence at the western edge of Milwaukee, not a business, and he remembered doing more than one dive for Edgar.

"I'll come out to the lake," he told her. "Same price as I gave him. And yes, I'll take you with me if you want, same places or different—your dime. You can dive? Good." He told her about his available equipment and what he'd charge for her to rent it. "How tall are you? How much do you weigh? Shoe size? How is next Thursday?"

It took persuasion, an offer to pay him an extra five hundred for his trouble and relying on her celebrity. The diver had seen her program a few times. He would join her at the lake tomorrow morning at nine, giving her his only day off this week.

She'd ask him then what he'd found for Edgar—if anything—and what, exactly, Edgar had him looking for. Face-to-face she might get more information than over the phone, especially since she'd be paying him. Then she called Rembert; it went to his voice mail and she left a message saying she'd check in with him early in the morning. Hopefully, he'd gotten enough video for Doug's promo pieces. She wouldn't be attending the conference tomorrow, would be standing up that fringe panel the organizers had put her on. She'd leave the other speakers to carry the load. It might hurt her reputation, but she could survive it. She'd be spending the day on and under the surface of Rock Lake…perhaps in pursuit of her own piece of "fringe."

It wasn't what she'd originally planned, diving the lake. She'd intended to go back to the conference and attack the murder investigation head-on. But as she looked out over Rock Lake, choppy in the slight breeze cutting across it, she considered that this was the right thing to do.

"What's down there, Edgar," she mused, "that maybe got you and Dr. Papadopolous killed? And how was Mrs. Hapgood involved with this?"

It was all somehow connected, wasn't it?

Lost in thought, she stood and stared so long her legs ached from not moving. The moon came out from behind a cloud, reflecting against the tiny waves and making it look as if sequins had been scattered atop the lake's surface. Lightning bugs appeared in the reeds along the shore, and the mist that she'd noticed near the bed-and-breakfast had crept to the edge of the water. There was a boat out there, not far away, small and with red and green bow and stern lights. From the shapes, it looked like father and son fishing, maybe for walleye, which fed primarily at night. This setting seemed wrongly tranquil and falsely placid, looking on one hand as if it could be displayed on a postcard, and on the other as if it could appear in the next top-grossing horror movie. "Come to Rock Lake," Annja thought that postcard might read. "Enjoy the scenery and watch your step." In her mind she saw Edgar's body broken and twisted, lying at the bottom of the stairs.

A beam of light along the shore caught her attention. Someone with a flashlight, not tall enough to be Detective Rizzo. She couldn't tell whether it was a man or a woman; the figure stood under the sweeping branches of a cedar that hung out at a sharp angle over the lake. The beam swung toward Annja, held on her and then went dark. In the moonlight, she could still see the figure, up against the trunk now, the mist wrapping around the person's knees.

Maybe it was nothing…someone else visiting the lakeshore on this early-June evening. It was a little bit of a tourist town, and it was a Friday night. Maybe not much else to do here other than find a tavern or visit this lake.

Still… Annja peered into the shadows, trying to separate them and make out more of the figure's features. Something prickling the back of her neck told her it wasn't a tourist.

There was a splash and a yip. She didn't turn her

head, but she guessed that someone in the boat had caught a fish. Voices carried over the water.

"Reel it in, son!"

"I'm trying!"

A loon cried, melodic and poignant, a long note that was answered by another and another.

"Look, it's a keeper, Dad!"

The figure didn't move.

Annja took a step toward the tree, the lake on her left and a couple of dark cottages on her right. Her shoes sunk into the sand as she went.

"Hello?" she called softly, moving closer.

Still, the figure didn't move.

Her cell phone chimed, startling her. Keeping her eyes on the figure, she reached into her pocket and brought it up, flipped it open and put it to her ear. It was Rembert.

"Where have you been?"

She quickly told him. "Do you have enough video for Doug?"

"Yeah, I guess. Why?"

She told him she would be in Rock Lake for likely all of tomorrow.

"Good," he returned. "No reason for you to attend a conference you registered for, right? No reason for you to show up for your Saturday panel, right?"

"You can go back to New York if you want."

"I think I'll stay for another day at least," he told her. "Room's paid for through Monday morning. Still have some money on my expense account. I could use a few days away from the family."

"Fine," she said. Annja hadn't intended to sound

terse; she was just focused on the mysterious figure. "Maybe I'll see you tomorrow."

"Maybe."

The line went dead.

The loons sounded again.

"Hello?"

The figure said something, words, but foreign and a language she didn't know. It was a husky voice, and so she guessed it was a man. Some part of her told her to leave, that she'd be coming back here tomorrow morning when the sun would be out and the shadows wouldn't hide anything. But Annja was curious.

"Everything is connected."

The voice came again, the incomprehensible words rushed and beautiful sounding. The figure stepped away from the trunk. Closer now, Annja saw more definition to the shape—a woman, either with hair very short or tied back. A very small woman.

"Hello." Annja tried one more time.

The reply was clipped, and Annja sensed anger.

Leave, that part of her mind told her. Find Manny and get out of here. Instead she went ever nearer, until she was practically beneath the big cedar's branches.

More words came that she couldn't comprehend. But Annja clearly understood the slashing motion the woman made with a knife that had come out of nowhere.

What the hell is going on in Wisconsin?

Annja felt the sensation of her sword's pommel against her hand as she called it, the blade looking like liquid silver in the moonlight that stretched down between a gap in the clouds. She thought the figure might run, but instead it crouched, as if to meet her, and made the slashing motion again.

Annja had no intention to fight, taking a defensive stance. But she did want to get a good look at the woman, find some way to communicate. Discover what—if anything—this woman's presence might have to do with Edgar.

"Everything is connected."

The woman—girl, Annja realized, probably a teenager—darted forward, slashing, hugging the shadow the tree provided. Annja backed up, calling to mind the three circles—not the gold coins, but fighting reach. The first circle was as far as her arm stretched out from her body. The second was how far her reach went with the sword in her hand. The third was how far that extended with one step. The woman's weapon was a knife, and so her three circles were much smaller than Annja's. The woman was forced to be quick, to dance in and out of Annja's circles, slashing viciously and retreating.

Annja made no move against her, other than to defend herself. She turned her sword so the flat of it caught the woman's knife, the long blade flexible and absorbing the impact. "Never meet edge with edge," she remembered Roux telling her. "Edges are not so flexible, and they are easy to chip and break." But once broken and re-formed, would Joan of Arc's sword break again? Annja parried blow after blow, inching back and trying to draw the woman out so she could get a look at her under the moonlight.

Finally, she was successful, and the appearance of her opponent surprised her.

The term *teenager* was generous. In her midteens,

at best, Annja guessed. Very young—too young to be knife fighting. Her hair was like ink, shiny and looking as if it was pulled back so tight it was painful. Her eyes were dark, wide and angry, the pupils big. Maybe on drugs, Annja considered; it could explain the wild behavior and the babbling that she had at first took to be a language.

The girl was dressed in cutoff jeans and a T-shirt that would have been baggy had it not been tied in a knot just above her waist, exposing a pierced navel. The writing on the T-shirt was faded.

"We don't have to do this," Annja said, meeting another blow. The girl was not as skilled as she, but was fast and agile.

"Yes, we do," the girl returned. The words were thick, making Annja wonder if she was indeed on drugs.

"I didn't mean to trespass." Annja wanted to keep the girl talking, get her farther away from the tree. "If I was on your property…" But she suspected from the sign it was a city-owned beach. "If I upset you—"

The girl had no answer to that; she just sprang in close and made a slash that cut Annja's waist. The knife went through her blouse as if it was paper and drew blood. It could have been worse had Annja not stepped away. The girl had meant to kill her.

That changed things, though Annja still had no desire to hurt the teen. She brought her sword down and around in an arc, the tip extending her third circle and forcing the girl back. She followed it with another swing, up and around and hitting the knife, trying to knock it from the girl's grip.

More unintelligible words came from the teen's

mouth. It was a language, a Native American dialect perhaps; the girl had a tan complexion. Annja tried to remember pieces of it, a word or two she could repeat later in front of someone who might identify the language.

Annja stepped in, swept shoulder high, turning the sword so the flat side would catch the girl in the arm… hurting but not cutting. If she could get the girl to drop the knife, she could dismiss the sword and tackle her, reason with her.

"You must die!" The girl caught the blow and stayed upright, kept her hands on the knife. "Die now!" She spun and dropped into a crouch, grabbing up a handful of sand. She flung it at Annja.

The grit filled Annja's vision and settled in her eyes, stinging like hornets. She hadn't been prepared for that, was concentrating too hard on not hurting her opponent. Annja had underestimated the girl and was paying for it.

The girl dashed forward, circling, coming at Annja from the side and jabbing. The knife tip went into her side, stopping at a rib. Annja clamped her mouth shut and didn't cry out.

"Hey! What's going on?" It was Manny's voice.

Annja blinked furiously and through her clouded gaze saw the girl race madly away. Annja would have chased her if the detective hadn't shown up, would have run her into the ground and fought against the sand in her eyes with every step. She would have gotten answers.

Now all she had was more questions.

She dismissed the sword to the otherwhere and dropped to her knees, bringing her arm in close to her injured side, one hand pressed to her waist where she'd been cut the first time.

"Annja!" The detective's feet thumped across the sand, his breath ragged. He stopped in front of Annja, gulping in air. "Was someone swinging a sword at you?"

Small favors, she thought. Manny hadn't seen just who had the sword.

"I think it was a big knife."

"Damn big knife." The detective looked in the direction the girl had run. "Don't see him. Fast sucker." He knelt in front of Annja. "We have to get you to a hospital. This place is too small, probably doesn't even have a clinic open this late. Want me to call an ambulance? I can take you in my car just as fast. Sirens and lights and—"

Annja gave a furious shake of her head. "I'm not hurt that bad." It was a lie, but she always healed quickly. "Got a first-aid kit in your car?"

He stood with some effort, then helped her up. "I dunno, Annja, that's a good amount of blood. I think I'm going to—"

"—show me that first-aid kit."

He escorted her from the beach. He'd parked about a block away at an empty spot near Copper Beach Cottage. She sat in the passenger seat, door wide open, feet on the gravel drive. He fumbled in the trunk and brought out a first-aid kit the size of a large tackle box.

"I can manage this," she told him as she picked through the contents and found eyewash. She used that first, working the sand out. She could see much better now, but her eyes would bother her for a while.

"Somehow I get the idea this sort of thing has happened to you before," Manny said. "Getting injured. Crocodiles, maybe. Snakes. Angry natives." He went around to the driver's side while she worked, thumbed his mic, said he was "too old for all of this" and called central dispatch to report the knifing. He was shocked when Annja told him it was a young woman but that she couldn't describe the girl, didn't get that good of a look at her.

Manny hadn't, either.

"I think she was on drugs, a teenager." At least, she believed that was true. "I think I just was in the wrong place at the wrong time, intruded on her private party, and so she came after me." Annja knew there was more to it than that, but saw no point in speculating or talking about hunches.

"Gonna have to fill out a report on this, too," Manny said. "I'm not going to miss all the paperwork. Two more weeks."

On the way out of town, Annja got the detective to stop at the diner again. After ten o'clock now, it was still open, with a dozen customers inside, all of them men, all wearing baseball caps and in T-shirts and patched blue jeans, of varying ages, but likely all from a softball team that had played earlier. Lakeside Hustlers many of the shirts read.

Manny hadn't gotten much information from either the managers of the bed-and-breakfast or the cabin, he'd told her. But it was a few more pieces for the puzzle.

Annja asked about renting one of the motorcycles on the lot as the waitress gave her a serious up and down over the bandage and the bloody blouse. "I'm coming back out here tomorrow," she told Manny. "And the bike will suit me better than a rent-a-car."

He pulled out of the lot after making sure her selection indeed ran: a 1964 Suzuki, the blue paint all flat and faded, and sad looking under the yellow parking-lot light.

The diner owner poured in a few gallons of gasoline from a can. "That ought to be more than enough to get you back to Madison."

She gave him a ten for the gas.

At one time the bike was probably a beauty. She paid a hundred dollars for it and would leave it at the airport or in the Arms' parking lot when she was ready to return to New York. The bike hadn't come with title or registration.

"Not good with paperwork," the diner owner said.

Apparently no one in Wisconsin likes paperwork, Annja thought. She slowly drove out of the lot, listening to the engine cough and spit. Everything Runs. She hoped it would keep running until she was indeed ready to go back to New York.

16

Saturday

The wet suit was almost too snug, but Annja squirmed into it, put on the hood and neoprene boots, the latter being a little too big, so they stuffed the toes with old cloths. She pulled on the gloves and checked the bright yellow tank.

"Air is good for thirty minutes, forty at the outside," said Robert Wolfe—Bobby, as he wanted to be called. "No longer because the lake's almost thirty meters deep here."

Annja nodded her understanding and inspected the tank regulator. He handed her a small bail-out tank to strap to her belt. It was a backup, in case they were down too long or the primary tank failed. He was a professional; she understood why Edgar had relied on him. He told her on the phone last night that in addition to teaching diving in Lake Michigan, he worked occasional rescue and recovery dives for the police department.

Bobby finished putting on his gear while she looked over a map of the lake he had brought with him. It was similar to the one Edgar had in the folder,

but had been encased in sturdy vinyl. Manny wouldn't
let her hold on to anything overnight, worried that he
needed it all back in place before his morning meeting with the chief. She hoped that meeting went well,
and she hoped to get another look at the contents of
the folder later to compare Edgar's map to this one.

Bobby had brought his own boat, a ten-foot flat-
bottomed aluminum one in which the center seat had
been removed to make it easier to stow all the diving
gear—including ten air tanks. He pointed to a spot
on the map.

"We're anchored here. This is the last place Dr.
Schwartz had me dive. Found some stuff for him
and got some pictures. Hard to believe he's dead, you
know. I just saw him last week. He wanted to go down
with me this last trip, but the shop didn't have a suit
that would fit him, and I told him that this early in
the season the water was too cold to go without one.
I didn't want the liability, an old guy like him getting
sick. Lawsuits and stuff, you know. Can't take the
chance." Bobby shuddered. "Should've let him come
anyway, huh? If he'd caught a cold, even pneumonia,
what would it have mattered? I feel bad, not letting
him go down with me."

Bobby had brought a pouch with him, filled with
pictures he'd taken for Edgar last week. He'd used an
underwater digital camera and had printed up the best
images. "Dr. Schwartz was going to come to my shop
Monday or Tuesday to pick them up. He paid me in
advance. Guess you can have them."

Annja glanced at them. They were shadowy, sections of mossy stone, no definition to them, and
blurry—though that might have been sediment stirred

up around them, not the camera's focus. She'd give them a closer look later. She was paying Bobby by the hour to dive, not to sit here while she tried to make sense of his photographs.

The spot he'd pointed to was roughly in the center of the largest section of lake. The map, marked with depths and asterisks to indicate a few topographical features, showed the lake to look roughly like a figure eight. The south part was labeled a protected marsh, and near it—Annja had discovered from a walk she'd taken early this morning—was a long stretch of vegetation that reached well out of the water and was the favorite haunt of the local loon population. The northwest area boasted a big sand bar where there were two fishing beaches and a series of docks for people who owned lakefront property and for one of the resorts. It was near where she had her run-in last night with the teenage knife-wielder. Manny had called her very late last night to say the sheriff's department had come up with nothing regarding the girl, and no one else had reported seeing her.

One more piece of the puzzle, Annja thought.

"Here," Bobby said, pointing to the south section. "This is the Glacial Drumlin State Trail. It runs across an old railroad bridge. A pretty walk, if you have the time. The trail is a sort of dividing line between the protected marsh and the rest of the lake. The first time I dived for Dr. Schwartz, it was near this bridge. It was too cold for him then, too."

"How many times?" Annja asked.

"He hired me on four separate occasions," Bobby said. "Nice fellow, obsessed, but nice. Two times he brought his Greek pal along."

"And he told you he was looking for—"

"Stone pyramids. Not the Indian mounds that anyone and everyone in these parts know are down there. They're stone, too. He wanted me to find actual pyramids, I guess like you'd see in Egypt." Bobby shrugged and tested his tank. "Real friggin' pyramids." He shrugged again and strapped his bail-out tank to his belt. "Like I said, he was obsessed. It was his dime, and I had the time. He booked me weeks in advance. What I found for him, what's in those pictures, should be right below us according to my GPS."

He eased himself over the side of the boat and held on to the edge. "So you said you've dived before."

"Many, many times."

"Lake diving? Or all salt water?"

"Mostly salt water, but I've done a little lake diving," Annja admitted. "I'll be fine."

"In Wisconsin? Ever dive in this area before?"

She shook her head.

"My second dive for the doc was off the Fremont Bar. Here." He stretched to point to a place on the map that had been circled in grease pencil. Annja noticed that there were four such circles, one marking the spot where their boat was anchored now. "The Freemont isn't as deep, and I found what everybody else finds who dives there, piles of rocks…rocks all roughly the same size and thereby interesting. If you go to Aztalan Park, you'll find mounds made out of rocks also the same size. But at Freemont, the lake has broken down whatever the rocks had been used to build. It's all just rubble there as far as I'm concerned."

"And the other dives?"

"The next time I went down, I found nothing.

Zip. Nada. I was using some dive charts from 1936, where fishermen had said they'd seen an underwater pyramid. So, they were off the mark, the lake had changed or maybe the fishermen had been drinking. Who knows? And then I tried a spot a local kook told Dr. Schwartz to dive on."

"And—"

"That was in the winter. Best time to dive the lake then. The water is the clearest you'll find. And I found some stuff, had a good camera with me, a dive buddy, and we wrote it up for a scuba magazine. It was choice, if you know what I mean. Good rocks, man-made, if you could call them that. Made money from Dr. Schwartz for the dive and made money from the article and pictures. Not that the pics were all that terrific, but certainly better than what I got last time. You see, Annja… Mind if I call you Annja?"

"Please."

"There are pyramids…well, buildings…mounds, whatever you want to call them…in the lake. Hard to find, despite all the high-tech equipment we have at our disposal. Still, we can't wholly map the bottom of this lake." He grinned wide like a mischievous boy. "Good that nature keeps some secrets, don't you think?"

Annja didn't reply. She didn't want the lake to keep any of its secrets. She wanted to find whatever it was that had been burning a hole in Edgar's soul and had started to burn one in hers. She wanted to do this for her dear friend.

"Well, let's get on with it. You're not paying me to jaw. Just understand that this particular trip is going to be a waste of time. But I told you that on the phone last night."

"What?" She couldn't hide her irritation.

"I tried to get you to do this Thursday, remember? Weather reports call for a clear, still day. Rained all day yesterday. Looks like more rain today. And if it starts lightning, we're out of here. Remember when we pushed away from the dock? I said we could only see the rocks and sand about five feet out from the shore. This is a Wisconsin lake, and it's not cooperating, all the rain. So prepare to be disappointed. But like I said, it's your dime." He put on his mask and waited until she was in the water. He stretched an arm into the boat and retrieved a flashlight, put the cord of it around her wrist and cinched it so it wouldn't sink away. He took a second flashlight and did the same for himself. A motion from him, and they went down.

Right below the surface was reasonably clear, and Annja saw a smallmouth bass swim past, his side a thick flash of silver against the gray-green water. When she'd dropped down ten feet, things became murky, as if she was swimming in silt. Particles made it look as if snow was swirling around her. Bobby gestured to get her attention and then began finger spelling. He seemed pleased that she understood him. Annja knew enough sign language to make out *D-i-a-t-o-m-s*. Some divers relied on sign language, the formal kind like Bobby was using, stock hand signals or gestures they'd developed on their own. In layman's terms, diatoms were algae, this just hatched and making visibility rotten.

Annja hoped the trip wasn't as worthless as Bobby forecasted.

Another ten feet or so down and she flicked on

the flashlight; all it did was brighten the silt-filled gloom. Bobby swam close enough and slowly finger-spelled again. *S-t-a-y c-l-o-s-e.* He dropped deeper and she followed, almost losing sight of him. Fish swam within inches, attracted by the beams. She saw bluegill and sunfish and a thin snakelike fish that she guessed to be a young northern pike or muskellunge. Noises came to her, but she couldn't identify them, a hum that might have been a motor from a boat crossing the lake, the sound of the bubbles from her tank—all of it could have been ghosts, it carried so hauntingly.

Although Annja had dived in lakes before, they'd not been anywhere near as cloudy as this one. The algae seemed even more numerous now. It was eerie and unsettling; she might as well have been on another planet. She only guessed at the time, that maybe five minutes had passed. She didn't have a waterproof watch, and Bobby had not brought one for her. Something brushed her leg and she swung her light down and around, catching site of a tail that might have belonged to a ten-pound something. Then Bobby was gently tugging on her ankle, bringing her down to the bottom with him, gesturing with his flashlight and nudging her closer. He finger spelled *S-l-o-w.*

They crept along the bottom. Annja looked up and directed her beam. The light traveled five or six feet, showing only a trail of diatoms. She finger spelled *E-i-g-h-t-y?*

He cupped his hands and then drew them apart. She took it to mean they were more than eighty feet down. *N-i-n-e-t-y,* he spelled. Then he turned his beam to the lakebed, which looked like mud. Each step shifted and multiplied the silt. One meter, two, three, and then his light hit a large round stone, and he brought his face mask in close to hers, his eyes wide. He nodded and drew her down to her knees, bringing the light in against the stone.

At first glance, it looked like nothing special to Annja. But as she stared, she noted a depression in the center of it. Altered by man. Annja suspected the stone had been used as a primitive mortar for grinding grain. There was another just like it nearby, though a little larger. She released her grip on the flashlight and it floated, still tethered to her wrist. Her hands free, she tried to lift the stone. She could budge it, barely, so she knew it would be too heavy to bring to the surface…at least not without a winch.

Bobby took her hand and led her in what she suspected was north. There was evidence of vegetation on the bottom here, surprising since she was certain no light from the surface made it down. Perhaps on very sunny days, she thought, there was just enough to satisfy the plants. Farther and there was a big bed of moss. The water was clearer here, though dark as night, the moss keeping the silt down. There were more stones, all roughly two feet in diameter and looking as if they might have been worked on to be so uniform. Most of them were moss covered, but some were clean; Annja suspected this was from divers handling them. She scolded herself for trying to lift the other stone. A good archaeologist disturbed nothing without the proper tools.

Among the symmetrical stones was an iron buoy weight with three feet of moss-spotted nylon rope hooked to it, undulating like a serpent. More searching revealed two more weights. Divers had been to this spot before and marked it with buoys, cutting the ropes when they weren't planning to return.

Bobby signaled for her to ascend.

Annja shook her head, wanting to see more. Round rocks weren't enough; they only tickled her curiosity and did nothing to help sate it.

He signaled again and pushed off from the bottom. Reluctantly she followed. On the surface, she could tell they'd traveled only about thirty feet from the boat.

"Stay here, all right? I'll bring the boat over."

The next dive would start from this spot.

Annja treaded water, setting her head back and looking up at the sky. It had been cloudy when they came out here, and it had gotten darker in places. It was going to rain again, and the lake would get even more silt filled.

During the second dive nearly a half hour later, they came across one of the notorious stone mounds. A quartet of mud puppies, two-foot-long salamander-like creatures, lounged on it. As Annja brushed away some of the moss, the mud puppies fled, stirring up algae and muck and cutting visibility to nothing, even with the beams.

Since their tanks were low on oxygen anyway, they surfaced, waited nearly an hour, then dived again. The muck had settled, and there was no sign of the mud puppies.

There was, however, next to the base of the mound, a steering wheel from an old car; a small boat anchor, which might have been attached to a buoy at one time; and the windshield from an old Model T or Model A, which had probably motored out on the ice more than a hundred years ago and broke through. There were no skeletons to indicate that the car's occupants had followed it to the bottom, but she did find a thoroughly rusted fender. Several large bass, which Annja knew any fisherman would give anything to catch, swam lazily above the worked stones.

Annja followed the length of the structure, aware that Bobby hovered nearby, present but unobtrusive. She didn't need him to keep such a close watch on her; she was probably as expert a diver as he was. But she appreciated his vigilance. She mentally marked off the distance, judging the "building" to be a hundred feet long and a dozen feet high. Perhaps it had been taller centuries past—Annja guessed the structure was roughly a thousand years old. The top of it was flat, and the stones here were worked smooth and mortared together…though there was little left of the mortar material. The years and the stones' weight held the structure together.

Suddenly the water cleared around her, and she could see all the details, the rounded corners on the stones to make them fit properly, and etchings on some. One stone at the very top looked to be carved into the shape of a turtle, and there were marks on the "shell" that could have been a language. Another had the shape of a frog. She cursed herself for not bringing a camera or asking Bobby to bring one. But she would come back tomorrow with the proper equipment so she could better document this.

She didn't touch the turtle stone, but drew her finger above it, as if tracing the marks. They weren't at all Mayan. Despite her knowledge of many ancient languages, she couldn't place this. But if she took a photograph and posted it to some of her contacts through the internet, she might be able to get it translated.

Annja touched very little, carefully brushing moss away here and there or moving things that were not in any way part of the ancient building, such as a concrete-filled coffee can that had probably anchored a buoy. Disturb nothing and leave only bubbles, she thought. The place had the "feel" of something sacred, maybe a burial spot. If there were more than one of these, as the stories about Rock Lake suggested, maybe the lake bottom was an entire city of the dead.

She could come up with an angle to make a *Chasing History's Monsters* episode out of this—which would give her a better reason to stay longer and to come back after Morocco. But for some reason she didn't want to sensationalize this. There had been enough publicity about these mounds through the years, according to Bobby.

Let the lake keep this secret. And if these were burial mounds, let the dead rest.

This couldn't have been what Edgar was so intent on. There was nothing Mayan about this place. It smacked of something European or Native American. She circled it again, finding no way in, further lending to her notion that it was a burial mound.

Bobby tapped on her shoulder and pointed up, gestured to his watch and pointed again. Annja nodded and reluctantly ascended. She could have gotten another ten minutes out of this tank, as she had been breathing shallowly to make the oxygen last. She also had the small tank on her waist for an emergency. But there was no reason to argue with her guide.

On the surface, she saw that the clouds had actually thinned out and the sky was brightening. She flipped up her mask. "You have underwater cameras, right?" Annja put the emphasis on the plural because it was obvious he'd taken pictures before.

He treaded next to her, reached up, grabbed the side of his boat and pulled himself in. He took off the mask and let the water dribble out of it. "Sure. I have three that are mine, the best a Canon 350D. The shop has more, has some for sale."

She pulled herself over the side and took off the tank and reached for another one. "When we come out tomorrow, can you bring two? The Canon and another? I want to get some shots of—"

"Whoa. Whoa. Whoa. Sorry. There is no tomorrow out here for me. I'm booked. Sunday through Wednesday, I'm booked. Like I told you on the phone, I have Thursday open. At least, I think I do. One of Dr. Schwartz's friends wanted to book Thursday, and I have him penciled in, but he hasn't gotten back to me."

Annja's throat tightened. "Dr. Papadopolous?" Was she going to have to tell Bobby a second of his clients had died?

"Not him. I know him, Dr. Papa-D. He said to call him that. But Papa-D didn't want to dive. I got the feeling he was claustrophobic. A lot younger than Dr. Schwartz. I wouldn't have had trouble taking him down with me. But he was chicken, even though he was excited about all of this. Excited like a kid, but he was scared. Maybe he was afraid of drowning. Who knows?"

"So if not Papa, who were you going to take out here Thursday? Maybe I know the archaeologist."

Bobby pulled off a glove and rotated his thumb. The joint was swollen; too young for arthritis, but that was what it looked like. "A doctor—" He thought a moment. "They're all doctors, aren't they, those archaeologists? I'm not too good with names, Annja. That's why I write everything down. It was…Dr. Cheepa, something like that."

Her eyes widened. "Chiapont?"

A grin. "That's it. But he hasn't gotten back to me. So if you want to lock in Thursday—"

Peter? She recalled their conversation at the jail. Peter had said he'd argued with Edgar, called him foolish for pursuing a crazy theory about Mayans in Wisconsin and evidence buried in a lake. If Peter had thought Edgar so foolish, why would he have scheduled a day with a diver? She was going to have another chat with her "old friend." And soon. She wondered if Peter was still in jail or if an attorney had gotten him sprung.

"Thursday? Anyone else from your dive shop available before then?"

He laughed. "This time of year, we book up pretty far in advance. You lucked out on today. I had a cancellation. And like I mentioned, I might not have Thursday if that Dr. Cheepa—"

"Done," she said. "I'll lock up your Thursday." Annja didn't want to wait until Thursday for another day to dive the lake, and she would certainly come up with another avenue to get back down tomorrow. There had to be places nearby that rented scuba gear and cameras; she'd buy them if she had to, other dive shops in Milwaukee. But she liked the idea of having a dive buddy who knew the lake and who had worked with Edgar…and who was going to dive with Peter. So she'd stay until Thursday if she had to just to get another diving day with Bobby Wolfe. She calculated that she could remain in Wisconsin until Friday night or early Saturday morning at the latest. Her flight for Morocco was scheduled for late afternoon that Saturday out of LaGuardia. But no matter what, she was coming back out here tomorrow.

"Fine, you've got me Thursday," he said, changing out his tank.

On their fifth, and what Bobby said was their final dive of the day, they located a second structure. It was close to one hundred and twenty feet long, which Annja judged based on the time it took her to swim from one end to the other. Not much taller than a man, and a dozen feet wide, it also had a flat top, but no decorative stones or carvings from what she could see. The lake had gone murky again, as if she was diving in pea soup, and the beams of their flashlights weren't sufficient to push past all the muck.

"Out of tanks and out of air," Bobby announced as he pulled up the anchor several minutes later. "But it was fun, huh? I never get tired of this." He marked the spot on a GPS device for future reference. "The pictures in that pouch I gave you are from the taller building…pyramid…mound…whatever you want to call it that we saw today. I'll bring my best cameras Thursday when we go down again, get you some more shots." He paused. "Hey, are you going to be doing something on this lake for your show…*History's Big-*

gest Monsters? You doing something on Her Snake-ship?"

"No. This is just for me, this dive. I'm on vaca-tion." Snakeship? So there was a monster associated with this lake? Maybe that was what Edgar was going to tell her about over dinner. Again, she remembered his email: "I have quite the monster for you to chase, dear Annja. We must meet for dinner tomorrow so I can give you my notes."

"Was Edgar…was Dr. Schwartz and Dr. Papadopo-lous looking for a big snake?"

"Nope. Pyramids. At least, that's what they told me."

She shrugged out of her air tank and added it to the collection of tanks in the center of the boat.

Bobby unzipped his wet suit and peeled the sleeves off his arms. "Hey, I suppose it is possible that they were after Her Snakeship. Maybe they knew better than to tell me that. I ain't diving in this lake looking for an imaginary serpent…even on someone else's dime. But Dr. Schwartz kept talking about pyramids. Never mentioned the snake." He shook his head. "Too bad. I liked the doc. Wish I would've let him go down with me last week." He started the motor. "I feel real bad about that. Shame."

Annja tipped her face up to the sun, which was shining bright now between gaps in the thinning clouds. "There's no way I can talk you into tomor-row?"

"Nope."

"Monday?"

"Nope. Persistent, aren't you? Or maybe you just didn't hear me the first two times. Annja, if there was a way I could swing it, I would. I love going with an experienced diver. But I'm booked. Thursday, like I said. Unless I get another cancellation. You're welcome to find someone else."

"No." She'd keep the Thursday slot with him, but she would absolutely find some equipment and come back on her own. Tomorrow. No way was she letting go of this. Somewhere, at the bottom of Rock Lake, was the reason Edgar had been killed. She felt certain of it.

"Gold medallions," she said as they neared the docks. "Did you find any gold coins…circles…on one of your dives? Edgar had some."

"Nope." Bobby grinned. "That would've been something, huh? Gold in the lake. Now, that would start a diving frenzy again. All I found were rocks. Rocks and that old car windshield. One of these times I ought to pull that thing up. Doesn't belong down there, you know?"

Annja would find something else, beyond rocks and car remnants, and along with it, she would find Edgar's murderer.

17

Annja thought her stomach was trying to claw its way out of her body, given how much growling it was doing. She'd had a light breakfast, figuring that would be better for hours of diving. And now she was famished. Three in the afternoon, a perfect time for "linner," and thinking of Rembert's term made her think of him. She called him after saying goodbye to Bobby; it went right to voice mail. Maybe he had gone back to New York.

She walked down South Main and into a restaurant called Blue Moon. The window advertised Creole-style food. Annja had been raised in an orphanage in New Orleans and had learned to love the flavors of all the restaurants on Bourbon Street. A cute kid, she'd been able to get samples from the cooks with a smile and a thank-you. She sat by the window and opened a menu, scanned it and waved for the waitress, who was reading a fashion magazine at the cash register.

"Lemonade," Annja started. "Pink if you have it. Deep-fried mushrooms for an appetizer, a Caesar salad, the Cajun chicken-breast sandwich and waffle fries."

The waitress wrote it down. "Anything else?"

"Pie of some kind, but I'll decide on that later."

Annja closed her eyes and pictured the stones she'd seen under the lake. Bobby said Edgar was looking for something different than those mounds—which were impressive and which she intended to research another time, if only through the internet. Real pyramids—supposedly that was what Edgar told Bobby he wanted to find.

Was Edgar chasing phantoms in his old age? And was Peter going to chase them, too? She frowned. Peter was keeping something from her, bare minimum his interest in Edgar's wild goose. Was he keeping anything else? *Priors.* That word continued to bob in her mind like the buoys on Rock Lake.

Peter had prior arrests.

She hadn't taken the time to search the internet and pull up the arrest reports—those were public, and she knew how to get them. She'd been so intent on Edgar's quest. Maybe she didn't want to know about Peter's past. Maybe it was none of her business. She did believe that Peter hadn't killed Edgar, and that might be enough.

But it might not.

Edgar had been a good friend, very good, just like she'd told Detective Rizzo over and over. And she owed it to Edgar to find out who killed him.

And why.

The why part, she owed that to herself. Annja couldn't let a mystery go unsolved. The who…she needed that, too. Even before she inherited Joan of Arc's sword, she had an ingrained sense of justice.

Four women wearing various shades of purple

came in and took the long table in the back. Two were wearing red ball caps.

"The usual!" the oldest of them hollered to the waitress.

Annja's lemonade was neither pink nor freshly squeezed, but it quenched her thirst. The mushrooms were on the greasy side—but weren't they always— and the Caesar salad was more of a mixed-greens assortment with overly large cucumber slices. But the Cajun chicken was so good that Annja ordered a second and passed on dessert.

"You a tourist?" the waitress asked when she slapped the bill onto the table. "Haven't seen you here before."

"Sightseeing," Annja said, which was the truth. "Diving the lake, looking around. Lovely downtown."

The waitress wrinkled her nose. "Lovely? I suppose. A bit of a tourist trap, if you ask me. I go into Madison to shop, once in a while to Brookfield Square in Milwaukee." She paused. "There's a carnival in town, way down at the end of the business district… well, what's left of the business district. Turn left at the lot of the grocery store that's closed. A couple of streets are blocked off for the rides. That'd be something for you to do."

"Thanks. I might stop if they've got a Tilt-A-Whirl." Annja left her a generous tip and strolled down the sidewalk, drinking in the small-town atmosphere. She caught site of the top of a Ferris wheel a few blocks away. It was so very different than her New York City home, this place. She hadn't heard a siren all day. In New York, the sirens were ever present.

People smiled at her and sauntered in the way

she'd expect them to in a quaint town like this. Annja peeked in shop windows, one an old-time drugstore that had a rack of comic books in front and a long, polished counter with an ice-cream fountain behind it. Maybe she'd stop there on her way back to where she'd parked her motorcycle. A strawberry sundae sounded good. There was a barbershop, but it was closed, only posting hours three days a week. A shoe repair shop, a dollar store—were they everywhere?—a tavern, a pizza place, a yarn shop that advertised knitting lessons and a wonderful big pale brick building on the corner. The sign read Fine Art Pottery. She stopped and looked up at a display arranged behind a high beveled glass window.

Intricately painted lady's slipper orchids appeared to grow up the sides of fluted vases. Annja thought she might buy a couple and have them shipped to her apartment; they would make lovely gifts. She liked to have gifts on hand for special occasions that would pop up…a wedding here, a birthday there. A funeral. Could she possibly get Edgar out of her mind for a few minutes?

An amazing vase with crackle glaze stood out; it was called Indian Summer. Annja thought she might buy that one for herself. A squat vase was called Garland of Wild Berries. It appeared that every piece had a name.

Annja went up the steps and wandered around inside, studying the shelves. She purchased an urn called Fall Rhapsody, a pair of ginkgo-leaf-shaped candle holders, a vase with a breathtaking whooping crane stretched along its length, a small bowl with a cat on it and another with a dragonfly. The pieces ran between one hundred and three hundred dollars each. Annja didn't bat an eye at that—the workmanship was impressive, and they would have cost her much more in New York, in any large city, for that matter. There was a massive bowl that almost made it onto her list, but it was seven hundred, and given what she'd already spent—on the pots, the motorcycle and on the dive—she reined herself in. She made arrangements to have her selections shipped home.

She was about to leave when a thin pitcher with an odd curved handle caught her attention. On its side was a half man, half jaguar, the tail of the beast forming the handle. Above it, on the highest shelf, was a bowl. She stepped back and tipped her head so she could better see it. Her breath caught. On the side was a stylized elk with a man's head. The image was identical to the one on the gold circle from Edgar's folder.

"That," she said, pointing straight at it. "I'd like to see that, and the pitcher beneath it."

The woman nodded. "Those are pieces from Joe, my favorite potter." She got a ladder and brought them down and sat them on the counter. "One of a kind, these two pieces."

Annja leaned in to look at them carefully, but made sure she touched nothing. The colors were beautiful. "The design, what… Does Joe like abstract art?"

"He did."

"Did. I take it he doesn't work here anymore. Retired? Is he still in town?"

The woman took in a sharp breath and shook her head. "Our dear Joe died early last fall. These are his last two pieces. Everything else of his has sold, though all of us here kept one. For remembering, you know. Now that I think about it, he didn't do abstracts. He liked Indian art, said this was Indian art. Excuse me, Native American. I keep forgetting to say *Native American,* politically correct and all. Came up with the designs himself. Said he saw them on some stones and wanted to put them on his pottery."

It was Annja's turn to inhale sharply. "He *saw* these designs?"

The woman tilted her head. "That's what he said. Joe pulled all of his designs from things he saw around here. Those dragonflies." She tapped the shelf behind her, indicating a row of vases. "Those are his designs, too. Not his pots, but his designs. The crane. Joe was responsible for a lot of the designs. Even the bats. Only made a few of these odd pieces, his man-beast pots. We never saved these designs, just let them be one of a kind."

"I'll take both." Annja didn't even look at the prices. So much for reining herself in. "You said he died?"

The woman looked pale. "Oh, yes. It was horrible. Found his body down at the beach. Some tourist had knifed him. Never did solve the murder. Not to this day."

Annja sucked in her lower lip. "Joseph Stever."

"Yes, that's right."

The name had appeared in one of the newspaper clippings from Edgar's folder, one of the unsolved murders, the most recent one. She hadn't read the article, just the headline, date and the caption under the accompanying head shot; she didn't know one of the victims was from right here in town. The rest had all been "from the area."

Was there a curse involving the lake?

Annja paid for the pottery with her credit card, the memory of the teenage girl with the knife surfacing. Could the mysterious teen have killed the potter? "Please, tell me about Joe."

The woman grimaced. "I'd rather not. Makes me sad, and there's enough sadness in the world, young lady. Be happy that you have the last two of his odd pots, as I call them."

"Please," Annja implored. "I just need—"

"Sorry, no." She shook her head firmly. "If you want to know more about Joe, you go to the other side of the street and talk to his cousin Sully. He'll tell you…though you'll probably have to buy something to get his lips to move. And that's provided he's sober."

Annja thanked her and left.

Everything's connected, right? Annja thought. The lake, the unsolved murders, the two men who tried to run her and Manny off the road, Peter Chiapont, and Edgar, and Papa and Mrs. Hapgood, and Garin. Well, maybe not *everything* was connected…. She didn't think Garin had anything to do with Edgar and his maybe-not-so-wild-goose chase. And what about the girl with the knife? Annja rubbed her temples and envisioned puzzle pieces floating on the surface of Rock Lake.

How did everything fit together?

Her sword appeared in the back of her mind, and she imagined it like a baseball bat, striking at each piece and forcing it into the proper order. The sword spun and…

A car honked and tires squealed. Annja turned to see that she'd stopped in the middle of the street and had nearly been run over. The bumper of a green Lexus was inches from her.

"Get out of the way!" the driver shouted. "You crazy, lady? Move your—"

Annja dashed across the rest of the way, the sword and the puzzle pieces vanishing from her thoughts. She jumped up onto the curb and stopped in front of a run-down storefront. The paint was gray, thick and peeling, curling and making the wood around the front window look like the scales of a fish that had been left to dry in the sun. A jumble of objects was displayed in the window…more like tossed into the window. Dolls sat crookedly atop stacks of books. Trains without wheels propped up trays of beads from a festival. Dishes, knitting needles, shot glasses, fishing lures and reels, faded baseball hats, dingy Christmas ornaments and more warred for her attention.

A sign painted on the glass read Sully's What-Nots. A piece of cardboard with oPeN printed in red marker hung on the front door.

She stepped toward it but was intercepted before she could go inside.

"OhmyGodohmyGodohmyGod!" The girl in front of Annja took out her cell phone and snapped a picture. "OhmyGodohmyGod!"

A teenage boy was with the girl, and he stared, dumbfounded. "What?" he said. "What, Keesh?"

"She's Annja Creed," the girl gushed. "*The* Annja Creed!"

Annja smiled politely.

The boy shifted impatiently and muttered, "Big whoop. Who's Annja Creed? Aren't we going to the lake?"

"Take my picture with her." The girl thrust the phone at the boy, then covered her mouth. "Oh, I'm sorry. Can Mitch take our picture? Would that be okay? I watch your program all the time. OhmyGod-ohmyGodohmyGod, no one's going to believe that *the* Annja Creed is in this hellhole of a town." She scrunched her face into an uncomfortable-looking expression. "Oh, no, I'm sorry. I didn't mean to say *hell*. Would it be okay to have a picture with you? Please?"

Annja smiled and put her arm around the girl's shoulders. The girl was tall and thin and she shook with excitement. "I would love to have my picture taken with you—"

"Keesha," she said. "My name is Keesha Marie Donaldson."

"Nice to meet you, Keesha Marie."

The girl's shaking became even more pronounced. "T-t-t-take the picture, Mitch. Take a bunch of pictures. I gotta post these."

"Sure. Whatever. Stand still, Keesh." He held up the phone to take the picture. "Still don't know who the heck is Annja Creed."

He handed the phone back to the girl when he was done. The girl, Keesha, was now rooting through her purse. "Here!" She handed Annja a small notebook and delved again, likely for something to write with. "Could you sign this? Could I get your autograph? Could you write *To Keesha* on it? OhmyGod-ohmyGod."

Annja obliged her, finding an empty page. She noticed that the other pages had sketches: an eye of Horus, an Egyptian-stylized bird, a crude rendering of King Tut's death mask. "You like archaeology, Keesha?"

"Like it? I love it. I live it. I'm going to be an archaeologist. I want to be just like you. I've seen every one of your episodes, and I have the DVD sets, too, the ones with the behind-the-scenes sections. OhmyGod."

"She's on TV?" This came from the boy, who suddenly seemed more interested in Annja.

"I've watched everything I could find on mummies, too. Egypt is going to be my specialty, the Karnak temples." She babbled on for several minutes, and Annja listened attentively.

Annja had learned to never be rude to fans, particularly ones with a real interest in archaeology. Every time she thought her *Chasing History's Monsters* was too sensational and not serious enough, something like this happened…someone showed her that the program made a difference or meant something to someone.

"And I've loved everything you've done on the Nile Delta and Kufu and—" Keesha came up for air. "I'm going to be a sophomore at Lakeside High, and we don't have much chance to study archaeology. But our library has a good selection, and the Milwaukee museum is wonderful. They had a King Tut exhibit and the Dead Sea Scrolls. Well, they weren't really the scrolls—they were reproductions. The real scrolls will never be put on display like that or let out of the country. But these looked amazing, and the tour was great, and some people thought it was horrible when they discovered they'd paid a separate fee to see the exhibit when it wasn't the 'real' scrolls. But they did have a real section of a scroll. A real piece of it. I went twice." She took another breath.

"So you're on TV?" the boy asked. "Is it one of those reality shows? Maybe I should have my picture taken with her."

Keesha just glared at him. "Are you on Facebook? I didn't think to look you up on Facebook. If you're on Facebook, do you think I could—"

"Of course you can 'friend' me," Annja said.

"OhmyGodohmyGodohmyGod."

Annja chatted with the girl for several more minutes, asking about her studies and recommending books. The girl soaked it in.

"So, why are you here?" Keesha asked. "In Lakeside? Are you trying to find the big snake? 'Cause I can tell you it doesn't exist. You'd be wasting your time." She nodded toward the shop Annja had been about to enter. "As silly as crop circles. You're not here for that, are you?"

"No, actually, I came to Madison for the Great Lakes States Archaeological Conference, and—"

"There's an archaeological convention in Madison?" Keesha squealed. "How did...? I didn't know... Where was it publicized? Can I get in? Is it expensive? I don't have a lot of—"

"Here." It was Annja's turn to reach into her purse. She pulled out her badge. "Use mine." She opened the plastic and stripped off the label that had Annja Creed printed on it. "Just write your name on it and see if it will work." The conference was quite expensive, likely out of the teenager's reach. If Annja wanted to get back in, she could buy another pass. But she suspected the conference was over for her. "I happen to know that there are two programs tomorrow on Egypt and the ruins they're finding under residential areas." Fortunately neither happened to be Peter's seminars, and so they were still scheduled, last she'd heard.

The girl covered her mouth again. "OhmyGod. I've read about that, homes collapsing because tomb robbers are tunneling underneath them." She looked at the badge. "I can go? Really?"

"It's downtown at the Madison Arms Hotel. Hopefully, the badge will work for you. Well, you'll have to find a way to Madison, but—"

"Mitch'll take me, won't you? Mitch has a license and a car and he can drive and take a book and read in the lobby while I go to the seminars and it'll be great and so very awesome." The girl's lower lip trembled. "OhmyGod." She shut her eyes for a second and took a deep breath. "But if I have your pass and you're in Madison for the conference, how are you going to go to the conference and—"

"I think I'm done at the conference," Annja said. "I think I'm going to spend a day or so here."

"Not on the big snake?"

"No, not on the snake."

The girl brightened. "Oh, the mounds in the lake!"

"There you go," Annja said.

"Awesome."

"Whatever." This from the boy. "Keesha, can we just—"

"Okay, okay, the beach, I get it. And then the carnival. But tomorrow you're taking me to Madison."

"Whatever."

"OhmyGod. Thankyousomuch, Annja Creed. Thankyouthankyou."

The boy tugged her down the street in the direction of the lake.

18

Annja finally pushed open the shop door, stepped inside and saw an incredible jumble of…stuff.

"Help you?" This came from a bearded middle-aged man with a bald head that gleamed in the overhead fluorescent light. He had a slight paunch, rounded shoulders and was wearing a Batman Lives T-shirt that had seen many better days.

The shop smelled fusty, and Annja forced down a sneeze. She walked across a wooden floor that creaked with each step, stopping in front of the counter. "I hope you can help. I'm trying to find out about—" The word *Joe* died in her throat. On display in the glass counter in front of her were coins. Most of them were quarters issued to commemorate the various states— and most of those were the Wisconsin variety—with a few silver dollars in the mix. There were a couple of silver certificates in plastic sleeves, and against a piece of velvet was a gold circle a little larger than a silver dollar showing a half-wolf, half-man figure— the same size as the circles Edgar had. She was surprised she spotted it, what with all the other items strewn around it.

She pointed to the coin.

"Oh, that's reeeeeeeeeeeeeal valuable," Sully said. "It's reeeeeeeeeeal gold. If it was for sale, well, that'd cost you a cool thousand. And it's not for sale."

"Do you have more?"

"Ones like that? I did. Sold them late last summer. Keeping this one for myself. It looks good in the counter, don't you think? Sentimental, you understand. My cousin gave them to me."

"Your cousin Joe *gave* them to you?"

"Yeah, Joe. Rest his soul."

"Them. Gave *them* to you. How many did you have?"

He gave her a mean look. "What's it to you? I'm not selling this one. Last real good thing I got of my cousin's. That and an ugly old pot that I'm using for a spittoon." He reached under the counter and pulled out a silver flask, unscrewed the top and took a long drink. "To Joe," he said as a toast, taking a second swallow then putting the cap back on.

Annja smelled the whiskey.

She glanced around. To her left was a shelf filled with political memorabilia, including a bobblehead Ronald Reagan, a plush Bill Clinton doll and a case of presidential campaign pins, some of them quite old— Harding, Coolidge, "Let's Back Ike" and a Landon Knox Kansas, whom she'd never heard of. Amid the junk, Sully had some truly expensive and valuable pieces. She hoped he had good security.

"Where did Joe get the gold circles?" she asked. "Do you mind telling me that?"

He shrugged.

Annja looked around for something to buy. "I'll take that old postal coupon. How much?"

"Twenty." He took it out of the case.

She paid for it and put it in her purse. "The woman across the street told me Joe was killed last fall."

"Sucked," Sully said. "Sucked a big onion, it did. Not just killed. Murdered. Still haven't caught the guy. Probably thought Joe was loaded."

"Because of the gold circles?" Annja pointed to the glass case.

"That and some other stuff probably." Sully folded his arms across his chest and shook his head as if he was disgusted. "But he wasn't loaded. Joe, he didn't keep anything for himself, you know. He was gonna be a priest at one point. Didn't work out, but he hung on to the poverty thing. Kept enough to live on, barely, and gave everything else away. Friggin' everything. Probably why some bugger thought Joe was loaded. Didn't even buy paperbacks. Checked stuff out of the library. Worked on the pots across the way 'cause he liked messing with the clay wheel, he told me. They didn't pay him much, not what he should've earned. He only needed enough money for food, rent and a few hobbies, is what he always told me."

"Where did Joe…where did Joe get them, the gold?" Annja tried to keep the excitement out of her voice.

"You want to buy anything else?" Sully raised his eyebrows. "I got some old gold rings and such if you have to have gold."

"How about that ten-dollar silver certificate? How much is that?"

Sully brightened. "I can let you have it for two hundred. And that's a bargain. Issued out of a LaSalle, Illinois, bank that doesn't exist anymore. In good shape."

She passed over her credit card and he handled the sale. This little trip was going to put a serious dent in her savings when it was all done. The silver certificate was in a hard plastic case and Annja added it to her purse.

"Do you know where Joe got them, the gold pieces?"

"Persistent as hell, aren't you?"

Annja smiled.

"You remind me of that big old guy who bought most of Joe's other stuff, him and his friend. They wanted to know where Joe got it all, too. Even went over to the pottery place and talked to Joe about it. Pestered the heck out of him, from what I understand."

Annja rested her fingers on the counter. "Sully—" She ran her thumbs in a circle against the glass. "The big old guy was a friend of mine, dead now, maybe dead because of those gold pieces. In fact, probably because of them. His friend, too, dead. Maybe your cousin died because of them." All connected, she thought once more. "So, I'd like to know where they came from. And if I were you, I'd put that piece of gold away, not leave it out on display. It might not be healthy."

Sully blanched. "He found the gold, young lady! Joe didn't steal it or nothing. He found it in the lake. That big guy and his friend, they wanted Joe to show them right where the gold came from. I don't know if Joe was gonna take them out on the lake or not. Joe didn't say. And then he was dead, Joe."

A car honked on the street, and Annja turned to see someone jaywalking.

"And that 'big guy?' Did you ever see him after he and his friend bought the gold? Did he return?"

Sully looked thoughtful. "I remember him coming back after Joe was killed, once, asking questions I didn't have answers to, and saying 'sorry for your loss' and all that. Looking for more of them gold pieces, they were. But I wasn't going to sell neither one of them the last one. Hell, between the two of them, they'd already bought seven of the eight pieces Joe'd given me. Even I draw the line somewhere. Kept the one for myself. I sold them the bracelet, though. Real pretty, it was, gold and silver and had jade on it." He smiled slightly. Annja wondered if he was proud of the fact he wouldn't cave and sell the last one or happy for the money he'd made off the other pieces.

"Sully, how much did you charge them for the pieces?"

"I might be overpriced on my stuff, but I wasn't gonna rob them blind. Three hundred for each coin, five for the bigger one with the bird on it. The gold in them was only worth, oh, four to five hundred by the weight, but they looked old, you know, and had pictures on them. Not coins, money, I can tell that, but old. Age has a value. The bracelet, now, I'd taken it to the jewelry store, and she offered me a thousand for it. So I brought it back, marked it at two thousand, and that fellow who was with the big old guy didn't bat an eye and paid me for it."

Annja felt clammy. She remembered word for word what Sully had said when she pointed to the coin he had left: "Oh, that's reeeeeeeeeeeeal valuable. It's reeeeeeeeeeal gold. If it was for sale, well, that'd cost you a thousand."

She kept herself from saying that thousand would have been a steal. If they were indeed Mayan, and indeed from Wisconsin, she'd guess the piece under the glass—and the three she'd seen in the police evidence bag—were probably each worth at least three to five times that much. Maybe not enough to kill over. But the bracelet? If it was Mayan, too…

He folded his arms. "The big old guy and his friend, they tried real hard to get me to sell this last one. Said name your price, they did. But Joe was family, and family is worth more than money, you know."

"Family is priceless." Annja had never had one. "Keep the piece close. For all sorts of reasons, Sully, keep that very close."

"Oh, I will. Hey, and I remember them asking for Joe's dive records. I couldn't help them there, either."

"So Joe was an avid diver? That's how he found the coins, going deep?"

"Yeah. One of his hobbies. He liked to dive the lake, liked the lake. He'd get pottery designs from the stuff around the shore and such. Me and Joe…we were always interested in the lake, obsessed maybe. Obsessed but for very different reasons."

Annja dropped her head, taking a last look at the piece of gold under the counter. "Those dive records would have helped," she said softly.

"Well, I couldn't help the big old fellow, not then. But I can help you now. I didn't have Joe's stuff then. But I've since got all of it…except for his clothes, I gave that stuff to the Saint Vincent DePaul center over by the church. Joe's old landlord dumped it all on me, not that there's all that much. A couple of cardboard boxes…that's what I kept. Diving logs are there. I hung on to them, thought that big old guy would come back. I was gonna sell them to him."

Annja gripped the counter. "Can I see them? Can you sell them to me?"

Sully got a far-away look in his eyes. "I heard that girl out in front of my shop, making a big deal about you. A TV archaeologist, she said."

Annja sighed. "How much are these diving logs going to cost me?" So Sully thought she was rich, that television equated to a lot of money. He was going to bilk her out of as much as he could. And she'd pay it.

"I heard her say you're a star on that program *Chasing History's Monsters*. Seen it, but I didn't recognize you."

"Yes," Annja admitted. "I'm with the program. But what about the dive records?"

"Oh, you can have them, but it'll cost you. I ain't looking for money out of this deal, lady. I'm looking for something else entirely." He unscrewed the top of the flask again and raised it to her in another toast.

Annja left the shop, a myriad of emotions dancing through her—she was anxious, exhilarated, tentative, hopeful and, overlaying all of that, unable to shake her grief over Edgar. Her old friend had to have known the pieces were worth more than what he paid. But she also knew he wasn't a wealthy man and probably couldn't have afforded to cover their true cost. And just what were they worth? What was the demand for Mayan pieces?

She'd check in with Manny, see what the expert from the Milwaukee museum had to say today. And do a little digging on her own at the hotel tonight, contact a few sources. But first… She pulled her cell phone out and punched in Rembert's number. Again it went to voice mail.

"I hope you're not heading back to New York," she said. "I hope you're still in Madison, Rem. I need you. I've got a project, and I desperately need your help." She hated to admit the "desperate" part, but she was. The mystery was burning ever brighter in her soul, just like it had in Edgar's. "Call me as soon as you get this message. Please."

19

In a spacious suite on the fifth floor, Garin stared at a shield that sat on a bureau protected with a starched white linen cloth. The bureau would normally have had a large-screen television on top of it. The room's occupant said he had asked for the television to be removed. He wanted flat spaces on which to display the wares.

"This man—" Garin indicated Rembert "—is my partner, and he will help authenticate it for me."

"I saw him taking video of the conference yesterday."

"At my request," Garin said. If Rembert had trouble with the ruse, Garin was pleased that he did not show it. "He is also here now at my request."

"Certainly, then." Willamar Aeschelman handed Rembert a pair of white cotton gloves. He was also wearing a pair.

It was a "heater" shield, so named by European museum curators because they thought the shape looked like an iron used on clothes. The top edge was flat and straight, two feet across, the side edges gracefully convex curving and coming to a point at the bottom, all of it forming a triangle about thirty inches long.

"It is genuine. I guarantee that."

"We shall see," Garin said. "Mr. Hayes?"

Rembert moved closer, bringing his face within inches.

"Not too close," Aeschelman warned. "I don't want your breath affecting it. A true museum piece."

"How old are you claiming this to be?" Garin did not take his eyes off the shield.

"It is from the 1400s, obviously French, obviously rare."

"Obviously," Rembert said. "Why do you think it is so obvious?"

Garin hid his displeasure. He'd told Rembert to say as little as possible, to nod and to pronounce the shield authentic and worth buying if Garin gave the sign.

The man snorted. "You test me? It is metal. That's what makes it obviously rare. Steel."

"Right you are," Rembert said.

Garin knew that to be true, as he had marched with men who carried similar shields, but they had been wood. In fact, most heater shields were—wood braced with iron, covered with leather or heavy linen. The one he had used was, and it hadn't lasted all that long. But the one who'd carried this shield had been landed and important.

"This style," Aeschelman continued. He looked at the screen of his iPad. "This style was used from 1200 until about 1500, but the supplier says this one has been successfully dated to being made between 1400 and 1430."

"And you were able to pin it down that closely?" This from Rembert.

Garin nudged him with a foot. *Be quiet,* he mouthed.

"The workmanship, and the pattern on its face. What you can see of the pattern dates it. And definitely French."

Garin mourned what the centuries had done to it. The steel shield had a thin piece of leather over the top, riveted in place and cracked, and the designs that had been painted on the leather were so faint he thought it sinful. Yet some care of it had been taken. The leather front was intact, and there was color to it. Still, he'd seen it when it was new; he knew what it once looked like in bright detail. A cross ran through the center of it, large and red like the Knights Templars had come to be known for. In the upper-left and lower-right quadrants were blue backgrounds with fleur-de-lis patterns in a yellow made to look like gold. In the upper right and lower left were each three white crosses on black backgrounds, representing the three crosses that had been placed side by side when Jesus was crucified.

"Yes, it is French," Garin said.

"My broker thought it might have been Scottish, as it is similar to the coat of arms of Sir Hugh Kennedy, a Scottish knight who fought with Joan of Arc. But it is not an exact match to that, the cross down the center making it different than the shield attributed to Kennedy and his men. But it fits with Joan of Arc's time. Perhaps it was carried by one of her knights. I don't have that much provenance on it. As I said, rare, especially given what it is made of. So few of the shields from that period are with us, and those that are…well, they're in museums."

"Is this from a museum collection?" Garin asked. "Liberated somehow?"

Aeschelman scowled. "How our little circle comes

by things is not up for discussion. You know that."
He reached a hand to his shirt, fingers resting on the
medallion Garin knew hung there. "We hold close to
our secrets."

"Secrets." Rembert visibly brightened at this.
"Not legal channels, that's for certain. Otherwise we
wouldn't be in this hotel room. We'd be at a public
auction house or—"

"I merely asked where it came from because that
would help Mr. Hayes and myself validate it." Garin
stared at Rembert. He should not have brought the
photographer into this, no matter how much he wanted
to rub Annja's nose in this artifact-smuggling operation.

"This particular shield has had several owners, the
last being old and divesting some choice pieces to pad
his bank account for heirs that do not appreciate his
collection," Aeschelman said. "So no, this was never
in a museum, from what I understand. But in passing
from hand to hand, certain laws were broken, and so
its ownership history is…best left to history." He adjusted his collar. "So, Mr. Knight, are you interested?
There are other pieces that we will be offering when
our sale opens at eight. Smaller, easier to take away
from this conference."

"Yes, I am interested in this shield. Mr. Hayes,
won't you turn it over for us? That should help us
authenticate it, yes?"

"Sure." Rembert carefully grasped the edges and
set it facedown on the bureau.

The back was dark, the rivets shiny from having
rubbed against something, perhaps whatever the shield
had been stored in. There were two leather straps that

had been preserved. The shield Garin had used had only one and so the shield's weight had not been as evenly distributed. But then Garin was not a landed knight and had not been as important as the shield's original owner. This one also had a longer strap that had run top to bottom, though the center of that piece of leather was gone. It had let its owner sling the shield across his back.

"Earlier, they used round shields, then kite shields, which were longer and afforded better protection," Aeschelman explained. "But these, these heater shields, were good for foot soldiers or mounted knights, more manageable."

"I understand the history of shields." Garin couldn't take his eyes off the piece.

"So do you collect them? Or medieval arms and armor in general?"

Garin didn't answer that. "The man who surrendered this from his collection…does he also have the companion piece, the helmet? It would have been made by the same armorer and at the same time. On the right side of the helmet were engraved fleur-de-lys and three crosses. I want to bid on that, as well."

"Not that I am aware of—"

"For what price will you give me the gentleman's name?"

Aeschelman looked uncertain, bordering on anger. "Double the price of what the shield goes for and I will *consider* it."

"I can do that."

"But I can't guarantee that he has—"

"I understand."

"And you will not talk to anyone about this."

Aeschelman's eyes were dark, and his fingers tapped the medallion beneath his shirt.

Garin remembered what Aeschelman had said about Mrs. Hapgood, that she was talking, talking, talking and that he "wanted to be rid of her" and so did her in. Doing Garin in would not be within Aeschelman's realm of possibility.

"I understand that, too," Garin said. "I know how to play this little game. I have been a part of your artifact-smuggling circle for nearly two years now." He turned to Rembert. "Well, is it authentic?"

Rembert turned to put himself between the shield and Aeschelman, then pointed to a spot on the rim. Garin had discussed the shield with the photographer before coming to the suite, told him where to look.

It was engraved, small and worn, and Garin doubted that Aeschelman even knew it was there. Two words: *Jeanne d'Arc*. Joan of Arc had engraved the shield at Roux's request. The shield had belonged to him, was made for him and signed by Joan herself at the armorer's shop. Roux had told Garin all about it, showed him the shield and the prized signature.

Roux had been a fool to tease Garin with what had now become a holy and historic artifact. But that had been centuries ago.

"You know, Captain America carried a shield with this shape, a heater shield," Rembert said. "The original Captain America, that is. Later the artists gave him a round shield."

"Thank you, Mr. Hayes," Garin said tersely. To Aeschelman, he said, "I don't suppose you can quote me a price and I can buy it right now?"

Aeschelman cocked his head. "You don't wish to attend our auction?"

Garin acquiesced. "Certainly, I will. There may be other pieces I want in addition."

"That's only two hours away," Aeschelman said. "I think you can wait."

"Two hours, then," Garin said. "I will bring my bank codes." He reluctantly left the room, Rembert behind him. He wanted the shield, and Aeschelman knew he wanted it. The piece was going to be very, very expensive.

Garin would give everything he had. Money was not important; it came and went. If he bankrupted himself to gain this very special shield, he would find a way to get more money.

But this shield…it carried Joan's signature. The shield was priceless.

And in two hours, it would be his.

20

"Sandra, my lawyer, doesn't think she can get me out until Friday. She's trying to get my bail hearing moved up. Got a formal arraignment coming first. She says that'll be Wednesday because the docket is otherwise full and one of the judges is up north." Peter stared at Annja with tired eyes, the circles so dark under them he reminded her of a raccoon. "So much for a speedy system, eh?"

"Friday." Annja learned a few minutes ago from Manny that Peter had been charged with manslaughter. They were going for the lesser charge, since the district attorney thought proving premeditation might be difficult. "Friday," she repeated. "That means you'll miss your diving session in Rock Lake with Bobby Wolfe."

Peter's eyes widened.

Annja had wanted to slip that bit in…that she knew about his plans. She was angry and made no attempt to hide it. "I met Bobby—dived with him earlier today, in fact. Nice guy. You were probably going to dive right where he took me. Down about ninety feet, to the mounds."

Peter's mouth worked, but nothing came out. He

regained his composure, but Annja went on before he could say anything.

"So you said Edgar was a fool, right? You said he was into fringe archaeology, that he didn't know what he was talking about…Mayans in Wisconsin. A wild-goose chase. But whatever it was that Edgar was looking for at the bottom of that lake, you wanted a piece of it, too. You booked his guide, and you were going to dive down. Bobby had your height and weight, had a wet suit picked out for you, knew where you wanted to go. You'd told him you were a friend of Edgar's—"

"I am a…was…a friend—"

"You intimated that you were part of Edgar's cadre. You and Papa. Except you weren't, were you? It was just Edgar and Papa, their research." Annja's face felt warm and she knew her blood pressure was high. She swore she could feel her heart thrumming in her chest. "You weren't part of it, but you were trying to horn in. You thought Edgar really was onto something."

Peter mumbled, but Annja couldn't hear the words. He'd held the phone away from his face to cut the volume of her rant.

"You found out…Bobby said he'd told you…told you that Edgar couldn't go into the lake, that he didn't want to take Edgar in, his age and weight, no suit to fit him. And that Papa was afraid to go, claustropho-bic, whatever. They were relying on Bobby to cement their great discovery. But you? You weren't afraid to dive a lake, were you? I know you, Peter. We've dived together, in cenotes in Mexico for crying out loud. You can dive."

He held the phone farther away and looked at the receiver, as if he might hang up on her.

She stumbled over her words, anxious to get them out, to make sure he heard her. "You were going to dive. You thought Edgar was right. You lied to me. You said you told Edgar he was a fool."

Peter held the phone close now and pressed the palm of his free hand against the Plexiglas that separated them. "I did tell Edgar he was a fool, all right? I said it."

"But you didn't mean it." She lowered her voice. "You really didn't mean it."

"The hell I didn't. He was a fool, an old fool. But a fool for telling me about his theory. A fool for not keeping his mouth shut. And look where he is now… the morgue."

Neither said anything for a moment. Annja thought Peter was going to cry. His shoulders had slumped forward, defeated.

"Dead is where it got him," he said finally. He regained a measure of composure and dropped his hand from the Plexiglas. "I don't know whether his theory was right, Annja, about Mayans in Wisconsin, but he showed me some of his research. It looked solid, believable. Plausible, in fact. He might have been onto something. I thought…yeah…maybe. Someone thinks he found evidence of Mayans in Georgia. They don't know if he's off his rocker or is valid. But if Georgia, why not Wisconsin, huh?"

Annja stared at him incredulously. "He was your friend, Peter. If you thought he had a good theory, why call him a fool? Why not support him?"

He was slow to answer. "He wouldn't let me in. He had Papa. It was going to be Edgar and Papa's find, with Edgar the primary. He let me get a taste, he teased me with the details out of our supposed friendship…teased me because his work was all so secret and compelling that he had to tell someone. Couldn't keep it to himself. It was eating away at him. He was so excited. So why not tell a friend, right? He showed me a piece of gold jewelry and said it came from Rock Lake."

"A gold circle?"

"Three, actually. I saw them Thursday. We got in about the same time. He showed them to me before I went on the Aztalan tour. I talked to Papa about their discovery when we were walking in the park. I thought if Edgar—"

"—wouldn't cut you in, that maybe Dr. Papadopolous might?"

"Something like that. I tried to talk Papa into including me in the hunt. I volunteered to do some of the research to help. I said I'd do the dives for them. Papa hated the water. His wife drowned in the city pool, you know. He was with her, couldn't save her. He never went in any body of water bigger than a bathtub after that. I'm surprised he went out on Rock Lake. That Papa would get in a boat at all convinced me that there was something to it." He paused. "Something. I don't know what, but something."

"And Papa wouldn't cave?" Annja talked softly now, trying to coax more information.

"Not on the tour. He wouldn't talk much about it on the tour. He was so busy spouting off about the mounds, showing people this and that. So I went to his house after dinner."

"Papa's house in town?"

A nod. "I was at Papa's house—" Peter stopped abruptly and hung up the phone.

"No!" Annja tapped furiously on the Plexiglas. "Pick up the phone! Peter! Talk to me!"

He looked to the door, as if he might summon a deputy to put him back in the cell.

"No!" She stood and leaned close to the barrier. "Peter!"

He relented and picked up the phone. "Annja, I shouldn't talk to you about this. Any of this. I've already said way too much. Sandra, my attorney, she said not to talk. To anyone. I'm like Edgar, huh? Saying too much when I should have kept my mouth shut."

"Please, Peter, will you just—"

"Just what, Annja? Tell you I don't have a significant find to my credit? I don't. Tell you I've drawn no great conclusion regarding Egyptian symbolism, my specialty? I haven't. That I've made no remarkable contribution to anything? That I've written no book in demand for college courses. That I've done… what…that I've done nothing significant in my life. I've piggybacked my whole career on other finds, followed other archaeologists, worked their digs, gotten grants by following up their projects. Never anything to leave behind. Nothing. Nothing. Nothing. Don't you understand?" He was shouting now and gripping the phone tightly. "And here my friend Edgar comes along and tells me about this 'amazing' theory he's been working on. That despite his arthritis and gout and all his other old-man ills he was going to put himself in the books. His name up in lights, as it were."

"So he told you out of friendship, because he wanted to share his joy," Annja said. The words were

a summation for her. "But he didn't want to share."
She shook her head. "I understand him, Peter. If it was
his discovery, his and Dr. Papadopolous's, he shouldn't
have had to share. You should have simply been happy
for him. Proud. Supported him."

"Proud? Wouldn't that be a kick, Annja, me being
proud? Of myself. I've never been proud of myself.
I've done some things—"

"What, Peter? What have you done?"

"I was at Papa's house Thursday night. Went a little after the tour, followed him home. Thought I'd
try talking to him again, thought I'd tell him how
dangerous the lake was and that he shouldn't go out
on it. That I would dive it for them, that they didn't
need the guide they'd hired. That their guide wasn't
good enough."

"And he told you their guide was good."

"Yeah, he told me about Bobby Wolfe. But he
wouldn't let me sign on with them, wanted to keep it
just the two of them, him and Edgar. He didn't want
to share the glory. Just like Edgar, he'd tell me about
their theory…that Mayans had come all the way up
here, that ultimately the indigenous people drove them
out, but that they left buildings behind. He showed me
some of the research. Just a little of it."

"And it was plausible." Annja recalled the underwater mounds. There was nothing Mayan about them.

"I gave up trying to convince him, though."

"Because he told you to leave," Annja guessed.

"Yes. So I did. I left, was in the car. I'd put the key
in the ignition and somebody pulled up. I waited. I
watched. I dunno why. I stayed out front and saw a
big man go into Papa's house, saw them together. The

drape was in the way, but I saw the silhouettes. I saw a struggle. I should have called the police, I know. Should have called right then and there. Should've gone back to the house and helped Papa. All that twenty-twenty hindsight, right? Instead, I drove away. Papa wouldn't let me in? Why should I help him? He wasn't going to help me." He started sobbing.

Annja realized that while she had considered Peter a friend, she didn't truly know him. Not at all. He wasn't as close a friend as Edgar, but still she thought she knew Peter's heart. Most of her relationships were casual, surface, not letting anyone too close. So she wasn't aware that Peter had a record—priors—and she never figured he was the type of man to try to take credit for another archaeologist's discovery…or hopeful discovery. To muscle in.

"I could have done the dives for them, Annja."

"But they had Bobby Wolfe for that," she returned softly.

"It occurred to me that maybe whoever had gone to Papa's house was also looking to get a cut, had maybe overheard us talking at the Aztalan mounds. So I drove around and came back an hour later. I was gonna ask Papa about his visitor. The car was gone, and I went to check on Papa. See if he was okay. I'd decided on another tactic to try to persuade him. The door was open, and so I went in. Papa…he was dead. I assumed whoever came to visit him did it and then put him in bed to cover it up. Then I called Edgar to warn him. Maybe it was about the gold. Edgar was in his hotel room, and I told him it looked like Papa's house had been searched. Papa's medallion—" He paused, letting out a great breath that steamed the

Plexiglas. "Edgar had showed me the three circles, clearly pieces of jewelry, clearly Mayan. He'd brought them here. And Papa…Papa had four pieces, one of them a bigger piece, a medallion that he'd said came from the same place, and a bracelet. I looked for the medallion at Papa's, found the box he'd had it in. But the medallion was gone, the circles and the bracelet, gone, as well as his research notes and computer. I told it all to Edgar. Annja, that gold was valuable. Seriously, seriously valuable. Not because…well, not because it was gold, but because of where it came from and that it hints there could be more."

Annja sat back, trying to absorb everything.

"Some of this will come out," Peter continued. "It'll show I didn't kill Edgar. Whoever killed Papa, well…"

Annja just stared.

"…I think whoever killed Papa killed Edgar." He switched hands on the telephone, wiped his sweaty palm off on his jumpsuit. "Problem is, nobody is looking at Papa's death as murder. He had a history of heart problems, and they think he just died in his sleep. The police don't know it's probably about the gold."

Peter could get them to look at Papa's death as murder, Annja realized; if it came out at trial about Edgar and Papa's research, the gold and the theory. But to do that, Peter would have to reveal that he was trying to talk his way into their clique, turn their duo into a triumvirate and take a share of the discovery. It would make Peter look bad…but could he look any worse than being charged with manslaughter?

"If you had called the police," Annja said, her voice a whisper, "when you saw the struggle at Dr. Papadopolous' house, maybe he'd be alive." She recognized too late how very hurtful those words were, that she'd put Papa's death on Peter. "Look, I—"

"You don't think I know that?" Peter's face was red with ire. "I know I screwed up…. If I'd done something, I maybe could've kept Papa alive." His voice faded to a mere whisper. "And maybe Edgar, too. If only I'd called the police right away."

"You're a fool," Annja said, not able to tamp down her anger. "Maybe Edgar was right about the Mayans. Or maybe he was on a wild-goose chase. In either case, he wasn't the fool."

Peter's shoulders shook. "Annja, I—"

Peter was a different man to her now. Not the archaeologist she had respected or the man she'd called a friend. He was defeated. Pitiful.

"Mrs. Hapgood." Annja remembered that people at the conference said Mrs. Elyse Hapgood was with Peter. "Does she have anything to do with this…with *any* of this?" Or was Mrs. Hapgood a puzzle piece that Annja wasn't going to be able to cram into place?

He shook his head. "Elyse."

"Not a coincidence, Peter. Everything's related."

He shook his head more vehemently. "Elyse had nothing to do with his. She is…was…a friend, a little more than a friend. But I told her about it, the gold and the theory, just in conversation at the park while I was hoping to talk to Papa again. I guess we all talk too much. But I swear she had nothing to do with—"

"Edgar, Dr. Papadopolous, your 'friend' Mrs. Hapgood. They're all related, Peter."

"Annja, no, maybe not. Maybe—"

"They all knew about the theory and the gold. And

they're all dead." She stood, still holding on to the phone. "I'd watch your back, Peter. I'd stay in jail, where you're safe. And I'd pay attention to your attorney. Keep your mouth shut." Maybe if he'd done that, at least Mrs. Elyse Hapgood would still be breathing.

21

Annja knew she had a temper, but she kept it under control most of the time. Now she wasn't even trying.

Right now she wanted to be angry, *needed* to be angry…over the death of Edgar, and Papa, whom she'd never met, over the death of a potter named Joe, who made works of art and discovered Mayan gold in a Wisconsin lake. She was an admitted adrenaline junkie, and her rage was giving her a welcome boost. She focused on it, felt her heart beating faster, formed fists as she walked from the police station toward the parking lot where she'd left her motorcycle. She could have parked closer, but after dealing with Sully, driving here right after, she wanted to burn off some pent-up energy.

Annja listened to the city as she went, the traffic shushing by, music coming from open car windows—rap, blues, country, rock. There was the loud belch of a bus that pulled up next to her, dispatching a few folks who were going toward an apartment building, probably headed home from work or possibly from dinner, judging by the time. She glanced at her watch; it was nearly seven. She'd hoped to find Manny after she was done with Peter, but he wasn't at the station.

"Out at the hotel and conference center," an officer told her. "Working a case."

His last case, she thought, wanting to help solve it for Edgar and herself, but also for the detective. It would indeed be a great note to end his career on. Two blocks to go and she caught a look at an old woman outside an antiques shop. She'd been looking in the window, the shop closed, but now she was looking at Annja, eyes wide and mouth open. Maybe a fan of *Chasing History's Monsters,* or maybe…

Annja spun, but not fast enough. A man had come up behind her, snub-nosed pistol in his hand. He jabbed her with it.

"In the alley," he growled. "Now, or I'll pull the trigger."

The sword was there in Annja's mind and she flexed her hand, ready to call it. But not here, right out on the sidewalk with all the people watching.

"No!" The old woman yelled and jumped back, hoping to shield herself. "Police!"

The old woman screamed. She was on her cell phone, calling the police, frantically describing the man with the gun.

"Damn." The man pushing Annja raised a hand with something in it just as they reached an empty alleyway. She breathed, and then the earth seemed to fall away and darkness reached up to swallow her.

She came to minutes later.

Annja knew she hadn't been out long, since the sky was still gray. She heard sirens, loud and close, likely coming in answer to the old woman's call. The man who'd clocked her now loomed over her. They were still in the alley. She'd been stuffed between two

Dumpsters. The guy was attempting to hide the both of them from the action on the street. He waved the snub-nosed gun at her.

"You!" he said.

Annja waited, tentatively reaching up and touching the back of her head, her fingertips coming away bloody. "Great." She was sitting on the ground, the back of her pants damp from whatever garbage he'd sat her in.

"You!" He pointed the gun at her and kicked at something on the ground between her knees. It was her purse, and he'd upended it. The contents were strewn among the litter. Her cell phone was in pieces beneath his heel.

"Great," she said again. The sword was there, waiting, almost as if it was demanding she reach for it. Annja held back. The man would have killed her if that had been his intent.

He touched his ear with his free hand; she noticed he had a phone bud. "Mr. A.," he said. "I have her. But the cops are here. Some old woman called them. Sirens going already. Yeah, I'll get it out of her. I'll get your gold. Stevie's bringing the van right now." He touched the bud again, disconnecting his call. "So, where is it, lady? The rest of it?"

Annja put on a surprised face and listened to the siren, which was passing by the alley. The car didn't stop. "The rest of what?"

He shoved the gun against her forehead.

"You know damn well what I want."

The guy was going to kill her, she decided, but not until after he got what he wanted.

"You know what. The coins. The gold your fat friend had."

"Dr. Schwartz?"

"Yeah, him." He pressed the gun harder; it hurt. "Quick, lady. Not in your purse." He moved his foot to step on the plastic enclosing the silver certificate. It snapped. "Not in your hotel room. Where is it and where did Schwartz get it? Tell me now and I won't have to dump you a long ways from here. Better if your friends find your body, don't ya think? Where did it come from, the gold coins? Where's the treasure? We know Schwartz was a friend of yours. Said your name all nice and pretty before he died—"

"You son of a bitch!" He'd killed Edgar. But the thug hadn't gotten anything useful out of Edgar in the process…other than her name. Her old friend hadn't mentioned Sully's What-Nots, nor the lake. She was planning to go along with the brute; he was clearly the muscle and not the brains. The brains had been at the other end of the earbud. That was who she needed to find—the orchestrator—to fill in the final puzzle pieces.

She wanted to yell at him some more, but she was mad and grieving, and suddenly, the sword was in her hand. She turned and swung with all the strength she could summon, hitting the hand holding the gun. She'd used the flat and the impact was loud, his cry of pain sharp. Still, he kept hold of the snub-nosed pistol.

The sirens roared louder. She counted two now. Were they doubling back? They had to be looking for her and this thug. She'd have to act quickly, to deal with the man and get some questions answered before the police found this alley or before Stevie and the van showed up.

She wasted no time. Sweeping the sword up, she rammed him with it. He staggered, and as she was clear of the Dumpsters, she had room to truly work the blade. She angled it again and drove it down, the flat cracking against his shoulder blade. She heard something pop—maybe his shoulder had dislocated, maybe she'd cracked a bone.

A string of expletives ran together as he jerked his gun in close and fired it.

Hot pain stabbed through Annja's thigh. He'd shot her.

"Where the hell…did you get a sword!"

She reversed her swing, and the blade caught him in the arm. "You bitch! Mr. A. says you gotta live… until you give up the gold." He quickly stepped back when Annja swung once more, slicing through his heavy shirt and drawing a line of blood. He fired again. This time the bullet connected with a Dumpster.

"Hey! What's going on down there? I'm calling the police!" The voice came from somewhere above them.

Tires squealed and Annja pressed her attack, rushing him and pinning him up against the opposite wall of the alley, bringing the sword up in both hands and hammering down with the pommel, catching him on the shoulder blade again.

"Who's doing this? Give me a name!"

His answer was to spit in her face.

Gravel ricocheted against trash cans and the brickwork, and tires squealed louder, heralding company in the alley. Annja looked now, expecting to see a police car, but it was a van, Army-green and speeding toward them.

A dog barked, more yelling and the sirens again.

The van was closing in.

Annja dismissed her sword to free both hands, and she sprung, grabbing the end of a fire escape and hauling herself up, her leg screaming in protest. The tips of her shoes bounced against the roof of the van; it had come that close to the wall, meaning perhaps to run her over.

Or to run over the thug.

She glanced down as she pulled herself up another rung and saw a flash of light from the passenger window. The sirens were too loud to hear anything apart from them, but she knew a gun had gone off. The thug caught it in the chest, and the van rocketed out of the other end of the alley, turning right so hard and fast it rode up on two wheels before disappearing from sight.

A police car followed the van, the sound of its siren so loud it hurt. A second car that was behind it, lights on but no sirens, slammed to a halt. Two officers jumped out, one leaning over the thug, the other standing next the car, mic to his mouth and looking up at Annja and motioning. She couldn't hear what he was saying. There was too much noise—sirens, shouts from the street, from someone above.

She lowered herself down the fire escape and jumped the last five feet to the ground, landing on her good leg and falling, but picking herself up before the cop could reach her.

"How is he—" Annja started.

"Dead," the officer answered. "One round in the chest, dead center."

More sirens. Annja pressed her palms against her ears and leaned back against the brick. "This has been a crazy day," she said.

An ambulance entered the alley from the opposite end, going nose to nose with the police car. Two paramedics hopped out, one going to the back and opening the door.

"No." Annja waved at them. "I'm not going to—"

"Ma'am?" This from the officer who had been checking on the thug. "We need you to go to the hospital, ma'am."

"It's Annja Creed," the other officer said. "The woman Rizzo told me about." He picked up the spilled contents of her purse and tried to make some order of them, then gathered her broken cell phone and stuffed it all in the purse. He nodded toward his partner. "Miss Creed, Larry here will ride with you to the hospital. Is there anyone we can call for you?"

She thought a moment, deciding not to argue and to accept the ride. Her leg throbbed badly, and her pants were wet with muck and blood. "Manny. You could call Detective Manny Rizzo for me."

"Yes, ma'am."

She closed her eyes when they helped her onto the stretcher. Its thin mattress felt comfortable. "You don't have to use the sirens," she told the paramedics.

But they didn't listen.

22

He liked the feel of her skin against his, slightly sweaty and perfumed, soft and smooth as porcelain.

"I have to leave, Keiko."

She sucked on his earlobe and draped an arm across his chest. "No, you don't *have to leave*. This is my vacation, Gary, yours and mine, and we can stay between these sheets until noon tomorrow if we want to."

He rose and checked the clock on the nightstand. "Sorry. I've an appointment," he said and padded into the bathroom for a shower, the steaming water washing away all trace of her.

Like money, women came and went from his life, but he was finding himself attached to this one. Keiko wasn't especially beautiful or smart, and he thought her overly skinny. But she had a charm, was good in bed, and he liked the way her eyes flashed with childlike wonder when she was excited over something… anything. Did she suspect that he would ditch her shortly? Not right after this conference, as he was going back to Chicago for a while and she would continue to provide a welcome distraction when he was not "working." But soon thereafter.

He'd fly out of the Windy City for someplace exotic, and he'd leave her behind. He would never see her again. Garin knew that he'd regret it.... It would be the first time in many, many years that he would feel sad—would feel anything—over leaving a woman. But he would leave her nonetheless. Women did not live forever...and even if they did, he couldn't imagine spending eternity with just one.

He toweled himself and changed into jeans and a tailored shirt, added a maroon silk tie Keiko had bought him this afternoon with his money. As an afterthought he put on a blazer, a very expensive linen-and-silk blend he'd paid seventeen hundred for. Fog-gray and adjusted to fit his wide shoulders, he fancied that it made him look professional, but not overly so, as the jeans kept his appearance casual.

"My handsome man," Keiko pronounced. "I like to watch you dress."

He came to the bed, leaned over and kissed her forehead. "And I like to watch you undress."

She giggled playfully. "I ordered wine from room service. Can't you wait until it gets here? Have a glass before you go to spend more time with those boring old anthropologists?"

"No, sweet. But I won't be gone all that long. Save me a few sips, will you?"

"And then I can watch you undress," she said. "I think I will like that even better."

He met Rembert on the floor above, not wanting the photographer to know what room he was in. Together they went up to the penthouse floor.

"Your camera?"

"Two, actually. My tie tack," Rembert said. He

fiddled with his tie to show him. "Neat, huh? Like something out of James Bond. Won't be the best for recording faces. So for that, I'm relying on this earpiece in my glasses. They weren't all that expensive, and I figure I can turn in a voucher for them. The quality? I don't know, not up to what I can get with my good equipment, but they're unobtrusive."

"No shots of me, understand, Mr. Hayes…until I ask you for such."

Rembert looked confused. "I thought you didn't want any—"

"And be careful in here. You said you valued your family and your skin. These men are…" He watched Rembert pale and left the sentence unfinished. The photographer got his meaning.

Aeschelman greeted them with champagne, which Garin declined. He wanted to remain alert, and he was pleased Rembert followed his lead. He stayed slightly behind the photographer's shoulder, ensuring that he wouldn't end up in the video.

There were a dozen others present, and even though the suite was large, the guests made the room feel uncomfortably close. Perfumes and scented oils mingled and made Garin's eyes water. A thin man was smoking, despite hotel regulations. The youngest was an archaeologist Garin had spotted yesterday trying to avoid the reporters in the lobby; he had the wide-pupil look of having just done a line of cocaine. There were two other men who'd been wearing badges earlier in the day. So Garin had accounted for the archaeologists in the circle who were attending the conference—two bidding and selling for themselves, one acting as a broker; he suspected the broker to be the cocaine boy.

All of the bidders were dressed similarly to Garin, the only woman in a long brown skirt that was not kind to her wide hips. He spotted Aeschelman's muscle, two men with thick arms who were pretending to look interested in the items on display. When they turned, he could see bulges under their jackets that were handguns of some type.

Garin nudged Rembert forward, past a counter that held an array of wines. Garin noted a pricey Pinot Noir from Santa Barbara that he adored. The assortment should surely cover just about anyone's palate and was far more than this gathering would drink, he mused. The appetizers represented everything he'd seen available from the dining-room menu: grilled flat bread, cheese and charcuterie, braised calamari, carpaccio of lamb, smoked-salmon rillettes, poached pears and tuna crudo.

Would the hotel be appalled if they knew what event they had catered here? He smiled at the thought and caught Rembert eyeing the food. He nudged him again, farther into the suite. It was the shield Garin wanted to see again, and out of curiosity the other items up for bid this night.

The shield was the centerpiece, in the middle of the marble-topped credenza.

One of Aeschelman's nattily-dressed goons started passing out white cotton gloves and telling the guests they could only touch what they were bidding on, and then only if they were serious.

"You don't like wine, Mr. Knight?" Aeschelman had moved up to Garin and gestured toward the display of drinks and food.

"Afterward," Garin said. "I find that alcohol clouds my judgment."

Aeschelman smiled, and in that moment Garin pictured the man as a crocodile in a previous life. "I understand, Mr. Knight. You don't want the alcohol to make you bid more than you've planned on, eh? And interesting that you desire the shield."

"Why?" This from Rembert.

"Shield, knight—the unintended humor is not lost on me." Aeschelman glided away to talk to the woman in the brown skirt.

"I never asked," Rembert said, keeping his voice to just above a whisper. "Why are you interested in the shield?"

"I am interested in a lot of things, Mr. Hayes."

Garin had a look at the other selections, careful to remain slightly behind the photographer. He noticed the way Rembert moved from one object to the next; the photographer was getting video of each piece. He'd already recorded the faces of the evening's participants.

The antiquities seemed to be Greek, Luristan, Chinese, Egyptian, Roman and French. Garin recognized an Old Kingdom limestone relief, an Illyrian Greek bronze helmet that must have dated to 500 BC, a Laconian dog, a Canosan pottery horse and an assortment of Ghandaran Schist pieces. On another table were two small vases; overhearing the young man, Garin learned they were from the Tang and Ming dynasties.

On the bureau where the TV had been were an Egyptian bronze Apis bull and the statuette head of an ibis.

"That, my good sir, is from the twenty-sixth dynasty." This came from one of the archaeologists Garin had spotted at the conference. He was pointing to the ibis. "I can tell you precisely from what dig I culled that. Everything in that tomb came from the twenty-sixth dynasty. It had better go for twelve thousand. The jewelry there, I brought those pieces out of an accidental find, following a tunnel under a neighborhood outside of Cairo. Most of it had already been looted, but we managed to knock down a wall and find an intact chamber. But that ibis, that's choice."

"I'm not bidding on that one," Garin said. "Egypt holds no interest for me."

The archaeologist huffed and turned to chat with one of the other guests.

There were several ushabtis, none taller than a foot. Rembert pointed to them.

"Funerary figurines," Garin said as explanation.

Near them rested Egyptian faience amulets of Isis festooned with carnelian beads. One featured the triad of Nephthys, Isis and Horus. Garin had said he wasn't interested in any of the Egyptian pieces, but the large amulet…if it did not go for too much, he would buy that for Keiko, a parting gift for her to remember him by.

Rembert shuffled closer, and Garin heard a faint click; not only did the photographer have cameras, he'd brought a separate recording device with him and likely had been turning it on and off to catch conversations. The admission of the archaeologist explaining that he'd taken relics out of Egypt should add value to Rembert's video.

There were pre-Columbian pieces on the desk, including three coin-shaped medallions similar to but smaller than the one hanging hidden from Aeschelman's neck. Two of them were placed together and had matching half-man, half-creature designs on them, probably earrings. The other was a stylized depiction of the sun. Garin turned it over to find a half man/half badger on it.

"Funny-looking," Rembert observed.

Garin could tell he'd reached into his pocket and clicked the recorder off, not wanting to pick up his own voice.

"Those little pieces, they look like deer or elk, don't they? And that one, a badger with a man's face. It's sort of like the mascot for the city's university."

Garin peered closer. "Indeed." Perhaps he would bid on those, as well.

The silver-and-gold bracelet, too, looked interesting. Dotted with jade and etched with more of the half-man, half-badger creatures. He doubted they were truly pre-Columbian, and in some cases he doubted the authenticity of several of the things for sale. Some craftsmen were so skilled that they could create objects that appeared to be centuries old, going so far as to find materials dating to those time periods; museums had paid thousands for pieces later proved forgeries.

Garin recalled reading an article in a current archaeology magazine before coming to this conference; he'd been trying to acquire conversational tidbits in the event he found himself trapped. It covered the controversial sale at a Paris auction house of a pre-Columbian stucco goddess. Nearly life-size, it had been dated to roughly 700 AD and went for more than four million. Mexican authorities contended that the artifact was merely a clever forgery and had been recently produced and artificially made to look ancient. However, the auction house stood by its experts. The article went on to quote European museum curators who said the Mexican government was merely trying to eliminate the trade of pre-Columbian artifacts from European markets. Garin wondered what the Mexican authorities would say about these pieces.

"These are beautiful pieces." This from one of the two men ogling the pre-Columbian selection; he pointed to the effigies.

Rembert had turned on his recorder again.

The gold effigies were each no larger than a golf ball, and they had been placed next to Colima pottery figurines and a pre-Columbian Moche stirrup vessel that Aeschelman said was dated to 300 AD.

"I acquired that very piece myself," Aeschelman told Garin. "We are ready to begin."

In the end, Garin acquired the shield for thirty thousand, not as much as he had expected to spend, but the only other interested bidder was the woman, and she had already purchased several of the Egyptian pieces. If the others had known that the shield had in fact been carried by one of Joan of Arc's knights… and had Aeschelman saw Joan's signature etched in the steel, it could have sold for ten times that amount.

And Garin would have paid it. He would have given up every last cent to get this, would have stolen it if need be. He knew when he saw it earlier today that he would not be leaving Wisconsin without it.

Garin spent eight thousand on the earrings, having been told that a pair of earrings of that age was exceedingly valuable. Often only one survived the centuries. And another two thousand on the small medallion of the half man/half badger; he intended to have it turned into a key chain.

If Rembert had been surprised at the money Garin was tossing at Aeschelman, he wisely didn't show it. Garin decided that it had not been so foolish a decision to bring Annja's photographer into this after all.

"Wine to celebrate your purchases?" Aeschelman offered Garin a toast.

"I have wine waiting for me in my room, thank you." And better company to share it with. He pictured Keiko stretched out, catlike, on the bed and could not help but smile. But he had one more stop to make before he could return to her. He paid Aeschelman and added thirty thousand to it. "The name of the gentleman who had the shield?"

Aeschelman provided a card; it would take at least a phone call to determine if it was the right man…an expensive risk. The auction host had also provided packaging material for each item. In Garin's case, the shield was carefully nested into an overlarge thin portfolio, the kind artists carried their paintings in.

"Perhaps I will see you at the next gathering of this circle," Garin said to Aechelman as he and Rembert left.

"Perhaps." Aeschelman turned his attention to the woman and put his hand against the small of her back.

At the elevator, Garin saw Rembert let out a deep breath and relax his shoulders. He opened his mouth, but Garin shook his head and mouthed *Later.* In the elevator, Garin waited until Rembert punched the button for the eighth floor.

"Are you sharing your room with anyone, Mr. Hayes?"

"No." Rembert gave him a puzzled look.

"Good. We will talk there."

Garin took the desk chair and rested the portfolio with the shield in the only other chair, leaving Rembert to sit on the edge of the bed.

"What did you think, Mr. Hayes?"

Rembert planted his palms on his knees, pointed his face toward the floor and rocked. "I think those are people with too much money and big egos. I'm going to sell my video to a major network and I bet they'll use it as a piece of a much larger exposé. Those people back there are going to be in a world of trouble. The police…hell, I think the FBI will come after them."

"And I think you will have solved some of your money woes and made quite a name for yourself."

Rembert agreed and raised his head to meet Gavin's gaze. "So tell me…at least tell me why you did this." He pulled the recorder out of his pocket and laid it on the bed. Garin could tell it was off. He took off his tie-tack camera and the glasses

"Did this? Did what, Mr. Hayes? Buy the shield and the trinkets?"

Rembert shook his head. "No. I know you're not going to tell me that. And frankly, I don't care."

Smart man, Garin thought. No wonder Annja liked working with him.

"Then what?"

"Why let me film this, record those people—"

"Those people with big egos and money?"

"Yeah. Why let me in? I don't buy what you told me earlier. There's more to it."

"Of course there is, Mr. Hayes."

Rembert seemed to be studying him.

"I told you at the beginning of this that you would learn nothing about me."

"Well, I have."

Garin got up, opened the portfolio and removed the shield. He left the white gloves in his pocket. "You've learned only that I have money and a big ego, Mr. Hayes, and now you will learn that I am a smug SOB. Your video camera, please. And do you have a spare memory card?"

Rembert went to his camera bag and rustled around in it, glancing up and keeping an obvious eye on Garin. "I do have a spare memory card. I wouldn't be much of a photographer if I didn't carry spares."

"Then film me with it, Mr. Hayes." Garin stood waiting, posing with the shield.

"This is weird," Rembert muttered. "All of this is weird. You're weird." But he complied. He videoed Garin from one angle and then another.

"You record sound with that?"

Rembert touched a button. "I am now recording sound."

"Keep it going, then." Garin resumed his pose and squared his shoulders, put his chin up. "Roux. I am in Madison, Wisconsin, a…boring, almost wholesome place, and in this boring, almost wholesome place I ran across something that used to belong to you. Do you recognize it?" Keeping his face toward Rembert's camera, Garin turned the shield around and held it by the sides. "Move in closer, please. I want my friend to see the signature."

Rembert came close and adjusted the lens.

Garin made sure Rembert captured Joan of Arc's signature. "See, old friend?" He paused and waited until Rembert had stepped back and manually adjusted the focus. "It is amazing what one can come across in America's Heartland. Oh, Annja is here, by the way." He paused. "Well, not here, not right here. But she is in the city. It is too bad she didn't find this first, eh?"

Garin's silence served as adequate signal to Rembert. He brought the camera down, opened the side, extracted the memory card and handed it over.

"Thank you." Garin carefully replaced the shield, feeling Rembert's eyes on him. He reached into the bottom of the case and brought out a small cloth bag, the one that contained the half badger/half man gold piece with the sun on the reverse side. Garin gave in to his impulsive nature and handed it to Rembert. "I don't need another key chain. That should net you a good bit, but take care where you sell it, all right?"

Rembert stared, slack jawed.

"Now I must be on my way. If you see Annja, give her my best, won't you?"

Then he was down the hall and into the stairwell, taking it down one flight to his floor. He hoped he hadn't been gone so long that Keiko had bothered to get dressed.

23

"Treated and released. I'm impressed." Manny stood just inside the Emergency Room doors.

It was nearly midnight. Annja had spent almost five hours here.

"Guess the officers wouldn't hand over their first-aid kit and let you fix yourself, eh?"

Annja thought he looked in worse shape than she did. He was visibly exhausted, his clothes rumpled, and she wondered if he'd slept any after coming back from Lakeside Friday night. Had he been working the case nonstop? She really liked Manny; respected him, too.

"Fortunately, the bullet only grazed me," she said. "I was lucky."

"They were after the gold, right?"

She nodded.

"That's why we were chased yesterday. Why *you* were chased yesterday."

Annja raised an eyebrow.

"The officers that responded to the alley questioned a witness who lives in an upper apartment and who apparently saw it go down. Overheard your conversation and regurgitated it apparently word-for-word, the guy demanding the gold from you."

"He killed Edgar, that 'guy.'"

"Your professor friend."

"Yeah." She ran her fingers through her hair, discovering it was riddled with tangles. "He did it, but he wasn't behind it."

Manny set his hands on his hips. "We know that."

"From the witness?"

A nod. "Busybodies are great with details. He even got a look at the woman in the van who plugged the guy that shot you."

"Stevie." Annja remembered what the thug had said.

"I'll wager either she was the brains, or—"

"No, the brains is someone named Mr. A."

"Okay." Another nod. "The witness mentioned a Mr. A. We got the guy's earphone and we're working on following the calls that came and went on it. He didn't have any ID on him, the thug."

Annja opened her mouth.

"And yeah, I'll let you know what we come up with."

"Thanks."

"C'mon, I'll take you back to your bike."

Like a gentleman, he opened the door for her.

"How'd your meeting with the chief go?" Annja asked as they left the hospital lot.

Manny gave her his trademark lopsided grin. "It went." He followed it up with a dry chuckle. "Good thing I'm retiring, he said. Damn good thing."

The chatter from the police radio was low. Annja listened to a report about a drunk driver sideswiping parked cars on Pinehurst Drive off Highway 14. Behind them a siren wailed, an ambulance going out on a call.

Annja was wearing a pair of scrubs a doctor had handed over. Her own clothes were filthy and torn, and were probably headed to the hospital's incinerator. She was looking forward to a long bath in the hotel… before she changed clothes and checked out.

"I'm going to Lakeside tonight. Um, that'll be tomorrow morning by the time I get there. I made a reservation at the beach cottage where Edgar stayed." She looked at the jumble of things in her purse. She'd have to get a new phone. "I had to book it for the week."

Manny didn't say anything.

"And I found out where Edgar came by the gold."

She had his full attention now. He pulled over and parked while she told him about her trip to Sully's What-Nots. She recounted everything from her day's activities…except what she'd already detailed to the police who took her report at the E.R.

"They want the gold, Manny, but not because of its value. Those little pieces aren't actually worth all that much. I did some checking, and the market for pre-Columbian relics just isn't all that high, not unless you have rare, large pieces."

"Then why do they want it?"

"They think there's more. Wherever those few pieces came from… I wager they're thinking a lot more. And that 'lot more' could include some very, very valuable things. Too, if they could find proof of Mayans in Wisconsin…that would be valuable, as well."

Manny let out a long whistle, pulled back onto the

street and took her to where her bike was parked. "I don't know, Annja, about the whole Mayans-in-Wisconsin thing. Sounds a little far-fetched. But I do know people got killed over the gold, and I intend to close these cases and go out on top. I'm going back to Lakeside tomorrow, too. But after I catch a nap. Arnie's still taking the hotel angle. All the archaeologists got another full day before they split. He might make some of them stick around."

"I can stay in the area through Friday," she said. "Then it's Morocco."

"Ah, the life of a—"

Annja got out of the car, then leaned in and put her hand on Manny's arm. "Thanks for the ride. Thanks for a lot of things. I'd give you my cell-phone number so you could call me tomorrow, connect in Lakeside. But it's in pieces."

He fished his card out of his wallet. It had his cell number. "In case you get another phone," he said. Then he handed her a jump drive. "This is a copy. And I'm not giving you this. Understand? You don't have this copy."

"Copy of what?"

"Something Arnie found in the stairwell of the eighth floor. It was jammed into the light fixture on the wall, had broken the bulb."

Annja recalled that when she entered the stairwell after first learning of Edgar's death, the landing had been dark, the landings below and above it lit.

"Belonged to your professor. A clever hiding place so the guy coming after him wouldn't find it. Smart, you archaeologists, but your professor would've been smarter if he hadn't run. If he'd have stayed put and called us…"

"Indeed," Annja said.

Then he was gone and she was on her bike. It protested starting, and so did her leg, but she shrugged off the pain, and the bike sputtered to life. She revved the engine; the thing was noisy, and it coughed exhaust. She hoped the police wouldn't pull her over for violating local ordinances—she was already in trouble for not having the registration.

Several blocks from the hotel, she found a twenty-four-hour pharmacy and bought a bottle of aspirin, a prepaid cell phone and a pair of cheap, relatively comfortable sneakers.

She called Rembert, cradling the phone on her shoulder.

"What?"

"Did I wake you, Rem?"

"No. Not exactly. Just got ready for bed. Where have you been?"

"Long story, Rem. I—"

"—don't want to hear it, Annja."

"I've an opportunity for you to pick up some extra cash. You interested?"

He didn't answer.

"How about doing some video for me tomorrow? I'll get Doug to pay you overtime, maybe double overtime."

Still no answer.

"Rem?"

"Yeah. Yeah. I'll think about it. Tell me where I'm going for this video, and if I show up, I show up. And I need to know if I'm getting double overtime."

Annja gave him an address in Lakeside. She started up the bike again and drove the last few blocks to the hotel, finding an open spot on the street. Her leg still ached from the grazing and the stitches, and the bandage felt tight. Despite that, she moved quickly, up to her floor, and discovered the thug had been right…he hadn't found the gold in her room. The meager contents of her duffel were strewn everywhere, and her laptop was gone. She stared at the jump drive in her hand. Rembert was still up, but all he had was an iPad. She wasn't about to wake one of the other conference-goers to borrow theirs.

That hot bath she was envisioning would come at the beach cottage in a few hours. She changed out of the scrubs, stuffed everything back into her duffel and gave a last look around the room.

She stopped at the front desk only long enough to leave her key card, check out and ask directions to a twenty-four-hour Starbucks. Somebody would have a laptop there. She only had to be polite and persuasive. Annja could be both when she worked at it. She patted the jump drive and headed toward her motorcycle.

24

Sunday

Thankfully, one of Madison's Starbucks was open even after midnight. She didn't have to borrow a laptop from one of the customers; the coffee shop had three available for use. She bought a zucchini-walnut muffin, thinking that bordered on healthy and would offset the double-chocolate brownie and the cinnamon scone that she'd already chosen. While her left hand was wrapped around one of the shop's signature drinks, the fingers of her right hand worked to key into the various folders on the jump drive.

"Talk to me, Edgar," she coaxed. "Tell me what caused all this mayhem and death." The drink disappeared before she'd realized it, and she ordered a second. She told herself that the caffeine would help get her through this, but more likely her nervous energy would power her past the fatigue that was pulling at her eyelids.

MAYANS IN GEORGIA. That was the first folder she delved into. It carried a report from December 2011 of an Atlanta-based couple who suggested that Georgia's highest peak had been the site of a Mayan outpost. One hundred miles from their home, the spot was similar to locations in Mexico and Guatemala that the Maya people had favored. The couple demonstrated that terraces on the side of the mountain were unique to the United States, yet identical to ones in southern Mexico attributed to the Maya. It was complete with pentagonal mounds. They further suggested the Maya had been mining the mountain for gold and that words from their language had crept into the vocabulary of Native Americans in the area.

The documentation looked both plausible and fantastical.

There were scans of newspaper clippings about the couple's contention and the subsequent controversy. Annja hadn't recalled reading anything about it before and made a mental note to bookmark some of the internet sites referenced…when she got around to replacing her stolen laptop. She drained her cup.

She thought about the aspirin and maybe stretching out on one of the couches here, just for a short while. But she thought of Edgar and…she didn't have time for that.

More clippings. The crux of the argument boiled down to one side claiming the Maya people had a connection to Native American tribes in the southern United States and the other side arguing against it. Some of the opponents, Annja extrapolated, had been railing against the notion their entire careers. And to be proven wrong would be disastrous to their credentials.

THE FLORIDA CONNECTION. Some of the files in this folder were duplicates, some scans of college newspaper articles. She raced through the material to get the gist of it. Near Lake Okeechobee, student researchers found early evidence of corn growing… before it had showed up anywhere else in the southeast, suggesting it arrived to the United States via people who brought the seeds by boat. Another article by a college professor out of Miami suggested the Mayans arrived in Florida first via boats and then migrated to Georgia. Lake Okeechobee had originally been called Lake Mayaimi, after a tribe that lived on its shores. The city of Miami derived its name from that. Interesting…Mayaimi…Maya.

Annja was fascinated and forced herself to skim things she wanted to totally lose herself in. There would be time for that later, maybe during her flight to Morocco; now she just needed the basics.

There wasn't a folder on Wisconsin or Rock Lake, so she kept going.

There was, however, a section on the Chontal Maya and their seafaring exploits. The people at one time dominated coastal trade routes along Mexico and into Central America. There were also records of their voyages to the Caribbean, and so Florida to Georgia wouldn't be all that much of a stretch.

Mayan jade was found in the Caribbean and on Antigua.

A historical tidbit that put Annja on the edge of her chair: Ponce de Leon's records mentioned that the people he met in what would become Florida were aware of the Yucatán peninsula and provided navigational headings.

"Fascinating. But what does this have to do with Wisconsin?" Annja said.

"Pardon?" a weary-looking barista gathered up Annja's empty plates.

"Oh, nothing. Just talking to myself." She took a break and got a third Frappuccino and a blueberry muffin, her sticky fingers trembling from the caffeine overload.

One section covered traditional history, and Annja glanced through it only to reacquaint herself with what she'd read years ago. The Maya people had the only fully developed language of the pre-Columbia people, were known for the architecture, art, astronomy and mathematical systems, their impressive calendar that some believe predicted the end of the world, and their interaction with other Mesoamerican cultures. Their civilization was recorded as stretching from 2000 BC through the arrival of the Spanish. The Maya never wholly disappeared, not like the Anasazi, whom Edgar had apparently given up on. They existed throughout Central America today, many pockets of population holding on to traditions and the language still spoken.

She knew there were disagreements to this day on when the Mayan civilization began. Carbon-dated Mayan relics in Belize dated to 2600 BC; a Mayan calendar held a date that equated to August of 3114 BC. The general acceptance of the first wholly Mayan settlements and structures were in the neighborhood of 2000 BC to 1800 BC. Between 250 and 900 AD, the Maya people numbered in the millions. They had empires and kingdoms, erected temples and held elaborate ceremonie, and perfected their intricate hieroglyphic writings.

Their gods were numerous and not stagnant, shifting between concepts of good and evil, neither trait necessarily admirable, some representing the sun and some the underworld, some of death and putrefaction. They believed heavily in the supernatural and that magic could be imbued in objects. They placed great importance on rituals and honored the destructive heart of their gods. Death rituals were numerous, and they believed that those who died in battle or by sacrifice or suicide were granted a route straight to heaven.

The civilization eventually collapsed around 900 AD, and speculation remained rife to the cause. Annja's eyes raced over the notes, trying to find some link to Edgar's Wisconsin theory and seeing only discussions about overpopulation, revolt, dissolution of trade routes, epidemics, climate change and foreign invaders. Highlighted was a passage about an intense drought, magnified by the deforestation the Maya people had conducted to expand their farm fields, which may have tipped the scales against them.

"There's nothing here. Nothing… Wait." Annja found folders within folders within folders, labeled only by numbers. A code Edgar had developed.

Annja's kidneys were arguing with her, but she forced herself to keep going. She felt so close to uncovering the crux of Edgar and Papadopolous's evidence and the meat of their hypothesis.

Maps of Canada showed jade deposits, including where people were mining today. Obsidian deposits were marked, too, as well as gold and silver deposits and present and past mining operations. The Maya people had historically treasured and used all of those things—jade, obsidian, gold and silver. There were more maps, and Annja clicked on each one in turn.

These were of Wisconsin, places in the north high-lighted, some in the central part of the state, right around the Lakeside area. There were accounts of veins of gold, silver and other minerals, and an article about early prospectors trying to coerce the Ojibwa people into revealing where the thick veins were. The research went on to say that the indigenous Ojibwa did not want the miners to dig out the sacred metals and so remained silent.

At the heart of what Edgar and Papa believed was that the Maya people did not originate in Central America and find their way to Georgia and Florida, but that they originated in Canada, migrated quickly to Wisconsin and from there went south. Edgar believed they had at one point mingled with the Anasazi…the connection that started his interest in all of this.

"Oh," Annja breathed, "is it…was it…possible?" The research could turn Mesoamerican history on its head.

There was more. They had collected old records from traders and trappers who worked this part of the country long before the United States was formed and Wisconsin's boundaries were established. In scattered segments pulled from explorers' journals and from reports by the French who traded for furs with some of the local indigenous people, Edgar and Papa had found the mortar for their theory. Local chiefs had passed down stories from one generation to the next. These tales were of a tribe that fashioned jewelry from gold, that traded in jade beads and that believed in blood sacrifices—a practice the natives thought "most horrid." Tales continued that they built a nine-step temple in which to bury their most honored dead and that "great treasures" were buried inside it, as well. They crafted items of supernatural power, including a green stone knife that would cut down any foe and that granted its wielder more strength with each drop of blood it drew.

One French trapper wrote of sharing a fire with a chief who regaled him of these tales long into the night and who said his ancestors feared the "hungry green knife," rose up against the blood-letters and drove them from these lands. But that they couldn't knock down the great temple. Eventually the gods did that, the chief said, changing the land and calling up a lake that grew bigger and bigger "and swallowed every last evil stone."

And according to Edgar's notes, that temple should be somewhere at the bottom of Rock Lake.

25

The room was dark, so Garin crept in and switched on the bathroom light. The glow bounced off the mirror on the closet and provided just enough to see by. He gently leaned the portfolio case that held his precious shield up against the luggage stand. Keiko was sleeping on her stomach, the sheet down to her hips. The tattoo she had of a cobra was partially hidden, making it look as if the snake was slithering up from beneath the covers, ready to strike whoever got too close.

The clock's blue numbers showed it was 1:00 a.m.; she'd probably drunk herself to sleep or got tired of waiting for him. He'd make it up to her. She had to be back to work Monday night, so he'd take her to Milwaukee later today, to the zoo to see the penguins then to a German restaurant he fancied. He ate there a few years ago when he'd visited the city.

First, he'd tend to the matter of Roux, and then he'd wake her, order a fresh bottle of wine from room service.

As silently as possible, Garin crossed to the desk and opened his laptop. The light from the bathroom didn't quite reach here, so he felt with his fingers, turning it on and angling it so the light from the screen wouldn't disturb Keiko. It took a little wiggling to get the camera memory card from Rembert into the slot. He ran his thumbs over the space bar, waiting for it to load, and listened to the soft chime the computer made to signify it was finished. Garin edited the clip slightly, taking out the part where he asked Rembert if he was able to record the sound. Satisfied, he sent it to an email address he hoped was still active. He'd know soon enough. Then he sent a copy to Annja so in the event the first email address was no longer valid she would get it to the right place...after she saw it and came looking for him. But Annja wouldn't find Garin unless he wanted to be found.

"Keiko, my sweet, we'll be checking out early," he murmured, deciding to avoid a run-in with Annja. He removed the memory card, closed the laptop and stored both in the thin leather computer valise. Then he picked up the phone and dialed room service, ordered the bottle of wine—they said it would be right up—and shrugged out of his gray blazer. "As soon as we finish the wine that's coming and have a bit of a... well, have a delightful bit of a—"

He took off the tie and moved to the bed, setting his knees against it and jiggling it. "Sweet, you said you liked to watch me undress. Keiko."

Garin reached behind him and found the desk lamp, turned it on and stared.

He crossed to the other side of the bed, turned on the lamp there so he could get a better look under brighter light. She appeared serene, peaceful, as if she'd just gone to sleep. But she wasn't breathing. He put his hand on her back and knew immediately that her heart had stopped. He set the back of his hand to her arm and held it there a moment. She was still warm, a barely noticeable drop in temperature. He carefully pulled back the sheet and saw that her toes were starting to turn purple and stiffening. Dead about three hours; Garin had seen enough bodies through the centuries to know when the soul had fled. On the floor, partially hidden by the bed skirt, was the bottle of wine she'd ordered from room service earlier. She'd drank it all, and it had killed her. She'd died shortly after the gathering in Aeschelman's room had begun.

He reached deep into the pocket of his jeans for his last packet of coke, rubbed the envelope against his shirt to take off any trace of his fingerprints and flipped it on the nightstand. Gary Knight didn't exist, but enough people had seen Gary Knight at this conference to get the police looking for him. Let them think she'd OD'd, as the poison that Aeschelman had somehow gotten into the wine would no longer be detectable.

Garin packed quickly, nesting his computer valise inside his rolling suitcase. He checked all the drawers and the bathroom, making sure nothing of his remained, pausing only to answer the door for room service. He wouldn't let the woman in the room, taking the cart himself and passing her a twenty for a tip. He hooked the do-not-disturb sign on the door handle and watched until she got on the elevator.

He looked at Keiko and scowled. She hadn't deserved that. He pawed through her suitcase to make sure she hadn't appropriated anything of his. She had—a packet of cocaine, which he wiped down and left there. Then he wiped down the rest of the room, everyplace he knew he'd touched and everyplace else as a precaution, fast and meticulous. His prints weren't on record and he didn't want them to be, even if they were connected to an alias.

Finally, he took the new bottle of wine, wrapped a small bathroom towel around it and managed to barely squeeze it into the suitcase, the zipper and seams protesting. He'd paid for the expensive bottle, and so he wasn't going to just leave it behind when he could enjoy it later. If, by chance, this wine was poisoned, too, it wouldn't matter; it certainly wouldn't kill him.

Though it could well appear that Keiko died in her sleep or of a drug overdose…the police would find at least trace amounts of coke in her system. The police would, no doubt, investigate her demise closely. There'd been too many fatalities at this academic conference.

Madison, Wisconsin, was no longer boring or wholesome.

Garin took the stairs to the next floor, leaving his suitcase and the portfolio in the stairwell. Rembert's room was only a few doors away, and that was where he went. He rapped quietly on the door, not wanting to wake anyone else. For a moment he thought that perhaps the cameraman had likewise succumbed to Aeschelman's clever poison.

"You don't like wine, Mr. Knight?" Aeschelman had said in the penthouse suite. Aeschelman hadn't been referring to the wine available to the bidders—Garin realized that now. He'd meant the wine Keiko had ordered from room service before the auction. Aeschelman had meant to kill Garin…for asking too many questions, perhaps, for demanding to see the shield in a private showing, for bringing along Rembert Hayes, who was not a pre-approved part of their little circle. Most likely it was the latter reason. And most likely Rembert was already dead, too.

He knocked one more time, turned away and…

"What? What's going on now?" Rembert was wearing pajamas.

Garin stared. What sort of man wore pajamas anymore?

"What?" Rembert yawned. "First Annja pesters me, then you—"

Garin moved so close he shared Rembert's breath. "Listen, this is a courtesy, one I don't owe you but one I am giving you nonetheless. You told me how fond you are of your skin, that you have a family to support. Consider this a warning, Mr. Hayes. Eat nothing, drink nothing in this hotel that does not come from a vending machine. You understand? If you want to keep living, pay attention—find Annja Creed and stay close to her until you're home again."

Rembert's lower lip quivered and he took a step back. Garin matched the step. "Annja's in danger?"

Garin shrugged. "Annja's always in danger. You implied you were done working with her because it was hazardous. Well, Mr. Hayes, you better revise that. You better stick to her like glue until you're back nice and safe in New York City and your video has been sold and made public. Right now…I'd say Annja Creed is likely the only one who'll be able to keep you alive."

Garin could tell the words were sinking in.

"The men tonight—"

"I told you, Mr. Hayes, they are not good people. They're behind the deaths at this hotel, every single body that's been carted out of here and every one that will be before this conference ends." He wondered if more people than Keiko were being culled right now by the madman Aeschelman. His earlier comment in the park of "I wanted to be rid of her," referring to Mrs. Hapgood, sent a shiver down Garin's back. How many people did he want to be "rid of"?

"They're behind this, those people from the suite?"

"Mr. Hayes, if you don't take care, your body will be added to their tally." Garin reached into his jacket pocket and pulled out a Glock, showed Rembert that it had a full clip and then gave it to him along with a second clip. "Mr. Hayes, my giving you this gun and a heads-up is an uncommon gesture on my part. Fortunately for you, I haven't been entirely myself in Wisconsin. See to it that you sell your video for a good price, and as I mentioned before, give Annja Creed my best."

Rembert started to say something, but Garin spun away and returned to the stairwell, grabbing his suitcase and the portfolio and taking the steps two at a time. As he was crossing through the lobby, he stopped at a house phone. "Mr. Aeschelman's room, please."

The hotel operator clicked a few keys. "I'm sorry, sir, Mr. Aeschelman checked out several minutes ago."

Garin would make connections and visit the smuggling circle again, another time, another city, perhaps another country. Eventually he would find Aeschelman, and he would settle the score for Keiko.

26

Annja recalled in vivid detail the exchange she'd had with Sully before she returned to Madison to be shot at in the alley.

"Tell you what," Sully had said. "I'll keep my word. I'll hand over Joe's dive logs, all of them. Give you his tanks.... I was gonna sell them. You'll have to get them filled up someplace, though. I won't charge you a penny for any of that. You can have them for free. But you have to put me and the boys on your television program."

"All right," she'd said without hesitation. She didn't need the equipment "for free"; she had enough to spend on it. But if the dive logs would get her closer to whatever Edgar had sought in the lake…the Mayan temple he believed was down there, she'd acquiesce to Sully. "All right, I'll get my cameraman out here first thing Sunday morning and we'll put you in an episode."

"But not about them pyramids," he'd said. "I ain't interested in the pyramids or the Indian mounds or any of that. That's all hogwash and no big deal."

Then about what? She hadn't found it necessary to pose the question aloud. He'd pointed to the wall behind him, to an assortment of very old newspaper clippings he'd framed. "I want to be on television about that," Sully had told her. "Nobody believes in the big snake, not anymore, but they will when you put it on that *Chasing History's Monsters*. They'll believe it then. People believe what they see on television."

Now Annja stood on the sidewalk outside Sully's What-Nots. It was a little later than she'd planned—9:00 a.m., an hour past when she told him she'd be here. But after Starbucks, she rode her motorcycle to the beach cabin, took a hot bath and lay on the bed for a nap. If her alarm had gone off, she hadn't heard it.

"Please, Rem, where are you?" She hung up the phone and tried again. "Rem?"

"Your photographer?" Sully had cracked open the front door, just as the Catholic church on the corner starting ringing its bell for the morning service. This early in the day, she was surprised to smell the whiskey on his breath. "Your guy's waiting inside. We're all waiting on you. Coffee's all gone. What kept you?"

Sleep, Annja thought in reply. A really necessary few hours of sleep.

Conversation filtered out through Sully's open door, and she recognized Rembert's voice. She was grateful but a little surprised that he had actually shown up.

She entered the shop and could tell immediately from the look on his face that he wasn't happy about being here. He pulled her aside…as much "aside" as the close confines of the shop allowed.

"I swore I would never shoot another episode of *Chasing History's Monsters* with you. Ever."

"And yet here you are." It was the money, she was certain, and Rembert needed quite a bit of it for his grandson's eye operation. Annja felt guilty for talking him into this. "Look, we're not going to shoot the entire episode today. In fact, I don't want to devote much time to it. Who knows if it will even turn into something? But we have to do this."

Rembert pulled a face.

"I'm going diving later this morning," Annja said.

"Diving?"

"In Rock Lake."

"In the lake? Why are you going to dive in a lake? Am I supposed to film you diving? And if I'm supposed to film you diving, why are we standing inside this junk store?"

She shook her head. "I need some maps so I'll know where to dive. And we have to do this segment to get the maps. A simple trade-off. I'd like you to film a little bit of the dive. It could add some color to our segment."

"Our segment on what? These guys won't tell me. They just smile and chatter about an upcoming bake sale and barbershop-quartet competition. They won't tell me anything, like it's a big surprise they're waiting to spring. Do you know what this is about?"

"The topic for this episode—"

"Yeah, the topic. Have you called Doug about this?"

"—is a little unusual."

"Not that anything else you've handled hasn't been for *Chasing*. Unusual, that is." He let out a long breath that hissed like steam escaping between his teeth. "I'm here. You got me here. Against my very best judgment you got me here. For all sorts of reasons you got me here." He lowered his voice to say, "You know how bad I need the cash. But maybe I'm going to be fine on the money end."

"Shouldn't take more than two hours," she assured him. "If that."

"Great. I can give you two hours. So, what are we calling this one?"

"'In Search of Her Imperial Snakeship.'"

Rembert's face contorted and he mouthed *What?* "Does Doug know about this?" he asked again. "You forgetting the conference and coming here? To go after a big snake? A lake serpent?"

"Rem, this is all on my time, remember? I'm not on Doug's clock this weekend. Besides, you said you have enough video for Doug's promo."

"Oh, I have some great video, though not of the conference."

She figured he was talking about the deaths. "And I did attend the conference."

"For not much more than an hour, from what I could tell." Rembert took a shot of her with the shelves filled with a myriad assortment of stuff as a backdrop. "Hey, I attended more of that conference than you did, and I'm not an archaeologist or interested in any of their moldy topics."

"We'll need some footage of the lake, certainly, maybe me diving, like I mentioned, so they get the idea I'm looking for Her Imperial Snakeship. Though that's not what I'm looking for. And I need a couple of shots of a big piece of driftwood not far from the swimming beach. Some of the locals say it's a serpent skull."

Rembert panned the camera around, taking in more of the objects. He raised it to get a shot of bicycles, canoes and deer heads that hung from the ceiling. Annja hadn't noticed them before.

"Let me introduce you, Annja, to the regulars at this little whatnot shop. 'The boys' Sully calls them. We've all been waiting for you, sucking down really bad coffee and wondering if you'd show up. They're part of a club I'd guess you'd call it. They get together with the owner of the shop and talk about—"

"Her Snakeship!" Sully interjected. He'd crept up to them, but the creaking floorboards had given him away. He had the silver flask in his hand. He took a drink, made a toasting gesture and replaced the cap. "Her *Imperial* Snakeship."

"This is getting better and better. No wonder you were all keeping the topic from me. Figured I'd bolt, huh?" Minutes later Rembert was taking still shots of the wall inside the whatnot shop, getting Sully and the others in the frame.

"Wisconsin is known for its critters," one of the old boys said. He identified himself as George Bamford, a retired fifth-grade teacher. "They popped up more often years and years back, a hundred years back, dumping boats over, scaring the crap out of fishermen, making the summer people flee back down into Illinois. Heck, one summer the beach shut down."

"Water dragons," said another, the youngest of the six men who had gathered. He went by Kip, no last name. "Lake serpents. I like Her Imperial Snakeship—that's what some newspaper once called her. She'd be as famous as that Loch Ness Monster if someone had gotten a good picture of her."

Annja leaned over the counter and noticed that Sully had removed the gold piece.

"Somebody did get a photo, remember? Was printed in a newspaper a long while back, but it was all blurry."

She could tell Rembert was actually getting into this, taking the camera from one man to the next, adjusting the mic to make sure he picked up every word. His expression had gone from disgruntled to one of genuine curiosity. The cameraman was far more interested in this than Annja was; she considered it only a means to an end. Satisfy Sully, and he'd give her the dive logs that might lead her to Edgar's temple. Hopefully, it would be more real than Her Imperial Snakeship.

Kip had been babbling, Annja letting the words drift through the crowded shop while she continued to think about Edgar and the Mayans. Sully's What-Nots was a worse floor-to-ceiling jumble of antiques, vintage toys and…stuff than she'd realized on her first trip. The wall near the counter, where the six old boys sat on folding chairs, was covered with framed newspaper clippings of Her Imperial Snakeship.

Rembert moved in closer to Kip, and Annja caught some of what he said.

"People—that's why you don't have many reports about Her Imperial Snakeship and the other lake monsters." Kip tucked his hair behind his ears. "More tourists, more fishermen, lakeshore development, people encroaching on nature. It all drives the serpents into hiding or into deeper lakes. Rock Lake here, they say at its deepest it's eighty-seven, ninety feet."

Rembert whistled softly. "That's pretty deep."

"Big Sand is over a hundred down in spots," Sully said.

Kip continued, "So the way we see it, Wisconsin's monstrous serpent population has moved to the really deep lakes, to remote places and such. They must live a long, long while."

Sully rose and tapped a framed clipping on the wall. One of his favorites, Annja guessed, because it was in a large gilded frame. "This article, and this one and this one. If you read 'em close, you can see that the biggest outbreak of lake serpents took place between 1860 and into World War I, mostly in southeastern Wisconsin. All of 'em stemming from right here in Rock Lake." He folded his arms in front of his chest, beaming proudly while regaling Rembert with his information. "I saw Her Imperial Snakeship myself thirty years ago, when I went swimming with my friends after high-school graduation."

Annja's heart sank. Sully had probably seen a plain old water snake maybe, but no monster. And so his deceased cousin probably never saw a temple in the lake, either…but the gold came from somewhere. Her stomach roiled at the thought that she'd gotten suckered into this deal.

Sully read passages from the clippings aloud, and Annja moved in front of the camera to stand next to him. It was reflex; she'd worked on so many episodes of *Chasing History's Monsters* that this was just one more assignment. Except it wasn't one of Doug's ideas. She'd come up with this winner all on her own, just to get another lake dive.

"Since you've done so much research about—"

"Her Imperial Snakeship," Sully said, puffing out his chest.

"Can you tell us when most of the significant, documented sightings occurred?" Annja asked.

His smile grew wide, revealing two missing teeth on the side. "For fifteen years, from 1870 to 1885, people saw her in the reeds. She hissed at people in boats. Fred here—" He moved over and tapped at another framed clipping. It was yellowed and had creases in it that had not been effectively smoothed out. "Fred hooked her. She towed his boat almost a mile. And another fisherman—" he tapped at another clipping that was horribly faded from where the sun hit it on the wall "—he speared it but couldn't hold on. She got away."

"Some called her the Rock Lake Horror," the retired schoolteacher added.

"Better and better and better," Rembert whispered.

"George, you got it wrong," Kip said. "That's the Rock Lake Terror."

George shrugged. "Some people think she stopped showing herself 'cause folks were trying to catch her or kill her. So she hunkered down at the deep part of the lake, got bigger and near the turn of the century got some revenge."

Sully pointed to another clipping, as if that news report verified George's story.

"They was in a rowing race," George explained, "a couple of men from here in town. And they said they saw a log stretched out in the lake, right in their path. Well, they'd been reading about Her Imperial Snakeship, and so they were careful."

"But not careful enough." This from Kip. "She dived and came up right next to 'em. Opened her mouth. Probably looked like that shark from the *Jaws* movie."

Sully took a turn. "Anyway, it was reported that a man on shore grabbed a shotgun, took his boat out and was taking aim when it disappeared again. Didn't show up for a week or more."

"Said it was longer than two boats," Kip said. "Two boats end to end."

Just in case this really did turn into an episode of *Chasing History's Monsters,* Annja injected another question.

"So where do you think Her Imperial Snakeship is today?"

"She ain't dead," Kip announced. "That's for damn sure. Someone would've found her body."

George cleared his throat. "Some say she slithered out of Rock Lake and through the woods to Red Cedar Lake, along the way eating dogs and pigs. One farmer reported half a dozen of his prized hogs taken."

"Their half-eaten bodies were found on the bank of Red Cedar," Kip said.

Rembert panned from one man to the next, recording their wide eyes and animated expressions.

"Said it was about fifty feet long by the time it made Red Cedar its home," George said. "Some were calling it a dragon."

"Got too big for Red Cedar." The oldest gentleman, looking over eighty, picked up the storytelling. He'd refused to provide his name. "Hitched itself over to Lake Ripley, took the route of a river that used to run between the lakes. The folks who owned summer cottages back around 1900 closed them up and went south."

George and Kip nodded.

"Folks hunted her fierce for some years," the old man said. "And she moved around…or maybe there were more than one of them. I'm pretty sure there was more than one. Could be one of her offspring still swims in Rock. Madison's lakes, Elkhart where she pulled a fisherman in, Pewaukee, Delavan, Oconomowoc and as far down as Lake Geneva. Heard tell that the one spotted on the shores of Lake Waubesa was more than sixty feet long."

"Credible witnesses," Annja said. "There were credible witnesses to Her Snakeship?"

"Her *Imperial* Snakeship. Oh, yes," Sully said. "Down at Lake Geneva. A lot of rich folks live there. Lots of summer homes. But back around 1900, there were more common people. A minister by the last name of Clark saw her when he was fishing. It was bright as day. And he said it was a serpent. The newspaper carried the story." Sully reached behind the counter and pulled out a scrapbook filled with old newspaper articles. He opened it to the one with Reverend Clark. "It says right here that people believed him, man of God and all and not having touched a drop of liquor in his life."

"Maybe it was a dinosaur," Rembert whispered. Annja could tell he'd gotten too caught up in all of this.

"Maybe she is," Sully said.

"Some say she escaped into Lake Michigan," the old man said. "But we don't believe it."

The men frowned as one. Rembert focused in close on the oldest.

"Mishegenabeg." Sully pronounced the word

slowly and with reverence. "That's the Indian name for her. Their legend says she has antlers and eyes like the moon, big and reflecting."

The old man straightened, his black eyes boring into Rembert's camera lens. "But some Indians... Native Americans they call them now...some call the big serpent Anamaqkiu. It means dark spirit."

"And you don't believe she's gone?" Annja stepped closer to Sully, a signal to Rembert to focus on the What-Not owner.

"No, she ain't gone. I'm not saying there aren't more serpents in the other lakes. But I'm saying that despite all the claims that she's moved on, Her Imperial Snakeship or her kin is still in Rock Lake. It's why I go out on the lake every chance I get. I know someday I'll see her. Someday I'll prove to everyone just how real she is."

"We're done," Annja pronounced.

"That's it?" Sully looked disappointed.

"Just done here," Rembert said. There was an eagerness to his voice, but Annja couldn't tell for certain if it was real or politely put on for Sully's benefit. "I want to get shots at the beach. Annja mentioned some people think there's a monster skull there. And then I want to get some video of her diving. I think you should close up shop and go out on the boat with us."

Sully grinned wide. "I'll go get the air tanks. Do you have a place to get them filled?"

Annja nodded. She'd already looked into that. She gave Rembert a foul expression; she hadn't planned on taking Sully along.

"Maybe you'll find Her Imperial Snakeship," Rembert said when they were out on the street. He walked backward to capture a picture of Sully's What-Nots growing smaller.

"Maybe I'll find something else."

27

The pontoon boat bore the name *H.I.S.* Annja knew it had a double meaning: the boat belonged to Sully, so it was *his*, but it also stood for *Her Imperial Snakeship*. *H.I.S.* listed to its starboard side, even when all three of them stood against the port. Rembert wore a life preserver, a discolored orange one that smelled of fish bait. There were two other life preservers, but they sat unused on a bench, their presence only required for safety regulations. Annja wasn't sure they'd work anyway. In fact, she was surprised Sully's boat floated.

The boat had not been manufactured by any professional company. It was hand built out of big metal cans that had at one time been painted baby-blue, plywood that was warped in the center and ringed with garden fence to serve for a railing. The benches were plastic, one new and still having a price sticker on it.

Sully sat in a folding latticework chair and finessed the motor, which was probably worth as much as a decent used compact car. It was a Yamaha F90JA ninety horsepower four-stroke jet drive with four cylinders a twenty-inch-long shaft motor. Annja got a good look at it. It was pristine; it had an electric start, tiller controls, three-blade aluminum propeller and ran on an external gas tank. Overkill for this pontoon boat.

"Just got it. Found it on eBay," Sully said, seeing her inspect it. "Low hours. Seller said it was used only a few times, had it hooked to a big lifeboat on his cruise ship. It was a steal at four thousand. Couldn't have touched it new for less than ten."

Annja wondered if he'd used the money he got from Edgar and Papa to buy it.

"Coffee?"

Annja shook her head. Sully had brewed a pot and poured it into two thermoses—and who knew how much he'd swallowed before that. It was close to noon now, as it had taken some time to go through the dive logs to judge where they needed to go. As the pontoon moved out across the lake, Sully kept one hand on the motor's rudder controls, the other wrapped around a cup of coffee.

He slugged it down and smiled, put the cup between his knees to hold it and unscrewed the thermos, adding in the contents of his silver flask, sloshing it around and then pouring another cup of "coffee."

"I'd mainline this if I could, Miss Creed. I was so excited, you coming to do a special on Her Imperial Snakeship, that I couldn't sleep last night."

She had no reply to that.

"I'm sure glad your photographer there thought I should come along."

Annja had no reply to that, either. She'd stopped at the dollar store across the street from the What-Not shop. Rembert waited while she made her purchases: two pairs of shorts, two three-quarter-sleeve T-shirts with Bucky Badger on them—the University of Wisconsin mascot—ties to hold her hair back, another pair of tennis shoes and a plastic slipcase for the dive logs so they wouldn't get wet. She wore one of the outfits now. It would have to do—Sully had sold his cousin's wet suit a few months past.

It was cool on the lake, the breeze working in tandem with the motion of the pontoon. Annja let herself enjoy the sensation of the air playing across her skin. She looked toward the bank. Lily pads were in force near the shore, bright white and pink flowers open. A bird swooped low over the tops, probably finding insects to eat. Two fishermen were fly casting at the edge of the pads, the lines whipping back and forth sending droplets of water in passing as the hooks touched down on the surface and rose again, no doubt hoping panfish or bass would mistake them for bugs.

It was in some respects a perfect place, this lake and town, Annja thought. Peaceful, a terrific spot to vacation or set down some roots. She saw Sully's expression, eyes lit with the pleasure of being in this place at this time. If only she could be here for another reason. Maybe Annja would come back here—or rather to a place like it—to unwind and to absorb something so very far removed from the violence and tragedy that had been dogging her since she'd inherited Joan's sword.

Rembert had been saying something, but she'd missed it entirely, listening instead to the purr of the Yamaha motor and the slosh of the water against the pontoon's barrels.

"Annja, I said how many bedrooms does your beach cottage have?"

She blinked. "Two, why?"

"Good, 'cause I checked out of the hotel this morning, and my bag is in the trunk of my rental. I'll crash with you tonight."

She didn't bother hiding her surprise. "Tonight? Rem, we're going to be done here after you shoot this." She noticed that he was doing just that, getting video of Sully happily steering the pontoon, then panning to catch the fly fishermen and the lilies before turning the camera off. "You can get a flight back to New York out of Milwaukee if you don't want to bother with Madison's airport, and—"

"I'll go back when you go back," he said flatly. "Open-ended ticket. Doug always gets me one. I'll just stick close and film you doing whatever. Do you have a problem with that?"

She started to stay something.

"Already called Doug. He doesn't have a problem with it."

"Fine," Annja said, gripping the pontoon's railing. Why was Rembert suddenly affixing himself to her like a shadow? Was it just for the money? Or was it something else? "All right, Rem. Just don't get in my way."

Sully had emptied his first thermos when the old railroad bridge came into sight, the one Bobby Wolfe had mentioned that the Glacial Drumlin State Trail ran across. In the distance, she saw the tall reeds. Sully cut the engine, took a drink from the second thermos and tried to add more whiskey to it. But the flask was empty. He cursed, stood and stretched. He tossed the anchor line over, then picked up a second, a buoy line, and set it over the side for good measure. "Okay, Miss

Creed. Those diving logs you picked through say Joe was working this area, right?"

"Yes." She and Sully had consulted the logs, and Sully deciphered most of Joe's handwriting. "We have to be close."

"Joe always kept good records," Sully said, "of everything. When we were kids, he kept a diary, even listing all the TV shows we liked and how many cans we shot with our new BB guns."

Annja looked through two pages in the logs again; on one of them Joe had mentioned finding the gold pieces, a silvery bracelet and an opening on the side of a pyramid. A note in the margin said he might come back to go inside if he got his courage up. "Willies," he'd written.

There'd been no opening on either of the two mounds she'd explored with Bobby. She remembered that Bobby had told her his first dive for Edgar was in this area. Edgar must have gotten the notion to look here based on talking to Joe. But Bobby or Edgar hadn't been privy to these dive logs and so were probably looking blindly. It was a big, deep lake, after all.

There were three oxygen tanks in the center of the pontoon boat, each with about a half hour's worth of air. There was no accompanying bail-out tank, and Annja did not have a waterproof watch, so she would have to rely on her instinct of time passing. She strapped on the tank and checked the gauge and mouthpiece. She'd checked both out earlier—she'd be diving alone and so was being extra careful. With no suit or neoprene boots, she'd have to be satisfied with her outfit and tennis shoes. She might get chilly, but she was made of stern stuff.

Sully had given her an extra boat anchor, which was a bleach bottle filled with concrete. She hooked it to one of the tanks and would take it down with her. Annja knew she wouldn't want to come up after just a half hour and so would switch out her tanks at the bottom. Then she'd hook the cement-filled bottle to the buoy rope so both could be pulled up, leaving nothing behind but bubbles, she thought.

"I'll be gone an hour," she announced.

"I brought a paperback," Rembert said. She'd seen him buy it in the dollar store, a Western.

"We'll be back in a half hour or so," Sully said, leaving the buoy rope but starting to pull up the anchor.

"What?" Rembert and Annja said simultaneously.

Sully gestured to the port side. "There's a little tavern over there with a dock. I didn't bring me a coffee can to piss in and I've gotta go bad. I could just hang—"

"No, you don't," Annja warned.

"I know. I know. I respect the lake…even though fish pee in it." Sully grinned. "So I'm gonna take me over there to the tavern and get us a couple of sandwiches."

It wasn't to use the tavern's restroom, Annja realized; it was to refill his whiskey flask. Sully had a serious drinking problem.

"I'm hungry." Rembert brightened at the prospect of sandwiches. "You want us to bring you back something, Annja?"

"Yeah," she said. "Something filling."

"She eats a lot," Rembert told Sully.

Sully let out a wolf whistle. "Not too much, she doesn't. Not with that body."

"Don't let him drink too much, Rem. I need you guys back here. Him reasonably sober." Annja dropped over the side, the weighted second tank helping to propel her to the bottom. She listened to the pontoon boat motor start again, the sound musical and disturbing as it cut through the water.

She was actually glad that they'd left. For a while it would be only her, the fish and whatever mysteries Rock Lake was trying to hold on to.

28

The soreness in her leg all but vanished as she dropped deeper and put on Joe's high-powered waterproof flashlight. Sully hadn't yet managed to sell it.

It was seventy feet deep here, according to the laminated map Bobby Wolfe had let her keep and the length of marked rope that had played out when Sully dropped the buoy. One of the grease-pencil circles, indicating where Bobby first dived for Edgar, was in the vicinity of this spot but about sixty yards closer to the railroad bridge.

Again Annja felt as if she'd slipped into an alien realm, a delightful, magical one filled with varieties of fish she couldn't put names to. She was more familiar with ocean species, which were more colorful, but she recognized a bass and a trio of sunfish. At the edge of her beam, a big turtle swam lazily toward the surface. She estimated her vision, with the beam, was about fifteen feet. Much better than her dive yesterday.

The water at the surface had been pleasant, probably in the mid-seventies. Now down about twenty feet—she could tell by the mark on the buoy line—it was getting cooler. A wet suit would have helped. After Annja had become a certified diver, she'd taken an advanced program for deep diving and cold temperatures. She well knew what she was doing and recognized that she was taking a few risks—no suit, no dive buddy, no bail-out tank. Some stupid risks.

But she remembered something a nurse once told her. The nurse had worked in a senior citizens center, where she often heard people say they wished they'd taken more risks.

Annja brought that conversation to mind whenever she was going beyond the realm of common sense.

Visibility improved after another twenty feet. The plant growth was sparse here, not thick like the reeds toward the railroad bridge or the colorful lily pads along the shore. The fish were numerous, however; a small school of minnows shot out of the murk straight at her, looking like pieces of quicksilver in the beam of her light. A second later she saw what had spooked them, a large thick-bellied fish, much bigger than she'd seen yesterday. Not a bass. A walleye? It stopped its pursuit of a meal to regard her. Annja held to the rope and stopped her descent, enjoying the moment. Its gills worked slowly and it turned ever so slightly, its eye holding hers.

A handsome creature, she thought, hoping no one would hook this one; it must have some age to it. After a few more moments, it swam away, and she continued her course.

At sixty feet, Annja directed her light straight below and saw the reason for the lack of vegetation. The lake bed about a dozen feet below was a mix of sand and mostly small rocks, helping visibility but cutting the silt and providing nothing for the plants to root in. Near the buoy rope was a massive boulder, at least

five feet high and twice that across. It was covered
with zebra mussels and moss. Annja's feet touched
gently on the floor and she rested the extra tank next
to the rock, not touching it, finding the mussel and
moss patterns artful. Leave nothing but bubbles.

She guessed she'd spent five to ten minutes coming down, as she'd allowed herself to be distracted
by the big fish. No more diversions, she admonished.
She didn't have enough tanks to allow for that. Using
the boulder as a marker, she glided to the south and
intended to go for about ten minutes before spiraling
back and switching out tanks.

Annja clamped her teeth tight to the mouthpiece.
It was cold here, maybe fifty degrees. A dry suit
would perhaps be even more appropriate. But she
was healthy, and she would not be down a terribly
long while. What would it be like diving this lake in
the winter, when visibility was at its best? she wondered, shivering.

She slipped past a field of rocks that ranged from
the size of a football to a beach ball. None were
worked, like the ones near the mounds, and she saw
no signs of them serving as tools. They were just…
rocks. Farther and she found a car bumper encrusted
with various growths, a mud puppy stretched out on
it. Farther still and she came across an old wooden
boat, a ten to twelve footer that had sunk maybe four
or five decades ago, judging by the degree of decay; it
had the look of being from the 1960s, when all-wood
boats were popular and appreciated. The depth and
the cold were helping to keep it from disintegrating.
Annja moved slowly around it, seeing a split in the
hull and noting that a school of small perch were mak-

ing a home of the center section. The boat had probably lost an argument with another boat. Its motor had gone down with it, the propeller bent from hitting the rocks at the bottom, zebra mussels covering most of it. She smiled; Sully would say Her Imperial Snakeship had pulled it down.

Another several yards and she swung to her left, what would be east if she'd managed to keep her bearings. She was starting her circle back to the boulder where the other tank was. More rocks, a traffic sign of some sort that an unthinking person had tossed in—a stop sign by the shape of it. She drifted past it and went another few yards when she nearly floated over a rent in the lake bed. She stopped and planted her feet, carefully knelt and aimed the light down. It was a crevasse, one that she was positive wasn't marked on the laminated map. Visibility was good here, and she was seeing thirty to forty feet with the light. But she couldn't see the bottom of the crevasse. The sides were a mix of smooth and jagged rocks, and the gap was only about ten feet across at its widest point and about twice that in length—easy to miss by anyone trying to map the lake even with equipment. She remembered the notes in Joe's dive book about "Bob the Boulder," which she took to be the very big rock, about the wrecked water-ski boat, followed by "Her Snakeship's Maw." She'd thought the last comment was a joke in reference to Sully's obsession. But now she thought it was in reference to this rent in the bottom of the lake.

Indeed, the gash looked like the crooked smile of some great beast. Annja shivered again, but this time with excitement. She found her way to the big boulder, switched out the tanks and hurried back to the crevasse. Curiosity tugged her down…that and the feeling that Joe had come this way before her.

Into the Snakeship's Maw, Annja thought as she descended slowly, swinging the light below, then across, where it easily illuminated the other side of the gash, showing more of the mix of smooth and jagged rocks. An earthquake might have been responsible; in fact, that could explain why the lake swallowed the mounds she and Bobby explored yesterday. An earthquake could have caused this fissure and changed the course of a river or opened up an underground body of water that subsequently came to the surface and created the lake.

She swung the beam up, catching the lip of the crevasse above her. Because visibility was so much better, she guessed that she was about thirty or forty feet down…at least a hundred feet below the lake's surface. Bobby Knight had made a passing comment about deep lakes in Wisconsin, the deepest being north of here and going down to three hundred and fifty. He said divers loved it. Rock Lake was supposedly eighty-seven to ninety, but that didn't take into account this apparently unmapped trench.

She fixed her eyes on a piece of stone that reminded her of a nose. Keeping the beam on it, she went down until the "nose" disappeared in the darkness. That put her down another forty. Holding on to a ledge, she turned the flashlight down again; still, it didn't show a bottom.

How deep?

And how much longer should she go? How many minutes of oxygen did she have left? And the deeper she went, the slower she would have to surface to avoid complications. Finding a spot to keep her eyes on, she went down what she guessed was another forty. A fish swam past her, caught in the beam of her light. It was huge…as far as freshwater lake fish went. What was it?

It was light with dark bands running down its long body. Its cheeks looked to be covered with skin rather than scales, and when it swam above her, she counted eight pores on the underside of its jaw. Its tail was pointed, and all of it was longer than five feet. It clearly didn't mind the cold temperature. Annja was shivering, however. It wasn't close to ice water yet, but this wasn't something she should stay in much longer. The fish twisted back and went lower, checking her out, slowly opening and closing its jaws as if it wanted to show her its row of teeth. The thing probably dined on small loons, she thought.

She pictured its image, trying to memorize it; she'd describe it to Sully. He'd know what kind it was. A fisherman's dream was what it really was. Imagine hooking that—it had to top fifty pounds. Perhaps this one had led to Her Imperial Snakeship lore.

When it apparently tired of her, it climbed, and she felt the water move from the force of its tail strokes.

Down again. When she finally saw a bottom to the trench, Annja guessed she'd descended a total of two hundred feet. She should go back, no bail-out tank in case she'd lost track of time. She should…but once more she recalled the nurse's line: "I would've taken more risks." There were only two directions to go in, right or left, and she chose left. There was another of the pale striped fish with teeth, this one a little more than two feet long, a mere baby compared to the giant of a few minutes ago. It didn't like her light and so quickly swam away. The bottom of the trench was sand the color of eggshells, and there was no garbage anywhere…no car parts or street signs.

She guessed she must have traveled fifty or sixty feet before the crevasse closed in front of her and she decided to turn back. But her beam touched on something different, and so she moved closer still.

It was stone, not the rock wall of the trench, but worked stone blocks that had carvings on them. She held the light close and saw the image of a sun…a Mayan sun.

Edgar, she thought, you were not chasing a wild goose. And where she thought the crevasse ended, it didn't. There was a gap between the worked stone and natural wall. She could squeeze inside.

But that would wait for another dive.

"I would have taken more risks."

But Annja wasn't going to throw her life away hoping she could hold out for enough air to explore any farther. She'd come back down later, with all three tanks full and with an underwater camera. She would prove Edgar right and get him that place in the archaeological annals he'd so wanted.

Annja breathed shallowly on her return. She came up along the wall of the trench where she'd found the building, discovered rock overhead, a ceiling of sorts, and followed it until it opened…until she crawled out of the Snakeship's Maw. Her visibility dropped suddenly, from the thirty to forty feet she'd been enjoying to about five. Yet the water wasn't silt filled, and there were no diatoms here. Visibility dropped even more; she couldn't see more than an arm's length in front of her. She refused to panic. It wasn't the lake; it was her flashlight.

She hurried along the bottom, instinct kicking in. She found the wrecked pleasure boat and spooked the school of fish making its home inside. From here she found Bob the Boulder, where she'd left the empty tank. The light went out. Annja's air was thin and she was seventy feet down. She'd be ascending faster than she planned. Still, she took precious time to unfasten the empty tank from the weighted bleach bottle, held her breath while she hooked the bottle to the buoy line so they could be tugged up together. Then she pulled herself along that line, taking occasional thin breaths, holding it as long as possible, moving higher.

She swore her lungs would fail her just as she broke the surface. Annja tipped her head back and took in gulp after gulp of fresh air, delighting in the feel of the sun on her face. She'd gotten so very, very cold down there.

Annja opened her mouth to ask Rembert for a hand up, but stopped herself. There was no sign of the pontoon boat anywhere.

A wave of panic washed over her.

29

The two men—brothers—who'd been fly-fishing near the lily pads gave Annja a ride. They were calling it a day anyway, it being late in the afternoon. It had taken her that long to reach the pair—swimming to the shore, an onerous task lugging two tanks that she refused to leave behind, slogging through muck and a tangle of weeds that tried to wrap around her legs and make her a permanent part of Rock Lake.

She'd passed two cabins, but no one was home, and she was starting to think she was going to have to walk all the way back to Lakeside when she spied the fishermen. Sully had said he was taking the pontoon in the opposite direction—but that would have been too far of a swim…since she wanted to keep the tanks. To Annja the tanks were gold—her chance to go back down this very afternoon to the Snakeship's Maw, as she was calling it.

She'd briefly considered just treading water when she discovered the pontoon gone, hoping for Sully and Rembert to come back or hoping to catch the attention of a passing boat. But once she'd opted for this route, she was committed.

Annja prided herself on being physically fit. But

between the dive and the swim, and the walk along the shore to find someone willing to give her a lift, she was exhausted. Her legs felt like lead when she climbed into the back of the brothers' pickup truck—joining a stringer of bluegill that sloshed around in a big bucket. The smell from the fish—and whatever else had been hauled in the truck—was strong, and she fought to keep down what she'd had for breakfast. The brothers dropped her near where Sully's pontoon boat originally had been moored. The boat wasn't there, but she hadn't expected it to be. A woman washing out a canoe on the bank was helpful; Annja described where Sully and Rembert had been headed.

"That would be The Office," she said. "The owner named it that about twenty years ago, called it that so when men wanted to get out of the house for a drink without getting in trouble with their wives, they could say 'I'm going to The Office.' It has a new owner now, but he kept the silly name."

The woman volunteered to give Annja a ride to The Office when she realized the *Chasing History's Monsters* star was in effect stranded. Annja had left a small pack containing her motorcycle key, beach-cabin key and her wallet on the absent pontoon boat. The woman gave Annja her business card in the event she needed further help: Jenn Walker, Bankruptcy Attorney. Annja would send her something nice as a thank-you when she got back to New York.

H.I.S. was tethered to the dock beyond The Office. Annja dropped the tanks near the full one by the bench and grabbed her pack and the plastic pouch with Joe's diving log…both of which had been left unattended. This late in the afternoon, that hazy spot between lunch and dinner, the parking lot had only two cars in it: the dented Impala she was familiar with, the other a Lakeside police car.

Rembert was at a table inside, talking to two police officers. Detective Rizzo, who was at the table behind them intently listening, politely got up when she entered and pulled out a chair for her.

Annja didn't have to ask where Sully was. Manny laid it all out while Rembert finished with the police.

Sully was fifteen miles away in the regional medical center, probably in serious condition. He and Rembert had been coming out of The Office with sandwiches and drinks when a teenage knife-wielding girl attacked them. She got Sully in the stomach and was going after Rembert, but he'd dropped the sandwich bag and pulled out a Glock. He didn't have to fire it—the threat sent her running. The Office bartender called for an ambulance, the local police were dispatched, and Annja had walked in just as the officers were wrapping up the report.

"A Glock?" Annja sat next to Manny, who gave her an up and down. She thought she probably looked like hell, her Bucky Badger shirt stained green from the lily pads and tall grass along the lakeshore, her hair a mess—she'd lost the tie somewhere in the lake—and her once-white tennis shoes the shade of canned mushrooms. She probably smelled like bluegills and night crawlers.

"Your friend there—" Manny nodded to Rembert "—has a real nice Glock."

"How the—" Annja didn't finish the question. She decided she didn't want to know how Rembert came by a gun, at least not at this moment. He hadn't brought it with him—he'd only brought the two carry-ons, and someone at LaGuardia would have spotted a Glock. "How…? Why…are you here, Manny? Isn't this still out of your jurisdiction?"

"Told you I was coming to Lakeside today, to see if I could find out more about your Dr. Schwartz and and his friend. Heard the call for a knifing and—" Manny laughed and gave her a lopsided grin. "I just knew I would find you here. Bet it's the same girl that went after you. But for the life of me, I can't connect it to anything else."

They sat silently while Rembert signed the report.

"Your buddy here did provide some crucial information about the murders at the hotel. *All the murders*. There's been one more. A young woman from Chicago, a waitress, not an archaeologist, but she was with someone attending the conference."

Annja sagged back against the chair, her mind suddenly as tired as her body. She wasn't going to ask Manny to explain further. She knew all she had to do was wait for it.

The Office bartender washed glasses and hung them from hooks above the bar, clearly trying to overhear the conversations.

Rembert watched the officers leave, then he joined Annja.

"So, Mr. Hayes here…while the local police scoured the woods for the teenager…told us about a man named Aeschelman who is probably behind the killings. Fits, eh? The Mr. A. your thug mentioned in the alley. Mr. Aeschelman." Manny gave Rembert the signature lopsided grin. "Said there's an artifact-smuggling operation that went on at the hotel last night, that Aeschelman ran it and that some of the archaeologists were involved. But Aeschelman's flown the coop."

Annja's eyes grew wide and then narrowed, as if to demand of Rembert, *Why didn't you tell me this?*

"Said all of it came to a head last night and in the wee early hours of this morning," Manny continued. "Quite a fellow, Mr. Hayes. He not only attended the auction last night but he got footage of Aeschelman and the archaeologists buying and selling things, all of it most likely illegal. Arnie wants him to come down to Central for questioning. However, we can't force him. He hasn't done anything wrong. Got nothing to charge him with."

"I told you what I know," Rembert said. "And I'll make a copy of the video for you." He adjusted the Glock so he could sit more comfortably. "And I'm not going to Central. I'm staying with Annja."

"And he's taking me in his rental to the regional medical center to—"

"—check on Sully Stever," Manny said.

And to ask his permission to keep using his pontoon, Annja thought, realizing she had never asked Sully his last name.

If he objected, she'd find another boat to rent, but she liked the notion of the pontoon as a diving platform. Then she'd get the tanks refilled and go right back down, likely early this evening…and after getting a new battery for the flashlight.

"Meet up for dinner, Manny? Say in—" She fished in her pack for her watch. The Office had one visible, but its hands hadn't moved since she'd gotten here, apparently permanently fixed at five. "An hour? Five o'clock?"

"Not going to be visiting with Sully Stever for long?"

"I'm sure he needs his rest," she returned. "Better make it an hour and a half to be safe." She picked Blue Moon, thinking about the Creole chicken.

Rembert wouldn't talk on the way to Watertown… not about where he got the gun or how he found out about Aeschelman and the illegal auction. All he said was "You'll see my video later. After I make my deal. I wasn't on Doug's clock for it. Or yours. My equipment, my time, my video."

The nurse said Sully was drifting in and out of consciousness, but he'd been upgraded, and given how filthy Annja was, they wouldn't let her in to see him. Rembert secured permission to use *H.I.S.* as long as they were in Rock Lake; Sully knew he'd be in the hospital awhile.

Annja cleaned up in a hospital restroom, bought a change of clothes at Award Winning Sports on Main and using Rembert's iPad found a place called Under the Surface, a nearby dive shop. It cost her, all totaled, eighteen thousand, but she picked up boots, a buoyancy compensator, a wristwatch that doubled as a dive computer, two lights, a dry suit, a bail-out tank, goggles, a camera that wasn't quite as good as what she had wanted and a semi-closed rebreather system that would let her stay down a long while. The rebreather, which had been developed and used originally by the military, was the only one the shop had, and it was responsible for the bulk of her bill. It took several minutes for the shop to determine that Annja had the funds. She could resell the stuff back to the shop before she left—but at a considerable loss. Or she could ship it to her apartment…the more likely outcome. She thought she could use the dry suit elsewhere.

"Expensive trip," Rembert said. "So you're going to be looking for overtime, too."

They were a few minutes late to the restaurant, and Annja wolfed down her meal—ordering less than she would have liked, but being careful because of her upcoming dive.

"Going back on the lake," she told Manny. "Or rather, into it."

"For your professor friend," the detective said.

Annja nodded, but really it was for herself now. Edgar's obsession had somehow become hers. She had a taste of it…seeing the building deep in the Snakeship's Maw, and she couldn't walk away. It was far too significant of a historical find to ignore.

"You going back to Madison?"

Manny shook his head. "Still poking around here, getting everything filled in, you know. Arnie's chasing down this whole Aeschelman thing. Gonna have to share it, but it'll still sound good for my swan song."

"I'll call you," she said, "when I come back up. See if you're still here." She passed him her new cell phone and he took down the phone number.

Annja grabbed the bill and dropped three fives on the table for a tip. "Any word on that girl with the knife?"

"Not a syllable."

"It's connected, Manny. Somehow it's connected to all of this."

30

"Still not going to tell me where you got the Glock? I know you didn't buy it. Never mind whatever the gun laws are, they're not cheap, so you wouldn't have sprung for it."

Rembert didn't reply. He sat on the lawn chair next to the tiller and looked toward the setting sun. She had to admit the sun was beautiful, coloring the water a molten orange, loons cutting low over the chop and sending out their mournful cries.

They'd dropped anchor next to the buoy Sully had put down earlier.

"Don't leave me, Rem. If nature calls—"

He picked up the "stadium buddy" on the deck next to him and dropped it back down. She'd bought it at the sporting-goods store where she'd gotten her change of clothes.

"And if any knife-wielding girl swims out here—"

He pointed to the gun that protruded from his waistband.

"I'm going to be down awhile." She didn't know how long, but the rebreather was a far better option than switching out tanks. "It'll be dark before I—"

He pointed to the pontoon's fore and aft lights and

to a battery light near the motor that he could use for reading, all part of Sully's *H.I.S.* setup.

"I hope you don't get too—"

He flapped the Western paperback and gestured to a small radio.

"Look, if you don't want to be here, you shouldn't have said that you'd—" She'd been talking to him while she put on the equipment.

"No, Annja, I don't want to be here. You know I don't want to be here. It is dangerous being anywhere around you. Me and Sully were across the whole lake and it was still dangerous. Sully got knifed. She was waving the damn thing at me, too. No, I don't want to be here, but I'm here. It's my best option right now, all right. That lesser of two evils. And no, I'm not going to talk about the gun—ever—or the auction or Aeschelman, who by the way is not a nice man. Not right now anyway. So go down looking for your friend Edgar's pyramid or Sully's Snakeship or whatever else you're after. And then when you're done with all of this…" He flapped the paperback again. "Then we can go home. I can sell my video, and I can go to work for another station and never ever film another episode of *Chasing History's Monsters* again or catch another equally lame assignment from Doug. So when you come back to this crazy town to finish up the Her Imperial Snakeship segment, you can bring some other idiot with you."

Annja wished she hand't prodded him; it was better when he wasn't talking to her. She dropped into the lake and embraced its otherworldliness, happy to get away from Rembert. The dry suit would keep out the chill, and the rebreather with it... She really wouldn't even be leaving bubbles behind.

She passed Bob the Boulder and the wrecked boat, saw a three-foot-long muskellunge swimming lazily along the bottom. That was what the giant had been that she'd encountered hours ago. She'd described the fish to the man at the dive shop, and he'd told her it was a muskie, more properly called a muskellunge, the most coveted game fish in these inland lakes, a trophy fifty or sixty inches long. Annja knew the one in the Snakeship's Maw was a trophy. Maybe in the secret depths of Rock Lake they just grew big.

Her visibility was good, at least thirty feet, no diatoms here and minimal silt. Despite that, Annja had difficulty finding the crevasse, even though she'd memorized the pertinent page in the dive log and thought she had exactly retraced her steps from earlier today. It took her close to a half hour, and at the end of that she'd worried that maybe she wasn't going to find it ever again. As far as the lake was concerned, the gash at the bottom really wasn't all that long or wide, like a thin scar on a man's chest. No wonder it had gone undetected. Joe had no doubt found it by accident. And without his dive logs...she would have never found it.

The dive computer told her she hadn't been far off her guess. The bottom of the rent was two hundred and ten feet down from the surface. Annja took the left, or what approximated the east leg of it, coming to what appeared to be a dead end until she aimed her light first one way and then the next, revealing the stone wall of a Mayan structure and a narrow gap between it and the rock wall. She'd thought about it on the ride to the hospital when Rembert wasn't saying anything. An earthquake seemed the most logical explanation. The ground had opened up and dropped the building into it, sealing it in a rocky embrace and at the same time creating the lake and covering up the Native American burial mounds.

Like the chieftain's passed-down tale of their gods changing the land and calling up a lake to take care of the Mayan blight, Annja recalled. She took pictures of the stone and where it practically joined the natural rock wall, focusing on symbols that had been worn thin by time and the water. Then she hooked the camera to her belt and slipped in the narrow gap, going only a dozen feet before she could no longer fit. Wiggling free of the rebreather tank, she kept the mouthpiece in and held the tank to her side and started squeezing deeper in.

"I would have taken more risks." The haunting, prophetic words returned. But how many more risks did Annja have in her? Pressed between the worked stone and the natural rock, her flashlight focused on the hieroglyphic symbols, Annja managed to tug the camera up, take a few pictures that she prayed weren't blurry and stuff it back. She looked down, seeing that she was no longer shuffling across the sandy bottom that had been part of the crevasse, but was on flat stone. It looked like a sidewalk, with its mortared segments every so many steps. Steps? She was on one of the steps of the Mayan pyramid.

Her heart raced and she felt her chest grow tight with excitement. All thoughts of Edgar and Rembert, Doug and Sully, and *Chasing History's Monsters* and Lakeside…all of it fled. There was only her and this moment of discovery, this amazing revelation, a once-in-a-lifetime happening. She felt euphoric.

It was a sensation she wanted to bottle and keep and imbibe over and over, an archaeological junkie on a high she'd never experienced before and perhaps never would again. Annja took her time. She crept through the narrow gap, touching the worked stone only when she had to, feeling the natural rock behind her. So much of what once must have been intricate and beautiful were mere suggestions, a hint of a sun symbol, a half man/half jaguar, then an elk with the stylized visage of a man.

A few of the etchings had been deeper and she could better make out just how detailed they'd been. Half men/half badgers, birds with their wings spread, symbols she didn't know the meaning of but that she managed to get pictures of.

Farther in, the gap widened and she could put the rebreather back on properly. Down and to her left the crevasse opened and descended even farther, and her light stretched about forty feet. Up, she could see the top of the pyramid. It resembled one she'd seen at El Mirador, which was one hundred and eighty feet tall.

She followed the structure down, using both her dive computer and high-powered flashlight for reference. She reached the bottom and took a reading. Three hundred feet below the surface. Rock Lake had held on to this secret for a very long time. She climbed back up, taking pictures along the way, especially of symbols that were the most legible, using her light and her computer and setting the height of the pyramid at about one hundred and fifty feet tall.

Once more she followed it to the base, but on a dif-

ferent side, taking more pictures, finding places where
the carvings looked as if they'd just been made. There
were more images of suns than of any one other thing,
half men/half animals, symbols she had no clue to
their meaning, images of death gods and depictions
of beautiful long-tailed birds that tugged at her memory. She knew a name for the bird, but it was escaping her at the moment.

The temple had nine steps, which was usually
symbolic of the nine layers of the underworld. Likely
members of a royal family were buried inside…along
with sacrifices.

Down and up again on another side, she found an
entrance at the midpoint. Her heart quickened, and
the euphoric rush skittered through her. A part of her
wished she could share this with someone—Doug
maybe, though he'd try to find a sensational angle
with it, wouldn't truly appreciate everything this represented. Edgar. Oh, she wished Edgar could have
seen his work become this reality. The old archaeologist couldn't have come down here, but Bobby Wolfe
or she could have been his eyes. Papa might have been
coaxed down, though even he would have had a tough
time squeezing through the gap.

"I have quite the monster for you to chase, dear
Annja. We must meet for dinner tomorrow so I can
give you my notes." Edgar hadn't meant a monster
for her program, not Her Imperial Snakeship or any
other fantastical beast. He'd meant a monster of a discovery. He'd meant his pot of gold at the end of his
archaeological rainbow.

She studied the opening more closely. It was
framed by an arch with numerous etchings of suns

31

Annja took a picture of the jaguar head and went inside. She made her way along a corridor that carried hints of painted designs. Annja tried to imagine what they'd looked like thousands of years ago—this structure had to go back more than two thousand years… four thousand more likely. Older? They'd used red paint, and some white and black, the suggestions of color intriguing. She took her time, recording as much as possible.

Among the images were death gods and gods of the thirteen layers of heaven, but always the death gods appeared on top, as if they were holding sway and were more powerful. Again there were more symbols she had no knowledge of, a language perhaps. There were bones—deer or elk, and pig, not typical of Mayan sacrifices, and so they were perhaps brought here for food. Next Annja discovered a chamber with a high ceiling. Her light grazed the top of it but could not reach to the other side. A massive room, then.

She moved at a snail's pace, not looking at her watch. In truth, she didn't want to know how much time she was spending here. Rembert said he would wait, and so he would, for some reason wanting to stay close to her....

She didn't want time to intrude on this magical experience. It would take as long as it would take…as long as she could drag it out and enjoy the enchantment of it all. Or at least until her common sense got the better of her. Rebreathers were amazing, but they did not let a diver stay down indefinitely. Annja calculated she had four and a half hours, maybe five at the outside. And she had the bail-out tank in case she got in trouble.

Along the walls were still more carvings, these not as worn as the ones outside the building. Annja had a working knowledge of the Maya, because of trips to Central America for *Chasing History's Monsters* and because of her overall fascination with anything archeological. Most of the carvings were of gods…the sun god; various gods of the underworld; Itzamna, an upper god or one of the creator deities. The depiction most prevalent was of Vucub-Caquix, a bird-demon that according to Mayan mythology pretended to be both the sun and the moon, father of Cabracan and Zipacna—two earthquake demons.

How appropriate, Annja thought. The being that the Maya people believed birthed earthquakes glorified in a temple that was swallowed by one. Was it possible there really was a divine hand involved with the watery entombing of this place?

There were more skeletons, and Annja's sense of wonder disappeared. No longer game animals—the skulls were small, belonging to children, in some cases babies, probably all sacrificed to accompany whatever royal personage was buried here to the afterlife. She focused the light elsewhere, illuminating whistles carved from obsidian, intact bowls, pieces of jade, marble carved into the shapes of animals… badgers and beavers, masks, effigy figurines, jade ear bores. Annja took pictures of all of it. Some of the ceramic pieces were exceedingly valuable, codex-style, black-line-on-cream decorated with images to show mythological events. The cold of the lake had actually helped preserve these pieces. She knew from attending legitimate auctions that some of these pieces could bring eighty to a hundred thousand each—worth far more than the coins Joe had brought up.

Mexican and Central American officials were trying hard to lock down the trade of Mayan relics, challenging pieces that came up for auction, proving some of them forgeries and asking for the return of things verified as genuine. But these pieces…would these all be arrayed in display cases in museums? Or would the archaeologists and explorers who came after her get them to the black market? Would these be worth more because of where they came from?

Undoubtedly.

Had Joe entered this pyramid? Had he been able to squeeze through the tight passage? Was she following his course? Or had he found the gold pieces elsewhere? No! He'd been here. The pitcher that she'd purchased in the pottery shop, and the bowl. She squatted and took pictures. They were right here…the originals. Joe had seen them and copied them to remarkable likeness, maybe copied others, as well. These pots, somehow preserved in the cold water at the secret bottom of Rock Lake, were exceedingly valuable. Worth far, far more than the pieces of gold Edgar had…but it wasn't those pieces Mr. A. had been after, was it? It was this *location* he'd sought, the place where the gold had come from. The thug had asked her that.

He'd demanded to know where the treasure was as he shoved the gun against her forehead in the alley.

This treasure chamber.

Either Edgar or Dr. Papadopolous, and most likely the latter—she told herself—had mentioned to the thug the possibility of more gold, of a Mayan hoard in Wisconsin. Or Peter. Maybe it was Peter. He was at the root of all the bad things, and probably oblivious to it. The clarity of it struck her. Edgar in his excitement had told Peter, Peter in turn had pestered both Edgar and Papa about getting cut in, had mentioned it to Elyse Hapgood…and who knew who she talked to? And once it was no longer a secret, the mysterious Mr. A. caught wind of it and acted. Manny said there was an illegal selling ring operating at the conference. So Mr. A. must have been primed and in a position to go for Edgar's find.

That was what they had been after, Mr. A. and his cohorts. Not the few circles of gold Edgar and Papa had, but the mother lode.

The old pot Sully had mentioned…she would ask to take a look at it. Maybe it wasn't one Joe made; maybe it was one he'd brought up from down here.

Nearing the back of the massive chamber, she found five intact skeletons, probably only kept that way because they'd at one time been wrapped in swaths of cloth that must have been elaborate. Now the cloth was in tatters, loosely keeping the bones gathered, strips of it floating in the water and looking ephemeral and insubstantial, like ghostly seaweed fronds. She took more pictures, the light touching the strips and revealing faint patterns that had been red—the color the Maya associated with death and rebirth. The five bodies were arranged facing north, aligning with where the Maya believed one of the entrances to the underworld could be found.

The treasure—the true treasure of this temple—was arrayed around the five bodies. Tucked in gashes and other small openings in the stone, there were wide gold and silver bracelets decorated with jade, massive elaborate necklaces that must have been too heavy to comfortably wear in life. The details were staggering, filigreed and engraved, images of suns and birds, of half men/half badgers, more symbols she had no understanding of. The more detail a piece of jewelry had and the larger it was, the more valuable. Annja recorded all of it on her camera and tried to touch nothing. Each of the skeletons had large headdresses, gold, serving in the stead of Egyptian funeral masks. She was struck with the notion…finding this temple, this chamber and seeing all this treasure.

The small gold pieces Edgar had in that envelope were insignificant next to this. Grains of sand in a desert. One of these headdresses alone could command more than a million, well more, given its condition and provenance. A fortune in just one piece. No wonder some archaeologists were tempted to take things away from dig sites.

She looked closely at the first skeleton, not finding its hands, then searching and searching with the light and catching sight of finger bones and jade and gold rings that had fallen off. This skeleton was the only one that did not have a necklace. Perhaps Joe had taken something from it.

Stepping carefully beyond the first skeleton, she looked at the others. Each body had so much jewelry and other trinkets buried with it. A very significant family, a king perhaps, the members of the family killed when he died. Two of the five skeletons were smaller, probably teenagers. Had one of the survivors ascended to the throne after the king's death, and had that survivor ordered the deaths of the other family members so his or her rule would not be contested?

Archaeologists would pull up the bones and study them, record their health, try to determine what they'd eaten and how they had died; it would all be fascinating and would take years. And it would be a major boon to scientists in the U.S., who would not have to ask permission from officials in Mexico and Central American and South American countries.

The chamber extended beyond the skeletons and was packed with treasures for the afterlife. Statues almost life-size, urns and bowls. Annja was dizzy, giddy, as if she'd just arrived at the wildest party and gulped down an entire bottle of champagne. Her knees quivered. There was an assortment of bowls that looked as if they'd been filled with so much blood that it had stained them—she'd seen their dry counterparts in Mexican museums. Finger bones were nearby. What sort of sacrifices and ceremonies had been involved? Had these people glorified Vucub-Caquix? Some of the larger bowls had the bird-demon's image carved in them, and one of the largest statues was of a man-bird with wings tucked close to his body.

Mayan gods were intriguing and complex; Annja

knew she would be reading voraciously about them
during her trip to Morocco and long afterward. That
good and evil vacillated in the deities was a concept
difficult to get a handle on. That a god could be per-
ceived as evil one day, good the next, its worshippers
not minding…that is, if she remembered her previous
research correctly.

Above all of that, she felt the pressure and presence of evil here.

She'd seen so much evil since inheriting Joan's
sword. She shook her head at the notion and continued to be mesmerized.

Jade beads, the currency of the Maya, a waist-high
urn, and there were weapons, too. Annja didn't know
enough Maya history to recall if they believed weapons were needed on the other side. There were dag-
gers made of obsidian and chert, obsidian arrowheads,
chert spearheads, the wood long since rotted away…
enough to have equipped a sizeable force.

Initially the Maya were thought to be peaceful.
Though the more historians and archaeologists studied the sites, the more they learned that there had
been struggles within communities for dominance
and with nearby communities. Some of the sacrifices
were believed to have been related to retaliation for
military strikes.

The bones, all the skulls…were they Mayan or Native American? Perhaps both. The scientists could
probably sort it out with time.

How long had she spent down here? Annja finally
gave in and looked at her watch. It was a little after
nine…not as long as she'd expected. Dinner had been
fast, and she was on the lake and in the water at six-

thirty. So, close to three hours. She imagined that Rembert was tapping his foot impatiently and wishing he'd bought a second paperback. She would go back at ten for his benefit and return tomorrow. She'd be rested and would find a place to buy another memory card for the camera. But just a little more now. A little farther.

At the opposite side of the chamber, which she judged to be more than a hundred feet across, she found a sloping passage that fell away into darkness. The pyramid had multiple levels, then. She'd been through several in Egypt, crawling on her belly through tunnels to access the various rooms. This passage was taller and wider and could accommodate her and the rebreather tank.

It led to another chamber and then another below it. There was more pottery and more weapons, more bones, more jade, and a few dozen pieces of gold and silver jewelry. Millions upon millions of dollars worth of relics. A shaft went up, and she followed it, using handholds that the centuries had worn away but that were easy for her given her buoyancy. It led to the very top of the temple, flat and with an altar. More images of Vucub-Caquix were carved all over it, with grooves to allow the blood to flow away.

It was enough for this night…but only because she felt the cloying fatigue, a sensation like she was walking through wet cement. A few hours of rest would serve her well, and as excited as she was by all of this, Annja knew she'd have no trouble sleeping. She would do a more thorough job tomorrow.

She returned to the thin gap between the rock wall and the temple, again taking off her tank to squeeze through the very narrow part. The archaeologists who would come after her would have to blast away part of the rock to access the temple, to take their equipment in and eventually the relics out…and to find if there were other buildings down here, too. Often smaller structures were built around something of this significance.

Her flashlight cut through the ink-black darkness. More muskies down here, not schooling by any means, but drawn by her beam and their curiosity. There were bass, too, the largest closest to the bottom. Over the wrecked boat were smaller fish, looking a little like muskie, but thinner. Northern pike, she guessed, not as prized as their larger brethren, but striking-looking nonetheless. She stopped at Bob the Boulder. She heard something…more than the purr of her rebreather, a staccato sound oddly muffled by the water.

She ascended along the rope, going slowly at first and then faster when she shone the beam up and saw lines of bubbles in the water…the trail of bullets. The staccato sound had been bullets.

She abandoned caution, worried about Rembert and swimming as fast as she could. Was he shooting or being shot at? Hand over hand up the buoy rope, feet kicking to propel her faster as more lines of bubbles laced through the water. Her head broke the surface as one more gunshot sounded.

"Annja!" Rembert had the flashlight pointed toward the shore, cutting a golden path across the choppy water. He reached over the fence railing and extended his free hand. His other held his Glock. He tugged her up and she practically fell over the railing, like a big fish landing unceremoniously.

"What's going on?" Annja dragged herself up onto a bench, unhooking her rebreather tank and tossing off her face mask. Her head pounded and she followed the beam, trying to see what Rembert had been shooting at. "Loons?" Had he been shooting birds? "What are you—"

He helped her get the tank off. He was out of breath and obviously frantic. "The girl with the knife," he managed between pants. "She came back again."

"Swam out here?" Annja staggered toward the railing, scanning the shore. Her vision was a bit blurry, but it was clearing. She only saw choppy waves in the light. Are you crazy? she wanted to ask him. "There's nothing—"

"Annja, didn't you hear me? I said *again.* This is the second time she's been out here. Yeah, swimming. I used a whole clip on her the first time. Wasn't trying to hit her, just scare her. And I did, the first time. Scared her off. Been jiggling the anchor rope, hoping you'd notice to get you up here. Four hours, Annja. You've been down there almost four hours. I thought you were maybe dead."

Annja peered toward land. There were lights from a few cabins and from the near-full moon overhead, but the area was primarily wooded and mainly all she could see along the bank were trees, birches close together, some weeping cedars and where *H.I.S.*'s big light struck lily pads; the flowers were all closed up and pointing to the sky.

A host of frogs were chirping, sounding like birds, loons called, the motor from a small fishing boat hummed somewhere to the west and Rembert continued to sputter.

"I'm not lying, Annja, and I'm not—"

"I believe you."

"About the girl?"

"Yes, Rem, I believe you. We should call—"

"Already did. I called the cops. Had the card of one of the men I talked to this afternoon. After she swam out here the first time and then went back, I called him. Said they would send a couple of units to the lakeshore. And then I called that Madison cop, but that was about a half hour ago."

"Manny?"

"Found his card in your pack.... Sorry for poking around, but I had to use your prepaid cell. My battery was too low and I couldn't get a signal."

"It's okay." Her eyes still trained on the shore, she started to peel off the dry suit. The cool evening breeze touched her skin and started to dry her hair. It was a pleasant sensation, but overshadowed by her headache. She'd come up too quickly and had a mild case of the bends. Not as bad as if she'd been on a deep ocean dive or using a regular tank rather than a rebreather, but still pretty bad. Only three hundred feet down at the lake's secret bottom, yet it wasn't just depth that played a part; time spent underwater mattered, too. And she'd been down a long while. Her joints ached, thereby confirming her self-diagnosis. She'd be able to shake it without help; she'd done so before—thanks to her amazing constitution, which was linked to having Joan's sword. It would just make her uncomfortable for a while. She massaged her temples.

"Guess it's good you have a gun," she said.

"Damn straight."

"Did you get Manny? On my cell? He still in town?"

Rembert helped her pull off her boots. She and Rem continued watching the shore the whole time, *H.I.S.* listing precariously from their standing together.

"He was almost to Madison but said he was turning around, something about the icing on his retirement cake." Rembert took the gun out and checked it, making sure he still had bullets left in the clip, this time putting it in his jeans pocket. "Your friend gave this to me, this Glock."

"Friend?" Annja finally looked away from the shore.

"Well, maybe not a friend, but he knows you. Gary. Gary Knight."

"I don't know a Gary Knight." But the moment the words came out, she remembered. She'd seen the name on a conference badge, the one pinned to Garin Braden…. She'd forgotten all about Garin.

She had to put him out of her mind again; she'd deal with that annoyance later.

"The girl, Rembert. I think she is after us."

"Really?" His sarcasm was unmistakable. "And just what would make you think that, Einstein?"

She gave him a dirty look and put on her tennis shoes, again keeping her eyes on the shore.

"Trying to kill us, Rembert."

"No kidding. You think I don't know that? She stabbed Sully and—"

"Us, specifically. We're not just random targets."

"I get that. After seeing her for the third time today, I really get that. But why?"

"Because of what's at the bottom of Rock Lake." The clippings she'd looked at, going back decades, the unsolved murders in this area. There was a common thread; she just hadn't looked close enough when she skimmed the articles in the diner. But she recalled that the first unsolved one in Edgar's file had been a WWII frogman. The last, Joe Stever, had been an avid scuba diver. She would bet every penny in her dwindling bank account that the victims documented in that folder had been diving Rock Lake.

And getting too close to the lost pyramid.

32

"Annja! There she is!" Rembert angled Sully's large flashlight to the north, catching sight of a silhouette under a tall birch. "That's her. I know that's her."

Annja couldn't see any details; the figure was a mere shadow. But she knew it was the girl, too. "Pull up the anchor, Rem, and take us to shore."

"No. Are you nuts? Are you friggin' nuts? I'm not doing that."

"And call the police. Tell them where she is."

"Okay, Annja. That I'll happily do. I set them up on your cell for speed dial."

Annja pulled up the rope and the buoy line with its weight. She didn't need the buoy any longer to find this spot. With the recordings she made on her dive computer, Joe's logs and Bob the Boulder, she could find the pyramid again.

She strapped on her fanny pack and went to the front fence railing. The girl had turned on a flashlight and pointed it first at *H.I.S.*, its beam not quite reaching, and then held it close, beam up, illuminating her own face. Horror lighting, photographers called it.

H.I.S. pontoon was too far away, but Annja understood the girl's invitation. She kept Sully's light aimed on her, wanting to get a good look at the girl.

"Take us to shore, Rembert, just close enough for me to get out."

"Seriously?" He mumbled something else, a string of profanity that would make anyone blush. "Your buddy Gary told me to stay close to you, that I'd be safer. I think he was full of crap, Annja. Being within thirty miles of you isn't safe." She heard him sit in the folding chair and start the engine. "But it's your funeral, right? Just don't expect me to go or to send any flowers."

He motored the boat closer, the girl with the flashlight not moving. Annja could see her better now. She had on cutoff jeans and a pink long-sleeved T-shirt.

"Hello, trouble," Annja whispered.

She revised her guess of the girl's age. At best she was thirteen, maybe even twelve. While the girl could be—and probably was—responsible for Joe's death, she couldn't have killed the others that dated back decades.

And why?

To keep people from finding the pyramid. Annja got that.

But why?

Annja had expected to hear sirens, but maybe the police were being circumspect, not wanting their lights and sirens to alert their suspect.

They were nearing the lily pads when Annja's phone chirped. Rembert still had it. She looked over her shoulder and saw him answer it, one hand cupping it to his face, the other still on the tiller.

"Who? Oh, Detective Rizzo? Annja's on the boat.

She's with me. That girl from before, she's on the shore in front of us. Looks like she's inviting Annja to come have a chat. And Annja's accepting, in case you're curious. Can barely see the Lakeside lights from here. We're on the east side, down from that railroad bridge. And the girl…just like I told the cops over lunch. She's really just a kid."

Annja looked back to the shore. The girl was still there, Rembert's comment of "just a kid" fitting. On a branch above her, a burst of color drew Annja's attention. The light reached the bird, setting its feathers to sparkle an iridescent, intense green and blue. It had a tail plume about two feet long that shimmered like the moon reflected on the dark lake. Its head, neck and chest were the rich shade of wet grass, and its lower belly and beneath its tail were bright crimson. There were violet streaks in its plumage, and when it took flight, Annja saw that the outside tail feathers were snow-white.

"Impossible," Annja breathed. The bird was a quetzal, rare and known to live in the cloud forests of Central America. Annja had seen them in pictures and once in Guatemala; the country named its currency after the bird. An endangered species, it would be impossible to find in Wisconsin.

But it was here.

The bird had been important to the Maya people.

Was it really any more impossible than finding a pyramid hidden in Rock Lake? This was the stuff of modern-day thrillers.

Annja stared closely at the girl. Was she Mayan? No, if anything she was Native American and had probably killed Joe and who was holding the long knife so Annja could see it.

"That's an invitation," Rembert said, his tone a warning. "She wants to get real close and personal with you. She could end up real close and personal to this—"

"Rembert, don't shoot the dumb gun. Have you ever had a gun before? Shot it before tonight?"

No answer.

"Here, stop here. This is close enough."

Annja slipped over the side of the pontoon, the water coming up only to her waist. The girl's knife looked green. A reflection in the water?

The girl said something over and over, but Annja didn't understand.

"Anamaqkiu."

Was it the girl's name? The bird's name? A challenge? Annja locked the word in her memory and would search it out later.

"Anamaqkiu!"

Annja edged closer, her legs catching in the lily pads. Determined, she moved forcefully, breaking them off with each step and feeling the uprooted stems catch around her legs. Her feet sunk into the lake bed and mud oozed over the tops of her tennis shoes.

"Anamaqkiu. Anamaqkiu."

"Who are you?" Annja asked. The water was to her knees now, and the girl was only a dozen or so feet away.

"Anamaqkiu."

"Is that your name?"

The girl smiled and nodded.

A name, then, odd and pretty-sounding at the same

time. She could see the knife better here. It wasn't a reflection; it was a solid piece of jade, similar to some of the ones she'd seen in the treasure chamber far below, but made of a precious stone rather than obsidian and chert.

"I know you don't want me in the lake," Annja said, creeping ever closer, the water to midcalf now, arms out to her sides and fingers spread wide. The breeze played through her spread fingers and she felt the pommel of her sword kissing her hand, waiting. She hoped it wouldn't come to that.

Were the police near? Behind her, Rembert was talking on her phone again. He was frantic, saying Annja was going to try to catch the girl.

"Anamaqkiu," she said again. "I am Anamaqkiu, and you trespass."

"You know the pyramid is there, don't you?" The water was to Annja's ankles now, the girl at the edge of Annja's third circle.

"I protect the temple," the girl said. "I am Anamaqkiu."

The girl's eyes were wide and dilated, like before when Annja had fought with her. She'd assumed it was the result of drugs, but now she had a different thought. Possession? Madness?

"Anamaqkiu," Annja said, hoping she'd pronounced it correctly. "Let us talk about the temple below the lake. Together let us come to—"

The girl screamed and lunged at Annja, dropping low and slicing at her legs, cutting through the material of her shorts and drawing blood, then retreating.

Annja was hesitant to call her own blade, knowing full well Rembert could see her in the bright light of the boat.

"Anamaqkiu, no!" Annja cried.

The girl snarled, made a slashing motion and ran into the trees out of the boat's light.

Annja sprinted after her, realizing the girl wanted to be chased. Annja wanted to lead her away from the light and Rembert's gun.

"Take the boat farther out!" Annja hollered, hoping Rembert heard her. She didn't want the girl doubling back and going after Rembert.

The girl was fast. It helped that she was clearly familiar with the property around the lake and knew her way through the trees. She sped north, and Annja caught sight of her now and again through gaps in the foliage that let the moonlight through. They approached a cabin with a light on.

But the girl pounded past that, past the cabin's rickety-looking dock and then past a few more cabins that were dark. She was outdistancing Annja.

Annja continued to chase her, eyes flitting between the diminishing form of the girl and the ground, leaping over a piece of driftwood…the skull of Her Imperial Snakeship? A canoe, a bicycle a child had left lying where a trail ended at the beach. The girl's feet slapped along the trail, and Annja followed, trying to set her stride in time with the girl's so she wouldn't fall any farther behind. It was dark here, the moonlight cut by birch trees that grew on both sides of the path. The scent of moss was strong and Annja stepped high to keep from tripping over exposed roots that in the faint light looked like corded veins.

Annja was a great runner and had once entered

a marathon in upperstate New York. But as good as she was, the long dive had exhausted her, and the girl was faster.

Annja felt the muscles in her legs burn. The ache in her joints from coming up too fast was gone, but the headache wasn't. It pulsed in time with her feet.

The trail came out into someone's backyard. They'd run so far they'd made it down the east side of the lake to the edge of town. Annja caught sight of her target slipping around the corner of a garage.

There was a police car speeding south, lights flashing. The occupants didn't see the girl, nor Annja's frantic waving.

"No!" Annja grabbed her side and reached deep, somehow finding more adrenaline…for Edgar, for everyone touched by this disturbing outcome of events. She hurdled a sandbox and managed to barely avoid snagging her foot on a screw-in post of a dog tether.

She luckily found more speed and whipped around the corner of the garage. It was brighter here, a streetlight in front of the house shining down and reflecting on shiny blacktop. The girl was just beyond the property, crossing the street and going in the opposite direction of the police car.

Annja could stop…. The girl clearly wanted to be chased. The girl was the predator, and yet Annja followed. A smart predator, maybe, tiring out her quarry, knowing her quarry would not let go of this.

Miraculously, Annja had gained a little on her. She reached deeper still, her legs pumping faster and propelling her forward. Then she was rocketing across the blacktop, taking in the stinging, stinking scent of the oil and feeling the slightest tug it made against the soles of her shoes.

Where were the police?

The girl disappeared from Annja's view as she sped past a large oak. But Annja saw her again when she cut across the street at an angle. The girl was rushing into a more dense residential area, an old one with a few smart Victorian homes among the saltboxes.

Around another corner and she met a downtown street.

On a Sunday night, going on eleven o'clock, Annja hadn't expected many people or cars. But the carnival was in town and still going strong. Over the hammering of her heart, she heard music and the squeals of happy children who'd been allowed to stay out late.

The girl with the green knife was headed right toward the fun.

33

Annja was nine years old the first time she went to a carnival. She and two friends had slipped out of the orphanage. It was after bed check on a Saturday night, and they couldn't resist the glaring lights or the strains of music. Not the blues or jazz so prevalent in the city in those years, but wild competing sounds overlaying each other and calling out to every imaginative kid within hearing distance.

Posey—that wasn't her real name, but that was what everybody called her—found a roll of tickets. She, Annja and their friend Lorianne divided them up and went on the Ferris wheel first, all three squeezing into one seat and screaming happily when their car stopped at the very top.

It was one of Annja's favorite childhood memories, that magical moment when she and Posey and Lorianne were poised above everything at the edge of the city. They were angels this high in the sky and so close to heaven, removed from the disappointment that so often dogged them. Annja didn't long for anything in that moment, not family or answers, and in subsequent years when things were bad, she recaptured those minutes in her mind, her and Posey and

Lorianne, just sitting there, rocking and taking everything in.

The rest of the tickets evaporated on the fast rides—the Tilt-A-Whirl, where Lorianne puked on her shoes; Pharaoh's Revenge, a great sweeping swing that took them up and around, spinning them until they were so dizzy they couldn't walk straight afterward; and finally the Salt and Pepper Shakers, where Lorianne got sick again and the ride operator cursed.

On the way out of the carnival, they stopped at one of the games of chance. One ticket left, they gave it to Annja, and she successfully hurled three baseballs at stuffed targets, knocking them over and winning a big stuffed purple dog that she presented to Lorianne.

It was the dog that did it.

They would have gotten away with it, even managed to get Lorianne cleaned up before they snuck back into the orphanage. But the stuffed dog was big, and Lorianne wouldn't keep it under her bed—she held it close and finally caved…telling one of the directors where it came from.

Annja and Posey and Lorainne were grounded for months, but the stuffed dog stayed, as did the magical memory.

Tonight, though, the carnival that beckoned in Lakeside promised nothing good.

Why had the girl led her here, rather than stick to the lakeshore, where the darkness could work in her favor?

The array of wild sounds struck Annja as she jogged to the edge of the midway. The girl had entered the carnival grounds ahead of her, obviously concealing the knife, as the only screams were of joy. Music came from everywhere, chaotic notes competing for her attention. Annja stopped and passed the ticket booth, ignoring the cries of the ticket seller dressed as a clown. Annja didn't need tickets for the attractions. She had only one thing on her mind: Anamaqkiu.

She was in the concession area; the rides rose up beyond and above it. Annja had lost track of the girl, and she scanned the clumps of giggling teenagers and found nothing. Signs flashed Pronto Pups, the Original Hot Dog on a Stick; Fresh Squeezed Lemonade; Fruit Shakeups; the World's Best Carmel Corn; Cotton Candy. Annja had hated the cotton candy she'd shared with Posey, all sticky sweet and drawing flies, and she'd never tried it again.

There! Annja thought she saw the girl dart around the corner of a vendor selling T-shirts. She raced forward. The proprietor was an old man with tattoos on his arms.

"A girl, young," Annja started. "Pink shirt, long sleeves—"

"Sold that top to her yesterday. She loves the carnival, practically lives here."

When she's not attacking people by the lake, Annja thought. But that was why the girl led her here—she was familiar with it, liked it, the noise and the lights.

"That way." He pointed down a line of games. "She was in a hurry."

A regular here, the girl knew the carnival and could confuse Annja, further tire her out, perhaps to persuade her to give up. Moreover, even though there were a few police and security wandering around, the girl could avoid them, hiding in plain sight. The police would have difficulty finding her amid the chaos and the crowd; she could slip away at her leisure to come at Annja again—here or at the lake. Annja would be going back to the pyramid.

Annja ran as fast as she could down the row of games, avoiding plowing into a toddler holding the hand of her father, and spinning past two teenagers locked in a kiss. The air was thick and cloying, filled with the scent of buttered popcorn and pizza and something sweet, maybe cotton candy. Her stomach roiled at the odors and her head still pounded, perhaps no longer from the bends but this riotous racket.

"A winnah!" bellowed a man who operated a balloon-bursting game. There was a policeman near him and Annja skidded to a stop.

"There was a girl with a knife at The Office this afternoon. Stabbed a friend of mine. You're looking for her, and she's here. In a pink long-sleeved T-shirt." It was enough of a description, and so Annja continued her frantic quest. The officer barked a question at her, but his words got lost in the cacophony.

The lights from the rides blazed ahead, and Annja spied the girl rushing for the Tilt-A-Whirl. The image of Lorianne puking on leather loafers rushed at her and she forced it down and sprinted. Each ride seemed to have its own music, and it was as if each ride operator wanted to crank the volume as loud as possible to catch potential customers' attention.

White strobe lights from the bumper-car attraction looked like a hundred cameras flashing. Red and green fluorescent tubes spun on the Kamikaze, and yellow and blue lights appeared to chase each other around The Whip. There was a house of mirrors, and

Annja headed toward that. The girl would go there, a place to hide and confuse, a place to tease and taunt.

A scream pierced the air and Annja whirled, distinguishing it from the squeals of delight. The Tumble Bug ride operator clutched his stomach, then dropped to his knees and pressed his hands against his stomach. More screams sounded, parents and children seeing the blood. The crowd pressed close to get a better look, and Annja forced her way through it and to the man. He had a radio and she snapped it up, pressed the button and called for help.

"At the Tumble Bug, get an ambulance. Now!" His face was sweaty from the heat the ride generated, but his skin felt clammy. "The girl—" Annja said.

He swayed and she helped him set back, with her free hand motioning the crowd to give him space.

"She had a knife. She was running. I was worried about the kids. I tried to trip her was all, just wanted to get the knife away."

"Where did she go?" The crowd was parting and two paramedics were pressing through. They must have been close.

"Dragon Wagon," he said.

The paramedics pushed Annja away, the tall one thanking her. She melted into the crowd, wiping the blood on her hips. "Dragon Wagon. Dragon Wagon."

"It's over there." A young man nodded toward a fresh burst of sounds and lights. "Just past the Freak-Out."

The Dragon Wagon was easy to spot, and it was filled with children. It was a roller coaster that sat on the flatbed of a semi, a vinyl red-and-white-striped skirt hiding eighteen wheels. Arcing above it was the

top of a castle, jester heads stretched across the top—
one missing an eye, another missing its entire face.
Flags flapped from the two plastic turrets, and the
coaster rumbled along, making an annoying clacking
sound that competed with the attraction's music. The
coaster was an eight-segmented dragon, and the toddler sitting in the last car was red-faced. There was
no sign of the girl, and this was the last ride in the lot.

"Papa!"

Annja whipped her head around. Papa was dead,
Edgar, too, and…

"Papa, look at meeeee!" It was a boy, in the lead
car of Dragon Wagon, hands flailing in the air and
trying to get his father's attention.

Perhaps the girl had fled the carnival entirely.
Annja felt anger and disappointment well up. Maybe
if Annja went back to the lake, the girl would show
up again…just to keep her away from the pyramid.

"She went under there." It was the young man from
a second ago. Annja recognized him this time. He'd
been with Keesha Marie, the girl who'd made such a
fuss over Annja outside Sully's What-Nots yesterday.

"The girl with the knife, that's who you're looking for, right?"

"Yes." Annja followed where his finger pointed.
Under the ride. "Great." Common sense told her to
stay out, but common sense and Annja had never gotten along well.

"Do you have a cell phone?"

"Yeah."

"Can you call the police for me?"

She saw him take her picture with it as she ran to

34

Annja's eyes had to adjust to the darkness, and in that moment, she was undone. The girl must have heard her coming and been waiting.

The jade knife sliced into Annja's sword arm above the elbow, cutting all the way to the bone. In reflex she screamed and opened her hand, thereby losing contact with the sword. It vanished into its otherworldly space, and Annja rolled to avoid a second blow. She knew she shouldn't have rushed in; she should have waited for help.

But too little sleep, a long, deep dive and then a race from the shore to the carnival had made any rationality disappear. Still, she shouldn't have second-guessed her instincts.

The pain in her arm was excruciating, fire chasing through her entire body. She felt the blood running from the wound, down her arm and over her hand, turning the asphalt beneath the ride slick.

The girl was smaller and more agile, skittering like a spider under the bed and between the wheels. She darted out and slashed Annja again. At the same time, Annja called for the blade and she swept it forward, knocking the girl's knife nearly out of her hand.

The girl regained her grip and rocked back on her haunches, snarling.

If the second cut hurt Annja, she couldn't feel it. Her arm continued to burn, and she could barely move it. Annja guessed the girl must have severed a tendon.

But the pain now seemed to help her focus. She used it. Annja hunched forward, sweeping the sword, her second circle.

If the girl had been winded from the run, she didn't show it. She did look wild, hair tangled and sticking out from the sides of her head; the light that came through the vinyl skirting outlined her as a shadow dancing madly in front of a backlit curtain. She jabbered, and Annja tried to make it out, but there was too much other noise—including, finally, a siren. One word Annja could make out from the girl's ranting was *Anamaqkiu*.

"That's not your name after all, is it?" Annja tried to draw the girl into conversation. She still held the sword in front of her, sweeping it slowly to keep the girl away. Though it was hard to maneuver under the bed, it was even more difficult now for the girl to find an opening, and so the confined space was working in Annja's favor. The girl could not physically get below Annja's swing. "What is your name?"

Annja couldn't catch the word the young girl hissed out at her. "But I am Anamaqkiu!"

"And what is that? A title? A queen?"

The girl laughed. She was so very young, really a child. It was a child's laugh that belonged in a schoolyard or on a merry-go-round. Annja wouldn't kill her, would do everything she could to avoid hurting her...

provided she could get out of this alive. The blood continued to gush from her arm.

"We have to finish this," Annja said as much to herself as the girl. It was an effort to stay crouched as she was, and her breath was becoming ragged. Did the girl know how badly she was hurt? "We can't fight under here. We shouldn't fight at all." That knife of hers shouldn't have been so sharp, Annja thought… it hadn't looked so sharp. And yet it cut through her flesh as if she were tissue paper. And the heat. The heat that it had somehow generated was still powerful.

"I will kill you," the girl stated, in that instant sounding very grown-up.

She knocked Annja's sword aside with her jade knife, blade to blade. The girl didn't know the basics of fighting, that edge to edge was the worst hit, that it could break the weapons involved. Annja pulled the sword forward again, holding it like a spear.

"Why do you have to kill me?" Annja asked.

"You know."

"To protect the pyramid?"

"Because I am Anamaqkiu."

"A god?" Was that word Mayan? Did it represent one of the figurines carved on the temple?

"A dark spirit. Anamaqkiu."

"And you protect the pyramid?"

The girl came at Annja again, rolling fast and kicking out, landing a solid blow against the sword and knocking the point against the undercarriage. A second kick caught Annja in the jaw. The girl stabbed with the knife, but Annja moved, slamming against a wheel and adding to the pain in her arm. Miraculously, the blade only severed a hank of hair.

She felt a rush of dizziness and recognized it: blood loss. Annja had been here before. She'd lost count of how many times she'd been wounded in fights, on more than one occasion wounded just as seriously as this. But in those cases her opponent had been an adult and she'd not been so hesitant to fight back. This was a mere girl, mad perhaps, misguided certainly...and a killer. But a child.

The clattering above them stopped and feet tromped across the metal planks of the semi, the sound booming underneath like elephants charging. There were more screams, none filled with pleasure, shouts. "Police! Clear the area!"

The blaring music kept going, threatening to drown Annja as surely as if she'd drowned in Rock Lake.

"The police are out there. You can't get away."

The girl looked one way then the next, scampering backward between the flatbed's landing gear, which was down to stabilize the ride above. "I always get away."

"How many people have you killed?" Annja wanted to keep her talking. She inched toward the girl, sword out like a lance. She was also concentrating on staying conscious. If she went down, the girl would finish her. "How many people have threatened your pyramid?"

The girl laughed. "Anamaqkiu kills, and his tooth drinks the blood." She waved the knife for effect. "His tooth gives me strength and purpose."

She was possessed, Annja was certain. Still, the girl was not old enough to be responsible for the deaths dating back to WWII. Someone else had done that. "Who gave you the knife?"

"Mother to daughter to daughter to daughter," she answered. "Anamaqkiu to Anamaqkiu."

"What a lovely family tradition." And one Annja meant to put an end to.

Give me strength, she prayed just as she launched herself forward, her head and back scraping hard against the undercarriage. The vinyl flap was raised up, revealing flashlight beams. The girl was caught in the glare of the light and Annja swung, not caring if the police saw her sword, caring only if she got rid of the threat.

Despite her training and the warning sounding in her head, Annja aimed the edge of her sword for the edge of the knife.

Edge to edge, where weapons should not meet.

The girl tried to escape, skittering farther back, but she was stopped by the wheel coupling.

The blades connected.

Annja had all her strength and determination behind the one blow. Left-handed, wounded, on the verge of collapse, she called for her last ounce of measure and severed the Mayan dagger.

"No!" the girl howled. Her scream reverberated under the truck bed and crescendoed to a piercing wail.

Annja shielded an ear with her good hand, letting go of the sword. In the wail she heard voices, all high-pitched. Mother to daughter to daughter to daughter.

"No!" the scream continued, joined by panicked calls from the carnival-goers. "No!"

It was a painful and brittle sound, one Annja would never forget, the chorus of names swelling up, whispers folding into it: "Anamaqkiu. Anamaqkiu. Anamaqkiu. Vucub-Caquix. Cabracan. Zipacna. Anamaqkiu."

On and on the mantra went, until the silly carnival music swept in and carried her away.

35

Monday

The man was easily in his seventies, white hair falling to just above his shoulders and a neatly trimmed beard that extended a few inches below his Adam's apple. Usually he wore the beard and hair longer; he'd had them trimmed recently. Under the hospital room's fluorescent light, his skin looked like worn leather, though she didn't notice a single extra wrinkle from the day she'd first met him. Despite his appearance, she knew him to be well more than five hundred years old.

"Roux." Her voice cracked at the word, and he handed her a cup with a straw in it. She drank the liquid, stopping herself from asking where she was. A hospital, obviously; she'd been in so very many hospitals since inheriting Joan's sword…either as a patient being treated for this or that wound or to visit someone who had been injured for being in her presence. She knew the smell of them…the antiseptic scent. She also usually smelled flowers in her room, but not on this occasion.

She pictured the sword in her mind. It was whole,

hanging there in its otherspace and waiting for her. She'd worried that she'd broken it, as hard as she'd brought it down on that damnable green knife, purposely hitting it edge to edge. Her precious sword was all right, not a knick on its blade that she could sense.

Roux had seen Joan's sword before it came to Annja. He'd been one of Joan's knights, like Garin. "In case you are curious, Annja, you are in the regional medical center, a private room."

Where Sully had been taken, fifteen miles from Lakeside. She waited; he'd tell her more if she just waited for it. The mattress crinkled as she made herself more comfortable. It had plastic on it beneath the sheet and was not soft enough to suit her. The pillow was good, though.

"I was told they brought you in after midnight, almost had you airlifted to Milwaukee. You'd lost a great deal of blood, apparently. You've had transfusions."

Wow. Transfusions. She looked at her right arm. It was wrapped in so much gauze it looked twice its normal size.

He continued, "Humerus broken. Severed tendon, severed artery. You could have bled to death."

The knife had been incredibly sharp.

"They stitched up your stomach. I got a look at your medical chart, and—"

Either because he charmed a nurse or looked like a doctor, Annja thought.

"—I could have sworn you'd been in a sword fight with a master."

"She was a kid," Annja stated. "A teenager and—"

"She wasn't."

Annja raised an eyebrow.

"According to the police report, she was twelve."

A kid. A murderer. Mad or possessed or… "How did you see a police report?"

"I didn't see a report, but I talked to one of the policemen at the carnival. He's in the lounge, waiting for me to leave so he can come in. They're allowing you only one visitor at a time. The doctors don't know you heal so rapidly. They think you're going to be here for several days."

"I'll leave tonight." She moved again and revised that. "Or tomorrow morning."

"A carnival, Annja, what were you doing fighting a twelve-year-old girl at a carnival? Under a truck in a small town at midnight?" He made a huffing noise and ran his fingers through his hair, messing it slightly. "Instead, don't tell me. I don't want to know."

"I want to know why you're here." Annja took another sip of water. She wished it was colder. "What brings you to the medical center? You couldn't possibly have known I was here. There is no way that you—"

"I flew into Madison last night. From London to New York to Chicago to Madison, rental car here— and not the kind I'd arranged for—all of it taking me sixteen hours because I had to wait for two connections."

"You didn't come here for me, did you?" He would have arrived before the fight at the carnival.

He pulled up a chair next to the bed and refilled her water glass. "I heard you were in Madison. Then from chatter on the internet, I heard you were in a place called Lakeside. Some girl posted your picture outside an antiques shop."

That would be her fan Keesha Marie.

He leaned back in his chair. It was vinyl-coated wood, easy to clean and old. It creaked under his weight.

"I was looking for Garin," he admitted finally.

She tried to sit up in bed, but a jolt of pain shot through her bandaged arm.

"Be careful," he cautioned. "They're going to put that in a cast this afternoon. Had to get the bleeding under control first."

"Garin." She'd almost forgotten he'd been at the conference. With the pyramid and the girl and the dagger and everything else, he'd been the least of her worries.

"But he was gone."

"I see. And you wanted Garin because…" She knew their history, or rather some of it. As much as both men had been willing to confide in her on separate occasions.

"He has something that belongs to me, and I'll leave it at that. So I take it you haven't seen him."

"Once. Briefly. Outside a lecture hall." Garin obviously hadn't been at the conference to see Annja, and yet he'd let her know he was there. It was something else for her to puzzle over…or something for her to forget about. Roux and Garin had their lives and dealings and she was better off staying out of them.

"And you haven't read your email?"

She laughed, discovering that her ribs ached. "I don't have a laptop anymore. Less to pack for my trip back to New York."

Roux rested his hands on his knees and dropped his gaze to the floor. "Be well, Annja. Take good care of yourself." He stood and gave her a small smile, the wrinkles deepening at the corners of his eyes. "Please take good care."

Manny came in after Roux left, setting a bouquet on the stand next to her bed. It was beautiful, and she knew he'd spent a good bit on it—a dozen orange gerbera daisies, a dozen yellow poms, hot-pink carnations and bright green button poms. Certainly cheery, it brought a smile to her face.

"I arrested a woman this morning at the hotel, Stephanie Granger."

"Stevie."

A nod. "I figure she was the Stevie you mentioned, the woman in the van from that alley. Got her and some hulk of a guy. They'd been seen with that Aeschelman character."

"Mr. A."

"Him, we couldn't find him. Not Sunday, not today. Gone before the sun came up Sunday morning, and couldn't find an airline anywhere with an Aeschelman on the passenger list. But Stephanie and her buddy had stuck around, waiting for the bank to open this morning. It was your photographer's description of the guy that helped us find them." Manny took a breath and rubbed at his eyes before continuing. Annja could tell he hadn't gotten much sleep in a while. "Played Stephanie and her buddy against each other. She was a toughie. In the end it was him who confessed everything. Admitted Aeschelman was involved in an artifact-smuggling operation and had killed the people at the hotel…or had them killed.

Stevie and her buddy will be in Wisconsin for more than a few years cooling their heels. We got Stevie for killing the thug in the alley."

"So you've wrapped it up."

A shrug. "Not all the way. There's still Aeschelman. Arnie'll be looking for him. The Feds, too. Me? I'll be looking out my back door at my swimming pool in Brownsville." He got suddenly very serious. "Thought we were going to lose you. The paramedics at the carnival—"

"You were there at the carnival?"

"Yeah, just as all the screaming started. Followed the racket 'cause I guessed I'd find you at the heart of it." He gave her the lopsided grin. "Paramedics there… they were good. Your heart stopped twice on them. Blood…lots of blood, Annja."

"I heal quickly," she told him.

"Good thing." He fiddled with the vase, turning it so the front of the arrangement was facing her. Then he moved the chair farther back from the bed to accommodate his long legs and eased himself into it. "Local guys got the kid out—the one with the knife. Your friend with the camera—"

"Rembert."

"Rembert Hayes. He went to the station this morning and identified her as the one who knifed Sully Stever. Holding her on two counts of attempted murder."

She'd killed Joe Stever and maybe others.

"They'll try her in juvie. She's only a kid." He shook his head and looked past her, out the widow. It was a sunny day. "Funny thing is, she's acting like she doesn't remember any of it, stabbing Sully Stever, going after you. Remembers going to the carnival, but only to buy a pink T-shirt. And if it don't beat all, we can't find her parents, any relatives for that matter. Seems she's been living by herself in a trailer park on the lake. No sign of any adult there, except for pictures of a Menominee woman, probably her mother from the resemblance. Twinkie wrappers, soda cans, things a kid would eat. Looks like she's been on her own a while."

From mother to daughter to daughter, Annja thought.

"So juvie's the best thing for her. Get her in the system. The system's not always bad, you know."

Annja decided she wouldn't tell the police about Joe, about the girl being the one who likely killed the potter. Being a twelve-year-old with attempted murder charges would keep her in the system long enough.

"The knife, Manny. She had a green knife."

"Funny thing about that knife, Annja. The local officers found it. In pieces. It was under that Dragon Wagon ride that they'd pulled you and her out of. That's what she got you with, that knife. Didn't find anything else under there that could have cut you up like that. And Mr. Hayes identified the pieces, said it was the knife she'd stabbed Sully Stever with. Must've swung it at you and hit an axel under that truck bed is what we're thinking. Shattered it."

"Makes sense," Annja said, glad that no one had seen her sword. Edge to edge, she could have lost Joan's blade. "Those pieces, Manny…"

"They'll stay in a box with the rest of the evidence. Her pink T-shirt, your shirt."

"Locked away."

"Yeah." His bushy eyebrows arched. "The knife looked old, like she'd stolen it from a museum."

"So they won't return it to her, the pieces."

The eyebrows arched higher. "No."

The mattress was feeling a little more comfortable.

"I'm getting out of here tomorrow, Manny."

He chuckled. "I'm surprised you're planning on staying that long."

"Have to appreciate the flowers, don't I?" She tried to match his lopsided grin. And she had to dive the lake one more time before the week was out, get a last look at the Mayan temple that she wouldn't tell another soul about. Leave Joe's dive logs deep down inside where the lake water could disintegrate them. She'd call Bobby today and cancel Thursday's dive.

"Coming back for my party?"

"I wouldn't miss it." She'd be done with her Moroccan segment by then. They sat together for a while, looking out the window. The clatter of a nurse's cart broke the silence. "Is Sully still in here?"

"He is. He'll be here through the end of the week, I'm betting. He might get himself cleaned up a little in the process. The local officers this morning showed him a picture of the girl. They said he was begging them to bring him some whiskey."

"Is Rembert out there?"

Manny's smile disappeared. "He left the station this morning after the cops finished with his report. I was there, checking in, you know, wanting to see how it all turned out. Said goodbye to him."

"Headed back to New York?"

"Yeah, he kept talking about a guy who gave him

a bad piece of advice, that the guy was wrong. Said it wasn't safer being around you after all."

"I'll see you at your party."

36

Three months later

Stuttgart was not Garin's favorite German city, but the capital of Baden-Württemberg in the south suited him better than any of the American cities he'd visited in the past year. It boasted a population of a mere six hundred thousand, making it Germany's sixth-largest city, but that was a deception. The entire metropolitan section topped five million. Stuttgart was a city surrounded by a ring of small towns, a densely populated area that was easy to lose yourself in. Garin was not easily found, nor had his quarry been.

Garin preferred the Rhine-Ruhr area or Berlin and Brandenburg. He fancied the nightclubs in those cities and preferred the museums…when he felt the need to indulge in something cultural. He'd just come from Brandenburg, where he played the part of a tourist visiting the castle, which he'd seen when the stone was not quite as worn. He'd spent a week at the Villa Contessa, eating fine food, reading and waiting.

Stuttgart was not without its charms, however. Two days ago he spent hours walking through the City Center, a collection of buildings that were architectural marvels—the baroque New Palace, the medieval Old Palace, the Bauhaus-style Weisenhof estate and the Art Nouveau market hall. He'd lingered the longest at the Old Palace because it held so many memories that he couldn't shake…and didn't want to.

He enjoyed his longevity, always fearful, though, that it would come to an end. In the mirror each morning, he checked to see if there were more lines on his face and wondered how tied to Annja and the sword his soul was. But his being around so long was a curse as well as a blessing, of memories anyway, and his remarkable mind held on to them with a vise grip that no amount of indulging could relax.

History recorded that Duke Luitolf of Swabia used to graze horses at the Old Palace more than a thousand years back. Stuttgart derived its name from the old German word *stutengarten,* which meant a stud animal, and its coat of arms bore a rearing stallion. Appropriate. It was Austria when Garin first walked these grounds, only becoming a part of Germany after 1534. It then became a seat of government for the region and a self-administered county. Stuttgart had evolved because of major European trade routes. Garin was here now because the trade route he had been following was stopping in the city tonight.

The city had spread across low hills and wrapped itself around vineyards, parks and valleys, adding to its sprawl with each century.

He was fond of the Green U park, first planted by King William I of Württemberg. Considered an English-style garden, it featured many old trees. Garin had watched them at various stages as he'd visited every handful of decades.

In a few hours, he would go to a program at the planetarium, escorting a young woman he'd met yesterday at the Wilhelma Zoo and Botanical Garden. Oddly, he'd gone to the zoo to see the penguins and had met her by accident. An attendant in the gift shop, Berdina fell for his smile and well-practiced lines, and spent the evening in his company. Not so inventive or athletic as Keiko had been, but she had the same look to her and the wide-eyed reaction to the world.

Later tonight he would take another stroll through Green U park, to an art gallery where his quarry would be receiving guests. Garin didn't have an invitation, but he would attend anyway.

Tomorrow would be his last day in Stuttgart; he would have a long lunch with Berdina and then go to the airport…a business matter to attend to in Belgium. One of his identities owned a fine apartment in an old building in Bruges on a quaint cobblestoned street across from a renowned chocolate shop. Roux's shield was on display there, hanging like a trophy on his study wall, a place of privilege.

It was a little after ten when Garin entered via the back of the gallery. The auction had been going for an hour, but there were still several pieces remaining. He helped himself to a glass of Riesling. It was delicately sweet and preferable to the other offerings on the table. Some of Aeschelman's guests were clearly not connoisseurs—several of them walked around with glasses of inferior blends.

Aeschelman registered his surprise at seeing Garin, but quickly recovered. He pointed to the next object for sale, a full close helmet, French, dating back to 1530. It was elaborate, embossed and etched with three crosses on each side, with an applied border to the faceplate and decorated by heat patination, and most importantly, it matched the shield in Garin's cozy apartment.

Aeschelman—who was known now as Dreschler—took a long swallow of wine, let the bidding commence and spoke in perfect German.

Garin won the piece, paying forty thousand Euros, much more than he'd expected it to go for, although much less than other items had cost. There were other collectors here tonight, and so he'd had to compete. Among the buyers, there was no one Garin recognized from any of the previous sessions he'd been to, yet clearly they all had considerable resources. Aeschelman gravitated toward him when an associate of his stepped forward to take over proceedings for the next piece, a bronze sculpture of a rabbit's head. Garin poured himself a second glass of Riesling.

"I thought you'd never been to Germany and didn't know the language, Mr. Dreschler."

"I thought you did not drink, Mr. Knight."

Garin watched as a middle-aged man in designer jeans and a thin gray turtleneck claimed the rabbit head at one million Euros.

"I drink," Garin admitted. "Usually when I am in the mood to celebrate something." In fact, he'd come to the auction with a slight buzz, having shared a bottle of champagne with Berdina in the park after the planetarium show.

He watched the same man buy the next two items: a bronze rat head that supposedly had been looted from China by the invading Anglo-French expedition in the nineteenth century and a bronze figure in good condition of Horus as a child, with an olive patina that was supposedly from the year 1000.

Aeschelman…or whoever he really was…took control of the auction and finished selling the remainder of the items, Garin politely waiting until the entire affair had concluded before paying for the helmet. They conveniently and carefully packed it for him in a motorcycle-helmet carry bag.

Then Garin quickly left.

But he waited.

He carefully selected a spot behind the gallery, more than a passageway and less than a street. It was clean and it smelled of old stone and rain; it had started to drizzle. Garin had never minded the rain. Aeschelman departed with two broad-shouldered men. Garin had watched the pair inside, the man's security, glorified muscle who were packing guns.

Aeschelman had sold Garin the name of a man who supposedly owned the helmet he now held. The man did not exist. Aeschelman had told lies and… more lies.

Garin didn't hate him for the lies or that he'd taken payment for the name under false pretenses. Everyone spoke lies…except dear Joan; she'd never lied to Garin or Roux, or to any of the other knights who had marched with her. Annja, who held her sword, she lied. Garin lied frequently—to the women he shared time with, to business associates, to himself.

No, he didn't hate Aeschelman because of his lies or the advantage he took when he saw it.

He hated him for what happened to Keiko.

Garin used a specially made silencer for his semi-automatic pistol, the kind often favored by the prime minister of India's bodyguards and used in the Afghanistan War. Garin liked guns, and this was one of his favorites. It had a range of fifty meters, but it could shoot accurately up to one and a half kilometers. He took Aeschelman down with a bullet to the back of his head from a mere two blocks away.

One of the man's thugs fled, and so Garin let him live. But the other remained, kneeling over the body—not to see if Aeschelman might be alive, but to pick up the valise he'd been carrying, probably filled with money and bank account numbers and transactions from this evening's sale. Garin assassinated this man, too. He approached them, listening intently.

He heard traffic on a nearby street, light at this hour and unhurried. No sirens. Windows opened onto this small side street, but apparently no one had heard.

Garin checked both bodies, a perfect shot each time. No doubt they'd died instantly, though he wished Aeschelman had felt it coming. He gripped the handle of the valise. No reason to let it lay here for a stranger to find and possibly profit by. He used the tip of his boot to turn Aeschelman over, and then he stretched down to the man's neck, feeling for the thin chain he knew would be there. One tug and the Mayan medallion was free. No use someone profiting by it, either.

It faintly glowed under the streetlight, as if it had some inner energy source. The disk was shiny and smooth, meticulously cared for, and the image of a Central American bird, a quetzal, had been deeply etched into the center of it. On the reverse side was a Mayan sun and in the middle of it an etched half man/half badger. The disk had a comfortable

37

Six months later

Vista Verde Memorial Park was located off Sara Road in Sandoval County not far from Edgar's Rio Rancho home.

All the grave markers, though of various sizes, were flat against the earth, the only raised structure a chapel that had compartments, looking not unlike gym lockers, on the outside walls where the cremated had been placed.

Edgar's grave, it turned out, had been purchased many years ago. It featured two plots; evidently, he thought he'd stay married and that his wife would join him in eternity.

Annja knelt in front of the marker, tracing the raised bronze letters and looking up. In the distance the mountains filled the horizon—purple-blue this early morning, tinged with snow. Breathtaking. No wonder Edgar had chosen this place.

She'd brought a small shovel and she now dug at the edge of his stone. Annja seemed to be the only visitor around. It was smack in the middle of the week, with cemetery workers busy nearby, preparing a grave.

She gently but persistently made a small hole in the earth. The ground was hard-packed and initially resisted her efforts.

When she had the hole about eight inches deep, she reached into her fanny pack and pulled out a piece of flannel, opening it up. The disk was smooth and reflected the light of the glowing sun. It had a good weight to it, and any museum would have welcomed it for a pre-Columbian display. Annja had nearly donated it; it was worth thousands.

The medallion had arrived last week in the mail, in a plain brown shipping envelope, insured and metered from Dairago, Italy. There was no return address and no name. But she knew, or rather suspected, it had come from Garin. The handwriting looked familiar.

The image of a Central American bird, a quetzal, was deeply and intricately etched into the center of it, beak open as if calling out. On the reverse side was a Mayan sun, and in the middle of that was an etched half man/half badger, like she had seen on the walls of the pyramid deep in Rock Lake.

The disk was unpleasantly warm against the palm of her hand and made her skin itch. As she held it, the image of Joan's sword came to the forefront of her mind and the sensation of its pommel against her hand tried to assert itself. The medallion, like the jade knife Annja had broken at the carnival, did not belong to the present-day world. They were things of ancient power, touched by dark spirits.

She'd wanted to be rid of it.

The medallion would be safe here with Edgar.

She set it in the bottom of the hole, which she filled in with dirt, pressing the brittle grass overtop it.

"Indeed, you had quite the monster for me to chase, dear friend." She wished she could have caught Aeschelman, the man behind all the murders. But someone would find him, the police or the Feds. There would be justice for Edgar and Papa.

A large colorful bird flew at the edge of the cemetery, circling once on an updraft and then moving on toward the mountains. Annja swore it was an intense, iridescent green and blue, with a tail two feet long that shimmered in the early light and a spot of bright crimson on its belly.

"Impossible."

She blinked and saw that it was only a common ferruginous hawk.

A moment later, it was gone.

* * * * *

James Axler

Outlanders®

WINGS OF DEATH

A legion of flying monsters spawns terror across Africa…

An old enemy of the Cerberus warriors unleashes Harpy-like killers on the African continent, hoping the blood-hungry winged beasts and their love of human flesh will aid in his capture of a legendary artifact: the powerful staff wielded by Moses and King Solomon. Except, the staff's safe in Kane's hands, and with the murderous rampage spiraling out of control and an exiled prince bent on unlocking the gates of hell, the staff is all that stands between the rebels and Africa's utter decimation.

Available February wherever books and ebooks are sold.

TAKE 'EM FREE

2 action-packed novels plus a mystery bonus

NO RISK

NO OBLIGATION TO BUY

GE13

JAMES AXLER

DEATH LANDS

SIREN SONG

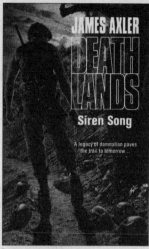

A legacy of damnation paves the trail to tomorrow

If utopia exists in post-apocalyptic America, Ryan and his companions have yet to greet it. But in the mountains of Virginia, their quest may find its reward. Heaven Falls is an idyll of thriving humanity harnessing powerful feminine energy and the medicinal qualities of honey. Bountiful and serene, this agrarian community is the closest thing to sanctuary the companions have ever encountered. But as they are seduced by a life they have only envisioned, they discover Heaven has a trapdoor that opens straight to hell....

Available January wherever books and ebooks are sold.